SOME GLOW BRIGHTLY

JOHN PALMER GREGG

Thistle Bound Press

Thistle Bound Press
www.thistlebound.com

Copyright © 2016 John Palmer Gregg
Cover painting by Tony Sobota
www.tonysobota.com

ISBN-13: 978-0-9979685-0-7

for Tina and Rohan
you have shown more patience than I deserve

Inevitable

There were two outs in the bottom of the ninth inning and the tying run was already taking a lead from first base. Fourteen-year-old Red Snyder stepped into the batter's box with the league championship on the line. Beads of sweat rolled into his eyes. It burned. He blinked them away. The pitcher reared back and fired the first two pitches right down the middle. Red had wanted to swing at both, but his body wouldn't respond. He raised his hand toward the umpire and stepped out of the batter's box.

The first storm clouds of August gathered above the outfield scoreboard. The metallic scent of the oncoming storm wafted through the infield. Two lights, like mocking, burning eyes stared accusingly from the center of the dark green scoreboard. Two strikes down, one to go. This was the moment he feared all season long. From the first foggy and cool mornings of league tryouts, he knew it was inevitable. Through the increasingly muggy afternoons of practices and games, this precise moment had always been ahead of him. He stepped back in the box, tapped home plate with his bat and tried to block out the twisting in his stomach.

Red's leather batting glove crackled as he tightened his grip on the bat. A dust devil, awakened by the breeze, danced over the pitcher's right shoulder between second base and the shortstop. Michael Lagos, Red's best friend, took two crouching steps off first. The next pitch came in too low. It hit the edge of the plate and ricocheted out of the catcher's reach. Michael ran toward second base, his arms pumping, a rooster tail of dust behind each footfall. The catcher threw the ball wide. The second baseman dove after it. Michael leapt over him like one of the hurdles during track season, his right leg held straight in front of him, his left tucked underneath his body. The ball bounced into the outfield grass. Michael rounded second, passing the dying dust devil, and made it to third base still standing. The head coach, who happened to be Michael's father, signaled for him to halt as the centerfielder made a perfect one-bounce throw to the catcher at home plate.

C'mon, c'mon, c'mon, you can do this, Red muttered under his breath as he closed his eyes and bounced the aluminum bat against the bill of his helmet. He turned toward the dugout and caught his father's eye. The only thing Red felt he inherited from his moderately famous war photographer father was his thick red hair. Red knew pressure meant nothing to his dad. The two shared a brief nod, and Red stepped back up to the plate.

Throughout the season, Red consistently held the best batting average on the team, one of the best in the whole league. He was definitely the best catcher, being somewhat stocky, but with quick hands and a good arm that could send the ball to second base with the speed and accuracy of a sniper. It was moments like these, however, these 'clutch' moments, that he knew he didn't have what it took. He would choke, he knew it. When it really mattered, his muscles would lock up and he would be forced to watch as everything around him fell apart.

Red saw from the first moment the ball left the pitcher's hand that it was going to be right in the middle of his sweet spot. He couldn't count the number of times he had smashed a line drive right up the middle off nearly identical throws. Normally he could have done it off muscle memory alone. All he had to do was let go of his fear, and let his body do the rest. The muscles in his arms and legs strained for their potential energy to be released. He brought his bat back further, like a scorpion prepared to strike. He shifted his weight forward then ... nothing. Nothing but a loud *thwump* as the baseball buried itself inside the catcher's mitt.

The first heavy drops of rain began to fall on the field as Red plodded to the dugout. His eyes were focused on the round drops throwing up dust from dirt still too dry to have turned to mud. He did his best to ignore the celebration that erupted from the opposing team. Mercifully, the rain hid any tears that might have been running down his cheeks.

***

Laurel Hollows, Tennessee was a city without purpose. Twenty years earlier, a new interstate had been built between Asheville, North Carolina and Knoxville, Tennessee, bypassing the treacherous winding highway that went through Laurel Hollows. In the intervening years, nearly all the industries and factories that had once called the city home moved their businesses and jobs to communities with easier access to the outside world. A few small-scale logging operations were all that remained. The population steadily decreased, the people leaving the once thriving city in busloads like the stout pine trees carried away by the logging trucks. The buildings that remained and the crumbling infrastructure were simply the outer trappings, a shell of what a city should be. But they still stood, empty vessels waiting to be refilled with new purpose.

Red relived the last moments of the season over and over as he watched the storm spend the last of its fury. He watched raindrops running down the windows of a renovated leather tannery given new life as a pizza parlor called The Tannery. Around him the rest of his team had already put the season behind them. They were as loud and wild as ever. Red ignored them. Instead, he watched as the individual drops on the glass were drawn to each other forming little rivulets that ran down the window. The tiny streams merged into even larger ones. With each meeting they flowed down the window faster and faster until they reached the bottom and dropped off the window's sill into a muddy puddle below.

A punch in the arm brought Red back to the party.

"Hey, Captain Gloom. Get over it," Michael said. He stood at the end of the table, gripping two sodas in the long splayed fingers of his left hand. "It's no big deal."

"It is a big deal. I failed the whole team," Red said. He turned in the booth and leaned against the window.

"Look, we wouldn't have made it even half as far in the postseason if it wasn't for you. You're the best player on the team," Michael said. He slid Red's soda across the table, pushed back his hair and scooted into the booth opposite Red. "You need to take a lesson from your elder, I don't let anything bring me down."

"You're only eight months older than me," Red said.

"Yeah, maybe, but those months were filled with wisdom and experience." Michael cocked a sideways smile, leaned back in the booth and mimed smoking a pipe. "You'll learn one day, young man. You'll learn."

In appearance, like attitude, Michael was nearly the polar opposite of Red. Where Red had short red hair, the same color as everyone on both sides of his family for as long as anyone could remember, Michael's was shoulder length and such a dark shade of brown that it was usually mistaken for black. He shared an olive complexion with his father and thirteen-year old sister Sara. It made them look like they were sporting a tan all year long, whereas Red was blessed with the pallid white skin of the Irish, a people that spent centuries under overcast skies. The only time Red even appeared to have a tan was when his generous supply of freckles merged together from too much sunlight. Normally he went from paper white to bright red. He looked like a cardinal with a flat top.

Sara slid into the booth on her knees beside Red and pointed out the window. Her hand was less than an inch away from Red's face. He felt blood rushing to his cheeks.

"It's a circus," she shouted.

Turning to the window, the three of them watched a convoy of brightly painted trucks make their way through the drizzling rain toward town. Each truck bore the name, *Circus Paenultimus*, in script on an arced scroll, and each one was gaudily painted with an advertisement for one of their acts. There were jugglers, acrobats, clowns, and everything one would have normally expected from a circus, including lions and a dancing bear.

"That is so lame," Michael said. "Did that one really just say

'Elsa the Dancing Bear' on it?"

"So?" Sara said. She sat down in the seat, crossed her arms and stuck her tongue out at her brother. "I think we should all go."

"I think Red and I are a little too mature for a circus," Michael said. He raised his eyebrows, stuck his nose in the air and slowly shook his head, doing his best aristocrat impersonation.

"I kind of want to go too," Red said. He was eager to spend an afternoon with Sara, and distract himself from the game. He watched their reactions closely to see how she responded, and to see if there was any indication that Michael had begun to realize Red had been developing a crush on Sara over the last several months.

"Want to go where?" Donal Snyder, Red's father, said overhearing the conversation on his way back from the pizza buffet.

"We just saw a load of circus trucks pull into town, Mr. Snyder, and Sara is trying to convince me and Red to go," Michael said.

"I don't know why you wouldn't want to go. A circus sounds like a lot of fun," Donal said. "I'll talk to Emily and Alexander, and I'm sure Claire will go if I twist her arm a bit. Tomorrow is a Sunday, after all; if they are set up by then we might as well go. I might even take my camera."

For several years the Snyders and the Lagoses made a near ritual of getting together on Sunday nights to eat dinner and play board games. The parents' friendship was initially brought on by their sons own friendship and the fact that they both lived in the same rural area outside of town at the edge of the national forest. Through the years, though, they had become like family. Since neither family had relatives nearby, or at least no relatives that they wanted to have anything to do with, they often shared holidays and major life events together.

Red watched his dad sit down with the other parents. As soon as he sat, they all subtly reoriented themselves toward him.

"You were saying that you were hiding in a bombed out school when the other army started shooting tear gas at you," one of the moms prompted Donal before he had a chance to take his first bite.

Red rolled his eyes and turned back toward the table.

"The circus is going to be great," Sara said. She smiled as she looked back and forth between Red and Michael.

Red loved how her eyes sparkled when she was excited.

"Yippee," Michael said flatly. He put two slices of pizza together like a sandwich, took a huge bite and spoke with his mouth full. "It is going to be so lame. What kind of circus would come to a podunk town like this anyway?"

The One Who Knows

Not far into the forest beyond the Snyder farm, an old logging road made a wide berth around a section of old growth. Ancient trees that had never felt the bite of an ax or the grinding teeth of a saw grew tall and thick. Maples, oaks, and black walnuts spread their twisting limbs out wide forming a latticework. Little light filtered through. Few things, save for a thick blanket of emerald green moss, grew underneath that greedy canopy, and no wind blew under the arms of the trees. The air, heavy with trapped humidity, smelled of wet leaves and decay. Huge boulders, left behind by glaciers ages ago, lay scattered and strewn around the forest floor. They were cracked and broken by time and the slow but incessant rending of roots. Darkness seeped from the edges of the old forest like the bleeding of wet ink across parchment. It was a melancholy place, filled with a kind of dark beauty that could at once enthrall and dismay.

It was no wonder that generations of Laurel Hollows residents had left that section unmolested. It was no wonder that stories told of spirits, kobolds, and other dark creatures who made it their home. It was no wonder because it was true, and the people who lived near were prone to seeing the world just a little more fully than other people. Only one person chose to call that malignant place home; The Hermit, the oftentime bogeyman of those stories. He was also the only man who knew why a circus would come to Laurel Hollows.

The large-knuckled fingers of The Hermit twisted the ends of a hand-rolled cigarette before placing it between his lips. He cupped one hand around the end. Sparks jumped from the tip of his middle finger to his palm - lighting the cigarette. After several puffs he blew the smoke out of his nose and leaned over the stew pot on his small cooking fire. The flames licked at the dingy scraps of cloth that hung like Spanish moss from his clothing.

This part of the forest was old when The Hermit first took up residence in the cave he called home. It was different then as well, but the changes occurred so slowly he had not noticed. The trees had grown more twisted, the boulders more bleached. However, he did notice when farms, like the Snyders, had begun creeping further and further up the mountain. The farmers had cut down trees at the edge of the forest, and tamed the land. With horse and plow initially, but now with tractors and bush hogs, men asserted their power over nature. They imposed their version of order on perceived chaos.

The Hermit was old when Red's great-grandparents put up the first frames of their farmhouse. He was old, but he had still known who he was. There had been some vestige of his former life left, although fleeting. Fleeting and small. Who he had been was eaten away by the passage of time, the same way that boulders crumbled and the serpentine paths of creeks changed their course. Back then he still cared for the man he was. He had once even harbored dreams. They were dreams of power, dreams of darkness, but they were dreams.

A fox, silver gray, flashed past The Hermit's fire and leapt onto a nearby rock. It looked expectantly at him.

"So, he has finally returned," The Hermit said, smoke falling from his mouth at each word.

The fox made only the slightest of movements as its master spoke, rearranging its front paws on the rock. Its eyes fixated on the steaming pot.

"He's back too soon!" The Hermit yelled. He kicked the pot at the fox which scampered out of the fire's light deeper into the cave. "I'm not ready yet. I must gather more spirits quickly. Straub will not be kind."

Grabbing a walking staff, The Hermit stomped to the mouth of the cave as the first rays of the morning sun vainly tried to pierce through the overhead leaves. The Hermit raised his staff into the air. He held it tight in his nicotine-stained fingers. Crackles of energy, like purple-fringed lightning, flowed up his arm and into the staff. It vibrated in his hand, nearly shaking free. He grasped the staff tighter until his fingers whitened and his knuckles glowed red. A low resonance reverberated from the staff through the forest, a humming so deep it was all but inaudible to human ears.

For ten minutes, he stood still. The energy twisted up his arm into his staff. His gaunt face and yellow stained beard flickered in its dark light. Birds, foxes, and other small forest creatures began slipping out from behind trees and rocks into the small clearing outside his cave. Several small, humanoid creatures came as well. They stood well out of the light at the very edges of the assembly, wary to even be seen by their master. As a solitary coyote arrived and sat on its haunches not far from The Hermit, he finally lowered the staff.

"My djinn, the time for secrecy is over," The Hermit said. He paused and looked over each of the assembled creatures in turn, assessing their condition. He saw too much of the animal in them, too little of the awareness of the original spirits he had placed inside them. Too long had they lived in such temporal bodies. They were slowly turning into the animals they had previously only pretended to be. Too long. Time had slipped away from The Hermit, a monotonous rhythmic cycle. The days and nights began to flash by like the flickering of an old movie reel. Now, he knew, his own greatly extended life would soon reach its climactic scene. As soon as the two worlds merged, he would hold a power in his grasp that few men dared dream of.

"Go. Find me some whose spirits are strong enough to be ransomed," He commanded them. "I will wring them from their flesh like wet rags."

The djinn, clothed in the flesh of animals, turned away. With squawk and howl they sped in all directions from the cave mouth. The small humanlike creatures, kobolds, slunk away through the trees.

It won't be long now, he thought. *I feel the interstice already straining to tear open.*

He walked into the wilderness burying the tip of his staff into the mossy ground at each of his long strides. Where his staff touched the moss it withered and turned black. He left behind an ever growing shadow with each step - a darkness spreading in an already dark land.

Circus Paenultimus

"You three stay together," Donal said to Red, Sara and Michael. He handed them their circus tickets. "We'll meet up outside the big top fifteen minutes before the show starts."

"Thanks. See you then," Red said. He watched as his dad put his arm around his mother's shoulder and walked through the entrance turnstile behind Sara and Michael's parents, Alexander and Emily Lagos.

"I'm still saying this is going to be lame," Michael said as they handed their tickets to the man beside the stile. Behind the ticket taker was a large canvas wall depicting the Circus Paenultimus logo. It blocked the view of whatever mysteries lay beyond.

The man tore Sara and Red's tickets, handing them back stubs. Michael held out his own ticket to the man, not bothering to face him.

"Why has it got to be lame?" The man asked. Instead of plucking the ticket from Michael's outstretched hand, he wrapped his fingers around Michael's own fingers.

The man wore a purple top hat, faded and threadbare. His striped suit and jacket, also purple, was tight around a thick torso that must have been several sizes smaller when the out-fit was tailored. Underneath long scraggly gray eyebrows, his narrow eyes were yellowed and bloodshot. Three layers of purple bags under his eyes gave them a sunken, almost skeletal look. From his chin dangled a sparse but wiry goatee, above which his thin lips turned down in a tight scowl.

"It's just that," Michael stammered as he looked up at the man for the first time.

"Hey!" Sara shouted, stepping up beside Michael and wrenching his hand free of the ticket taker. "Leave him alone."

The man stood up straighter. His scowl fell away leaving an insincere smile underneath. Taking off his top hat, the man bowed briefly with arms stretched wide. His thinning hair slid out of his hat and hung in swaying, greasy clumps.

"I am so sorry young masters," he said addressing Sara. "Forgive me, for I meant no disrespect. We here at the Circus Paenultimus are rather proud of whatever meager talents we possess, and it pains us to hear someone, even one so young as your dear friend here, dismiss us so curtly without first giving us the opportunity to prove ourselves. Which is, of course, our most primary of concerns. I, Arthur P. McCoy, the Third, do personally guarantee that we will both delight and amaze, or I will personally refund double the price of your admission."

With a deft motion, McCoy grabbed the proffered ticket from Michael's fingers, tore it in two and held the stub out to him.

"Yeah, uh, thanks," Michael said. He took the stub and shoved it into the back pocket of his jeans.

"Wow," Red said after they walked out of earshot. "That might have been one of the freakiest people I have ever seen."

"Circus people are all weirdos," Michael said. "Let's go see if there are any carnival games. Dad taught me the trick to busting balloons with a dart last year at the fair."

The three of them walked around the edge of the canvas wall and immediately stopped, dumbfounded at what they saw.

The midway of the Circus Paenultimus was designed to overwhelm the senses. Just in front of where they stood a banner was stretched wide. In large florid letters it read: 'The Circus Paenultimus Midway: A Congress of Unusual Mortals.' Gigantic painted banners, each about fifteen feet tall, advertised sideshows, refreshments and acts from the circus. The banners lined the left and right sides of the midway. There were advertisements for a headless woman; a real live caged werewolf; the world's fattest woman; Troy the half man and dozens of other sideshow acts. The banners tapered at the far end toward an imposing purple and yellow striped tent.

The sideshows were a myriad of smaller tents and cages in the same garish purple and yellow stripes. They were scattered around the pasture field turned midway in small clusters of three or four. The edges of every tent and cage were rimmed with flashing lights and fluttering pendants. A barker stood in the middle of each cluster shouting at every passerby to come inside whichever attraction had the smallest line. Loud circus music blared from a steam calliope that continually belched rings of vapor into the air. The pungent scent of animals and wet hay was intermingled with the aroma of popcorn, funnel cakes, and fried foods. Clowns, jugglers, and stilt walkers made their way through the bewildered crowd.

"Whoa," Red said.

"Yeah, whoa," Sara echoed. "This is like something from the dark ages."

Michael looked around the midway at the various tents. "So, no games then," he said and walked toward the nearest grouping. Sara and Red followed behind him trying to take it all in.

The four tents all faced toward a common center. One was Troy - the Half Man, which advertised him as being the top half of a mustachioed man, cut off just below his torso. He stood on his hands with his waist dangling several inches off the ground. The second tent was for The Beautiful Esmerelda, the Mystifying Gypsy Sorceress from the Dark Forests of Romania, the third was for Django, a dog that could supposedly read your mind. The final tent advertised Synesteria, the Sultry Snake Woman. Painted on that tent's side was the scaly body of a snake with the upper body of a beautiful woman. The snake portion was coiled like a cobra whose green scales melted away into the pink flesh of a woman wearing a snakeskin bikini top. Her arms were stretched out in a belly dancer's pose. Her eyes were painted the same shimmering green as her scales, her brown hair was blown wildly about. It was this painting that caught Red's eyes. At the moment it also had the shortest line.

"Step right up and prepare yourself for this once in a lifetime sight," the barker in the center of the ring of tents bellowed. "She was bred, that's right I said bred. She was bred in a tiny village outside Agra, India in the very shadow of the Taj Mahal. She alone survived being drowned by the locals. Her mother was a witch who couldn't have her own children, so she weaved an incantation on a snake in order for it to have human babies. Her brood mates were all abominations, some more snakelike than the others. It was a stroke of pure luck for our Synesteria that our illustrious ringmaster, Rinthim Straub, was there on holiday to save her."

Red took several steps nearer the barker away from Michael and Sara. The barker saw him edging closer and spoke directly to him.

"Oh, men and boys, you have never in your life seen anything like this before. Her scales are those of an Indian cobra, her face one of exotic and enthralling beauty. Synesteria will turn your stomach for the vile abomination she is. Synesteria will turn your heart for the sultry beauty she is. She'll both sicken and tantalize you." The barker wiggled the tips of his fingers at Red as he spoke the last sentence. He turned away from Red back toward the passing crowd. "All for only a dollar, ladies and gentlemen, all for the price of a candy bar. A delight that will melt away on your tongue in just a few sweet moments, leaving you wanting more. For that very same dollar, you can see Synesteria, and the memory will both haunt and excite you anytime you wish to recall her sinuous form."

The barker turned toward Red and took off his hat. "So whad'ya say kid, it's only a buck." The man smiled and winked once at Red before turning away again. His teeth were brown and rotten, several were missing.

"Let's see the snake woman," Red said as Sara and Michael came up beside him. "She seems as good as any of the rest."

"Yeah, okay," Michael said. "Only let's go see the sorceress next. I'll bet that one will be pretty cool."

"I thought all this stuff was lame," Sara said, elbowing her brother in the ribs.

The three of them handed their money over to a squat man

outside the entrance and walked into the small tent.

Inside, a small knot of adults blocked their view of the snake woman. The air was still. Clouds of smoke hung in the air like fog. It was nearly dark, save for a shimmering light coming from somewhere in front of the gathered adults and minuscule daggers of sunlight streaming through tiny holes in the tent's roof, piercing the smoke filled darkness.

"It's just some trick with mirrors and the like," a man said as he moved away from the red velvet rope separating the crowd and the snake woman.

Red squeezed through the crowd, filling the space the man left as he exited the tent. He grabbed the rope to stake his claim. He felt Michael come up behind him. Sara pushed her way through the crowd and came up beside Red as well. Her fingers brushed across his as she grabbed the rope. A tingle rushed up his arm and through his entire body.

It took several moments for Red's eyes to adjust to the darkness. The first thing he noticed was that the shimmering light came from a large brass oil lamp, shaped like the kind genies are supposed to come out of. Smoke hung around and above a figure laying on a chaise lounge. A slow movement beside the lounge caught his attention. The light from the lamp was reflected in iridescent ripples which slowly resolved into a giant scaly, serpentine figure. His eyes followed the undulating form upward until the scales faded, disappearing into the soft pink skin of a woman's stomach. Unlike the painting outside however, the woman was not wearing a top. She was nude from the waist up. Thick wavy black hair fell over her shoulders down to her navel, covering much of her upper body. Her narrow eyes glinted in the lamplight as she blew smoke out of her full-lipped mouth. The smoke traveled just a couple of feet in front of her until it merged with a cloud of smoke engulfing a tall hookah. Red could not take his eyes off her. He was startled by a voice right beside his ear.

"There is no way that is real," Sara said. She squinted and leaned over the rope for a closer look. "I'll tell you one thing. Our parents are not going to like us seeing this kind of stuff."

"What are you worried about?" Michael asked. "Everyone knows it isn't real. It's just makeup and dim light. It is no different than going to a movie."

But it did seem real, to Red at least. He studied the intersection where scales and flesh met, looking for the trick or some kind of seem. *It's flawless,* he thought. His eyes kept betraying him, straining to see beyond the flowing hair. He turned away from Synesteria. He felt self-conscious staring at a half-naked woman with Sara standing beside him.

"Come on, let's get out of here," he said.

The eyes of the snake woman followed them as they made their way through the crowd and out the rear exit. The light outside momentarily blinded them as they pushed the flap aside. Before their eyes adjusted to the brightness they nearly walked into their parents.

"I don't know what kind of place this is," Red's mother, Claire, said. "But I do know I don't like it."

"I don't like it either," Emily, Michael and Sara's mother, said. "Maybe this wasn't such a good idea. I don't know if the kids should see this kind of stuff."

"It's fine," Alexander said to his wife as the three kids joined them. "It's just silly sideshow stuff. None of it is real these days. Besides, the actual circus will be starting pretty soon."

"Mom," Red began, but was cut off by his mother as soon as she realized he was there.

"Listen Red," Claire said. "I don't think it's a good idea for you to go to anymore of the freak shows."

"It's okay, Mrs. Snyder," Sara said. She gave Red's mother her sweetest smile as she walked up beside Red. "We just want to go see the magician anyway."

"Claire," Donal said. He reached up and laid his hand on Claire's shoulder. "It's not a big deal. Let's all go see the magician or sorceress or whatever together, then we can go find our seats. After that it will be time for the circus to start anyway."

"I don't care too much for magic tricks," Alexander said. "I'll go ahead and get some popcorn and save us some seats."

The tent for Esmerelda the Sorceress was larger and brighter than Synesteria's dank den. Bleachers lined one canvas wall facing a small stage that was bare except for a simple wooden magician's box, no larger than a briefcase, on a pedestal in the center of the stage. The two families settled into the first row. The remaining seats were quickly filled. Once the final seat was occupied, the tent flap dropped closed – plunging the guests into darkness. A row of stage lights flickered hesitantly on at Red's feet. When the lights all finished pinging, and popped one final time, they revealed a beautiful teenage girl standing behind the magician's box. As the crowd clapped, she took a formal curtsy. Two doves appeared in her hands as she rose, stirring a second round of clapping.

Esmerelda wore a long-tailed purple jacket made of a material that shimmered as she flourished her hands. Underneath the jacket was a white corset and cummerbund, also purple. Coins and beads were woven into thick brown dreadlocks which were tied back at the nape of her neck. They sparkled and jangled as she moved. It was an effect she used to her advantage. It confused and misdirected her audience during the performance. Her movements were smooth, and each gesture ballerina precise. She never wasted an ounce of energy on unnecessary movement.

"This is much better," Claire said to Donal behind her hand. "I'm sorry about before, but you know how nervous I get in crowds, and those sideshows were creeping me out."

Donal reached over and took his wife's hand in his. He stroked the back of it with his thumb. "Don't worry about it. You're doing fine."

At the touch of his hand, Claire visibly softened and a tightness she had felt in her neck and shoulders melted away.

"Tank you all so very much for coming to enjoy my show," Esmerelda said through a thick Slavic accent. "I am Sorceress Esmerelda. I am pleased to perform my magics for you."

Michael leaned forward on the bench, all thoughts about how lame the circus might be were forgotten.

Esmerelda's act turned out to be more of a traditional magic show than any kind of exhibition of sorcery. She performed card tricks and a few small-scale appearances of doves and rabbits. Five minutes into the performance the lights dimmed, and a man wheeled an upright box just over five-feet tall onto the stage. The box had the figure of a woman painted onto a door in the front of the box. A hole was cut out where the woman's head should be. Esmerelda walked up to the box as the stagehand left the stage taking the pedestal with him. She opened the door and pulled out three swords.

"Now is the time for a volunteer," she said.

Michael's hand shot into the air, his bottom raised several inches off the seat. His enthusiasm shocked even himself. From the moment Esmerelda first appeared on stage, he had been transfixed. He followed every movement she made without blinking. Her every gesture was poetry in motion. The glint of her jewels in the stage lights, and the flashing of her coins only served to him as a most unwelcome distraction.

"My, you are an eager one," Esmerelda said. She waved her hand, motioning Michael to join her on the stage. "You are brave too, I am hoping."

Michael stood and stumbled forward as Red pushed him from behind. He didn't take his eyes off Esmerelda. His knees were gelatin as she took him by the hand leading him to stand beside her on the stage.

"Please to tell me your name," she said.

It took Michael a moment to realize she had spoken to him, and a moment longer to realize he was expected to respond.

"Michael," he finally managed to say.

"Michael," she repeated. "If you would be examining this sword and letting these people know it is a real sword."

Michael took the sword and held it in his hands. He turned it over and tested its weight. "It feels real to me," he said. "Though I don't hold too many swords."

He felt the heat of the light on his face as a few people in the audience chuckled. It was difficult to see the crowd, but he managed to make out Red and Sara wearing huge smiles on their faces.

"I would be hoping not," Esmerelda said. She took the sword back from Michael's hand and walked over to stand beside the box. "As you see, this box is not being very large." She grabbed a handle on the side of the box and walked in a circle providing the audience a view of the apparatus from each angle. "It is just big enough for me to stand inside it."

She let go of the handle and turned again toward Michael.

"Michael, these swords are for you. You are to be stabbing me with them while I am locked inside the box," She said and handed all three swords to him.

"You want me to do what?" he said.

Several more people in the audience laughed. Esmerelda almost did as well. She had to put her hand in front of her mouth to hide her smile.

"Stab me with the swords," she said. "But wait until I am inside the box and tell you I am ready. Now, if you would be so kind to help me into the box." She held out her hand for Michael.

Michael felt himself blush as he took her hand and helped her into the box. He hoped that the sweat he felt on his palm as he held her hand was hers and not his. He fought the urge to let go of her slender fingers and wipe his palm on his jeans. Once she was situated inside the box, she told him to close and latch the door. He fumbled with the latch, only able to use one hand while trying to hold the swords in his other.

Esmerelda's face appeared from the cutout above the female figure. One of her hands came out of another hole cut into the side of the box.

"There is a slit on your side of the box. Please be putting the first sword through it," she said.

Michael's hands were shaking as he tried to slide the sword's point through the narrow opening. Finally, he managed to get it slotted in. He pushed on the sword's hilt until it met resistance. He felt her movements through vibrations in the sword.

"The sword is now against my hip," she announced to the audience. "Now, Michael, you are needing to take a deep breath and push it all the way through me."

Michael took a deep breath and pushed the sword, first tentatively, then with his full weight behind it. At first he felt resistance, which gave way suddenly. His shoulder rammed against the wood.

Thunk.

The tip of the sword emerged from a slot on the opposite side of the box. Esmerelda grunted. She grimaced as if the sword went through her body.

"Are you okay?" Michael shouted, momentarily forgetting that this was all an act. He hurried around to the front of the box. There was more laughter from the audience. Esmerelda had to hide her mouth behind the cutout to keep her own amusement from showing.

She had him shove a sword through a similar slot on the other side of the box, and a third that was located in the back. The final sword came through the front of the box right where her chest should have been.

She gave a small shriek instead of a grunt this time, and Michael hurried back to the front of the box again.

"Before you are asking, Michael, I am fine," she said before he had a chance to speak. The audience laughed louder than any other time in the performance so far.

Michael felt his face redden again. *Why do I keep embarrassing myself around girls?* He took a step away from the box, unsure what to do with himself while the audience clapped.

"There is one more thing I am needing you to be doing," she said. She spoke through gritted teeth as if each syllable caused nearly unbearable agony. "Take me by the hand and be spinning the box to show audience that there is nowhere for me to be hiding."

Michael rubbed his now very sweaty palm on his pants before taking her hand. He walked around the stage in a circle like she had done moments before turning the box around. Halfway through the spin, during that brief moment when he was unable to see the audience, everything went dark. The world began to swirl and spin. Unseen hands pulled him through the wall of the box like it was made of nothing more substantial than smoke. "In you go, funny boy," Esmerelda whispered in his ear. He thought it was her, but he couldn't be sure, she didn't sound quite right and the whole world seemed somehow wrong.

As he came back to his right mind he found himself staring out of the box at the audience. Esmerelda quickly pulled the swords out, threw them to the floor and flung open the door. She reached inside and, grabbing Michael by the hand, helped him out of the box. He was still bewildered as she pulled him down into a bow.

First Red, then Sara, and soon the whole audience gave the performance a standing ovation.

"Michael, ladies and gentlemen," Esmerelda said. She let go of Michael's hand and nudged him back toward his seat. Michael stepped off the stage and stumbled back to the bleacher entirely unsure of what just happened. He felt Red slap him on the back. He nearly fell out of his seat.

***

"You have got to tell me how you did that," Red said. He walked backwards in front of Michael toward the big top at the end of the midway. "Were you in on it? How did you know what to do?"

"Look, I don't know," Michael said. "It just sort of happened."

"What do you mean it just happened? Come on, I'm your best friend," Red pleaded. He stumbled as one of his feet slipped on a discarded popcorn box.

Michael reached out and grabbed one of his flailing arms, but Red weighed too much for him. The two fell on the trampled grass.

"Steam roller!" Michael yelled. He crossed his arms in front of his chest and rolled over Red. The two lay side-by-side on the ground laughing. The crowd, forced to walk around the two boys, gave them disapproving looks.

"I can't believe I'm willing to be seen in public with you two," Sara said. She kicked Michael in the arm as the two friends stood back up.

"You're embarrassed to be seen with us?" Michael said rubbing his arm. "You're just a little girl that follows us around like a lost puppy."

"Whatever," Sara said, her face flush. She gave a momentary glance at Red. She spun around and stomped ahead of them into the tent, turning off to the one side behind the bleachers as soon as she went through the opening. Hidden in the shadows and surrounded by the scuffling feet of people taking their seats, she wiped her eyes dry with the hem of her t-shirt.

"Why do you always have to give her such a hard time?" Red said.

"She's my sister. She can take it," Michael said.

"I don't know. I think that really upset her."

"She's got thick skin," Michael said. He put his arm around Red's shoulders and together they walked through the tent's

26

opening. They didn't notice Sara standing just a few feet away in the dark beneath the bleachers. "I don't know why she insists on hanging around with us all the time anyway."

In the last few minutes before the big show, the circus squeezed a few additional dollars out of the waiting crowd by offering elephant, camel, and pony rides inside the three rings. Along the edge, between the stands and the animal rides, were souvenir and refreshment stands. Candy butchers weaved their way expertly through the crowd, hawking their treats. As the Snyders and Lagoses made their way to their seats, an announcement said the show would start in five minutes.

Lights, ropes, and various safety equipment hung from the scaffolding encircling the three rings. The animal trainers ushered those still waiting in lines back to their seats. Stagehands cleared away their equipment and the managers of the souvenir and refreshment stands wheeled their carts out of the tent. The lights dimmed as the last stragglers found their way to their seats.

Sara squeezed her way past Michael in their third row seats and sat down on the other side of Red, away from her brother.

"Hey," she said.

"Hey. Listen," Red said. "Don't worry about what Michael said. He's just…"

"Forget about it," Sara said cutting him off. "Let's just enjoy the circus."

The tent flaps were lowered and the lights went dark. A deep booming voice reverberated through the darkness, shaking the very insides of the capacity crowd. Spotlights waved wildly around the stands.

"Ladies and gentlemen, boys and girls of all ages. Welcome to the Circus Paenultimus," the announcer said.

The spotlights stopped their dance and focused on one end of the wide tent. Animals and their trainers, clowns, acrobats, and jugglers paraded into the tent. A band from the other end broke into an overly goofy version of *Entrance of the Gladiators*. Sara leaned forward in her seat to get a better look, absent-mindedly pushing off Red's leg with one hand as she did so. She jerked her hand back, hoping he hadn't noticed.

"Please direct your attention to the center ring for the master of ceremonies, the illustrious and illustrated ringmaster, the grand general and devious director of the Circus Paenultimus: Rinthim Straub," the announcer's voice bellowed.

The spotlights shone on a tall figure striding purposefully toward the center of the ring. He too wore a purple jacket with matching slacks, but they were much fancier and ornate than any Red had seen so far. The material shimmered with embossed symbols and intricate designs. His jacket sleeves, rolled up beyond his elbows, revealed sleeves of brightly colored tattoos. His round-rimmed glasses reflected the light making it look like he had two glowing circles where his eyes should have been. High cheek bones over sunken cheeks stuck out from underneath his glasses. He was weak chinned and wide mouthed with flapping lips like the collars of a disco jacket framing his wide mouth. Red thought he looked like a piranha.

Rinthim Straub took off his gray and purple striped hat and spun it between the fingers of his left hand. His right hand held a baton, which he crossed over his chest as he bowed deeply to the audience. The front and top of his scalp was bald, but the rest of his greasy black hair was long and tied back in a ponytail. He stood and tossed his hat spinning into the air. It flipped twice and fell neatly into place above tiny ears.

"Thank you, thank you, thank you," he said. His voice was thick and oily.

"For centuries untold, traveling circuses have entertained, enthralled, and enticed millions with daring displays of human feats that mortal men find impossible. For generations, the implausible has been shown to be reality. The improbable revealed, and a myriad of humanity's oddities showcased." Straub spun slowly in the center ring with his arms outstretched. He spoke the beginning of each sentence quickly and loudly, slowing down and speaking softer as he went along, stretching out the last few syllables of each pronouncement.

"Our endeavor this afternoon is to continue in that vaunted tradition. We promise to amaze you. We promise to surprise you. We will," he stopped spinning and went silent. The spotlights shut off save a single light that shone at a side entrance. "Thrill you," he finished.

A large tiger, alone in the spotlight, stepped into the nearest ring. It roared once. In the center ring a large hoop burst into flame. The tiger lowered its head and ran full speed toward it. It took only a couple of seconds for the large cat to reach the center ring. It bounded through the flaming hoop just as the lights were brought back up. It leapt to a nearby pedestal and sat on its haunches. Two lions and another tiger were already at their places in the ring. Their trainer, a small man with a long curled mustache, walked in circles between them cracking his whip.

For several minutes the trainer performed with the cats. They jumped through hoops, roared on command and finally left the ring with their front paws on the shoulders of the cat in front of them in a conga line. The original cat led the way out with his paws on the trainer's shoulders.

Red watched jugglers, clowns, and other acts each make their attempt to thrill the audience. Following a brief intermission, a trainer walked several elephants through a particularly boring performance. The elephants left the ring in a long line as well, each one holding the tail of the one in front with their trunk. Following the elephants, all three rings were filled with clowns. They acted out a baseball game as the announcer read the poem *Casey at the Bat*. For a moment, Red was caught up in their silly, exaggerated motions, until he remembered that at the end of the poem Casey struck out and dashed the hopes of Mudville. He was thrown back to his own less than stellar performance the previous night. He was reliving that final pitch when he felt an elbow at his side.

"Hey look. Isn't that Michael's new girlfriend?" Sara said loudly so that her brother would be sure to hear her.

Red looked up and saw three acrobats swinging on wires high in the air. There was no safety net underneath them. It definitely looked to him like one of them was the magician from the sideshow earlier. Instead of a magician's outfit, she wore a tight trapeze suit and a scarf tied around her head. She hung by her legs from a man on a swing. As he swung her toward the center of the room, a woman swung toward them from the other side. The man released the girl. She rolled through the air with her knees tucked under her chin, and right as Red thought she would not be able to make it, she unfurled herself and clasped the hands of the woman.

"The Hibbard Family Gypsy Flyers," the announcer said. "Luca, Nadya and their lovely daughter Esmerelda come all the way from Romania with their high-flying acrobatics."

"That is definitely her," Red said.

Since sitting down in the bleachers, Michael had been lost in his own thoughts as well. He had been replaying the final scene with the magician and her spinning box. *What could it have been if it wasn't magic?* He kept asking himself. There just didn't seem to be any other option he could come up with. He was outside the box, then he felt hands and a jerk, sudden darkness and then poof - there he was inside the box looking out at the audience. Red jabbed him in the side.

"I said, there's your girlfriend," Sara said leaning across Red.

"She's not my girlfriend, and I told you I never saw her before," Michael said.

"So you really aren't going to tell us how you did that trick then?" Red asked.

Michael rolled his eyes. The crowd gasped. Turning back toward the show Michael almost leapt out of his seat. Esmerelda was barely hanging onto her mother's hand by the tips of her fingers. Her legs scissored wildly in the air as she tried to bring her other hand up. It took several seconds and a full arc of the swing before she managed to grasp her mother's wrist. The audience let out their held breath simultaneously as Esmeralda's feet touched down on a small landing in the scaffolding.

The lights went off quickly and the band, caught off guard by the sudden ending, sputtered to life out of sync. As the band finally got into rhythm, the ringmaster made his way hurriedly into a spotlight in the center ring.

"We hope you have all enjoyed the show! We have done our best to impress. You've seen daring feats, and even. ..." He paused and gestured toward the scaffold where Esmerelda was making her way down. "Moments of dire distress. Please, if you enjoyed the show, tell your friends and tell your foes – to come see us, the Circus Paenultimus.

"Performances will be held nightly throughout the week, and two shows each Saturday and Sunday before we must sadly speed our separate ways," Straub said quickly as the full house lights came on and the tent's flaps were thrown wide.

Coyote Runs

"**D**onal, I'm going to ride back with Emily and Alexander," Claire said as the two families walked through the field filled with cars. "Take Red with you and pick up the hotdogs and hamburgers, we'll get everything else ready for tonight."

"Will do," Donal said. He gave a quick salute to his wife. He and Red stopped at their car as the rest walked on to the Lagoses minivan.

"Good, this gives us a chance to have a baseball chat," Donal said once they sat down in the car.

Red felt the hair on the back of neck stand at attention. He absolutely did not want to have this conversation. He just wanted yesterday done and forgotten.

"Look, I just screwed up. I don't know what happened," Red said.

It was just like that time he and Michael were playing in the woods. They were trying out their homemade slingshots made of a cut-up inner tube when they spotted a paper wasp nest in a tree. They could not resist testing their marksmanship with such a fine target. Red had been the first to make a hit. A black hole appeared on the gray nest. The two boys gave a high five as the nest fell at their feet. Michael had taken off like a firecracker at the first angry buzz, but Red had stood there immobilized as the cloud of wasps swarmed his bare legs. It took several seconds and several dozen stings before he could make his legs work again.

"Are you talking about last night?" Donal asked.

"Oh," Red said caught up in the memory. "I thought that was what you wanted to talk about."

"Don't worry about that, it happens to the best of us," his dad said.

Red was sure it would never have happened to his dad. He kept silent, hoping his dad would forget he mentioned it.

"What I wanted to talk about was next year. You know Michael will have aged out of the under-sixteen league."

"Yeah," Red said. He wasn't sure where this conversation was going.

"Well, Alex asked me if I would consider taking over as coach." Donal eased the car into the traffic heading back toward town and the grocery store.

"Why would he ask you? You aren't going to do it are you?"

"Why shouldn't I? You're not embarrassed of your old man are you?" Donal asked.

"I'm not even sure I'm going to play next year," Red said. He had no idea where those words came from. The thought hadn't crossed his mind, at least not that he was aware of, until the words were out of his mouth. They hung in the air as his father drove down the highway.

"Why?" Donal asked. "Is this because of the game last night?"

"No," Red said. "It's not that. I'm not sure why I said that. It's just that next year is still a long way off. I just haven't thought about it is all."

"Fair enough," his dad said.

Red tried to imagine his dad as coach. He was a little worried that everyone might think that the only reason he started every game was because he was the coach's son. But then again, the other assistant coach was Bill Weather. His son Riley desperately wanted to play shortstop even though he was scared to death of a line drive and couldn't read a ground ball to save his life. Red was also sure that if Bill was the coach, then he would no doubt start Riley each game and blame every other kid on the team when Riley chalked up error after error.

"I guess you would be a pretty good coach," Red said. "You would be better than Riley's dad anyway."

Donal laughed, reached across the seat and slapped the bill on Red's hat. It fell down over his eyes, pushing his ears out.

"Dad, quit it," Red said. He laughed along with his father, despite himself, and they talked strategies and possible player positions for the rest of the drive to the grocery store.

***

"Are you sure you don't need a hand getting things ready?" Emily asked as she leaned out of the passenger window when they let Claire off at her house.

"No, I'm fine. I just have a couple quick things to take care of. Come on over whenever you're ready," Claire said.

She fumbled with her keys, worried despite her words that she wouldn't have enough time to get everything in order before they returned.

The house was spotless inside, as always. She made sure of

it. She had grown up in a messy home. Messy both literally and figuratively. Her parents had been hoarders, even saving years of old newspapers until they piled up like snowdrifts in the den, leaving only a path to the couch and to the television where her father sat from the moment he got home until the moment he lumbered off to bed. Although he had never beat her or hit Claire, her father had found ways to be subtler in his abuse. He never missed an opportunity to point out her mistakes, tell her she was stupid, spoiled, and not worth the cost of the food he slaved at his crappy job just to put on her plate. Her mother didn't make her feel any more welcome either. She was too timid to stand up to her husband and constantly kept her eyes focused on her toes. She made Claire feel like a burden and a shame. Claire shared her mother's timidity, and one of her worst nightmares was that she would one day turn into the same woman.

At the first opportunity, Claire did what she had always wished her parents would do with the trash, she threw herself out. The day after she graduated high school she took a job as a waitress at a roadside diner and rented the cheapest apartment she could find. She vowed to make sure no one ever saw any kind of mess in her life, neither literal nor figurative.

She took her time going through every room in the house. She kept a mental checklist of where everything should be, one that she ran through anytime company was expected. Her and Donal's bedroom was fine, but she ran her fingers behind a picture frame on the dresser just to make sure there was no dust. Satisfied, she went through the living room and the kitchen, fastidiously rearranging photographs and various bric-a-brac. She saved the second bath, the one that Red used, and his bedroom for last. There was always something there that needed to be tidied up.

She picked up Red's catcher's mask from the bathroom floor and took it to his room. She placed it gently into the bin beside his closet where all his baseball gear was stored and was surprised to find he had actually made his bed that morning. She walked over and sat down on the side of the bed and picked up a photo from his nightstand. It was her favorite family picture. Emily had snapped it of all three of them one Sunday during a picnic in the park. It reminded her of one of the photos that was already in the frame when you brought it home from the store. A perfect family in a perfect place, everyone seemed so happy.

She was getting the paper plates out of the pantry when the doorbell rang. She hurried through the front room, looking it over one more time as she did, and opened the door for the Lagoses.

Emily handed her a plastic shopping bag of potato chips and salsa.

"I'm going back to the car to get the pie," she said. "And just in time too. I see Donal and Red coming over the hill."

Claire looked down the road and saw their car coming toward the driveway. From the other direction she heard a logging truck rumbling down the dirt road toward the bend at the bottom of their driveway where the pavement begins. She could tell from the sound that it was going way too fast. It sped down the hill, bouncing from one side of the rutted road to the other. She watched it careen around the corner. As the chains snapped and the logs flew off the trailer, the shopping bag slipped from her fingers. The glass jar of salsa tumbled out of the bag and shattered on the concrete. The porch and her shoes were splattered in a brilliant red.

***

The sky was a cloudless blue edging toward purple. A lone coyote sat at the crest of a knoll on the Snyder farm, her fur was gray and mottled. It was thinning in large patches across her flanks and stomach. Her pitch black eyes were rimmed with a pale-pink inflammation. Across the fields and across the road was the forest she called home, the forest where The Hermit had claimed mastery over her years ago. He had for many years now neglected his duty. The djinn, like herself, roamed the woods and fields like common animals each one slowly wasting away, the long years taking their toll on their borrowed bodies. She was no longer entirely sure where the animal left off and her own self began.

As she sat sentinel on the small hill, she spied down the road in one direction while her ears were cocked toward the forest's edge in the other. She felt a change come over her. A renewed sense of purpose and meaning welled up inside her chest. It felt like life. She imagined she could feel her gray coat growing full once again. She curled back her lips and growled, snarling for the sheer pleasure of it. To once again have something meaningful to do was as intoxicating to her as the animal pleasure of a fresh kill, the copper flavor of warm blood trickling down her gullet.

The logging truck she had been listening to coming down the side of the mountain for the last ten minutes neared the edge of the woods just as the Snyder's car came around one of the many curves in the road. It was just about half a mile away. The timing could not have been better. When The Hermit had sent them off to find spirits to sacrifice to the interstice, she had claimed this man for herself.

She threw back her head and howled. A black cloud of birds rose out of the hay field across the road like a small tornado spinning out of the tall grass. The birds coalesced into a swirling knot and sped off toward where the logging road entered the forest.

The coyote took off down the hill. She dashed back and forth between scrub pines and prickly thistles, covering whole yards with each bounding stride toward the sharp curve where the dirt met the asphalt. The logging truck rumbled out of the shadow of the trees as the phalanx of birds swarmed the cab. *Thwump, thwump, thwump.* Several of the birds sacrificed themselves against the windshield. Others flew through the open windows and set themselves upon the hapless driver. He frantically waved and swatted at the birds. He slammed on the truck's brakes, forgetting the nearly 40 tons of pine logs mere feet behind his head. The truck jittered, skidding down the dirt road. The load was too much. The brakes failed and the truck sped unhindered down the hill, bouncing from one side of the road to the other. The birds flew out of the cab and off into the forest as quickly as they had arrived. Their job accomplished.

"Dad, look out!" Red shouted. He pointed toward a coyote leaping out of the roadside brush. It landed fifteen feet in front of their car, only halfway between their car and their driveway.

Donal slammed his foot on the brake, screeching to a halt. The coyote bared its teeth and ran toward the car. It leapt onto the hood, its claws scritched and scratched across the slick hood as it tried to find purchase. It was large for a coyote, almost entirely obscuring their view. It glared, first into Donal's eyes, then into Red's. There was a glimmer of triumph reflected in the shining black eyes. Its lips rippled as it bared its teeth and snarled before bounding over the top of the car and taking off behind them.

"Oh no," Donal said. All the color drained from his face.

At the bottom of the hill, the truck driver pulled the steering wheel hard to the right, throwing himself onto the passenger seat. The turn in the road was too sharp. The momentum of the heavy load on the trailer too great. The truck managed the sharp turn, but the trailer jackknifed on its hitch. The whole assembly flipped on its side.

Even as Donal spoke, his fingers found the release button on his seatbelt. He threw his body across Red's.

Over his father's shoulder Red saw the chains holding the logs snap like old rubber bands. The logs flew off the trailer, still impelled by their tremendous inertia coming down the hill. They twisted and flipped through the air toward their car. The first log fell like a hammer on the car's front bumper. The entire vehicle bounced off the asphalt and tilted forward. The second log spun slowly toward the windshield. Red felt like a baseball hurtling toward home plate. The log spun around like a bat swung by an invisible giant with his eyes on the outfield wall.

Time slowed. Red watched the log hit the windshield. Cracks like spider webs spread tinkling across the glass. He heard a metallic crunch. The whole world went black.

The Hospital

Red had never experienced darkness like this before. It was heavy and dense like liquid. He swam through it, soared through it. He felt buoyant and free, but soon he grew anxious and chilled. The dark took care of him, though. It wrapped around him like a heavy blanket. It became comfort and warmth, a cocoon of contentment and safety. The darkness was his security from all danger and harm.

He slept.

Red drifted in and out of consciousness for what seemed like lifetimes. It was both beauty and bliss. Eventually the sedatives began to wear off and he became aware of the external universe once again. Slowly, feeling returned to him. His feet tingled as if they had fallen asleep, they were tightly wrapped in warm dry cloth. He tried to wiggle his toes, but he couldn't make them move. The tingling moved up his legs, then to his hands and arms. Soon his whole body tingled and tickled. He laughed involuntarily, stirred in the hospital bed and cracked open his eyes.

He saw the coyote staring back at him, snarling at him. Saliva dripped from long fangs between quivering lips. Its black eyes burned into Red's soul. The eyes were deep wells, his every instinct strained for him to lean further into them to see what mystery lie at their depths. Red fell into them, lost. Deep down was movement, a twisting, spinning shape speeding toward him. He gasped. One moment it was the shape of a baseball bat, the next a pine log. It flickered back and forth – bat, log, bat, log, bat, log – as it came hurtling toward him.

He squeezed his eyes shut again. The vision disappeared. He felt cold and clammy. His breathing slowed and steadied. He became aware of beeping and buzzing around him. Hazarding to open his eyes again he found himself lying cold and sweating in a hospital bed. He looked down at his body. It was wrapped almost entirely in bandages, and the parts that weren't wrapped were in casts. Wires and tubes ran from what seemed like every part of his body to a wide array of machines and drip bags.

His eyes soon grew heavy once again, and he sank back into sleep.

It was the rhythmic beeping of the monitors that greeted Red as he came to again. As he woke he realized someone was holding his hand. He opened his eyes. There was no coyote. Turning his head to one side, he saw his mother sitting beside his bed. She gently stroked his hand.

"Hi honey," Claire said. She smiled at him. She released his hand and cupped his face in her hands, rubbing the tips of her fingers across his brow. "How are you feeling?"

"I - I think I'm okay," Red said. He tried to sit up, but the effort made him dizzy. He rested his head back down on the pillow.

"No, don't try to sit up. Just lie there for now," she said. "The nurse should be here in a little while. You need to try and eat something when she comes, it will make you feel better."

"What day is it?" he asked. "How long have I been out?"

"It's Monday morning. You've been asleep since the ambulance brought you here last night."

As Red lay drifting in and out of sleep, he let his mother softly pet his face. *It must have been the drugs that caused me to have such a weird dream,* he thought.

***

For Red, everything about hospital food was terrible. It was all either mashed, a liquid, or some type of gelatinous goo. The only thing that had any flavor to it was the applesauce, and all Red could think of as he swirled it around the bowl with his spoon after giving it a tentative taste, was that it looked and tasted like cinnamon flavored snot.

Red was doing his best to swallow the horrid stuff as the doctor came into the room.

"Ah, Red. Good to see you up and eating," the doctor said. He punched something into a tablet computer, pressed the power button on the side, and dropped the computer into a large pocket of his white jacket.

"I'm Dr. Cayson," the doctor said. "I'll be the one in charge of your care while you are with us."

"Thanks," Red said. He felt stronger and more aware after he had some food inside him.

"Mrs. Snyder," he said, turning toward Red's mother. "I hope you are holding up alright. I know this is a lot to go through. We do have a multi-faith chaplain in residence if you wish to speak with her."

Claire pulled a tissue out of the purse on her lap and nodded at the doctor as he spoke.

"No, no. I'm fine," she said. Her voice was shaky.

Dr. Cayson gave her a brief nod and rested one hand on her shoulder. Claire let out a brief sob at the touch.

"I know everything is going to be okay. I'm just glad Red wasn't as badly hurt as Donal."

"Dad! What's wrong with Dad?" Red asked. He pushed the food tray away, knocking over his cup of half-drank orange juice. "Can I go see him, is he okay?"

"Oh Red, look what you've done," Claire said. She grabbed a handful of napkins from the tray and bent down trying to daub the orange juice off his blanket.

"Don't worry about it, it's nothing. It was just an accident," she said sweetly, realizing that her nervousness might have came across as anger to Red and the doctor.

The doctor hadn't noticed. He was busy looking over the displays on the machines encircling Red. He gave a cursory examination of Red's casts and bandages, pulled the tablet out of his pocket and typed on it for several seconds.

"Everything seems on the up and up," Cayson said cheerfully. "Are you in too much pain?" He asked Red.

"No, I'm sore all over, but it isn't too bad," Red said. He watched as his mother threw away the wet napkins and sat back down in her chair, wringing her hands.

"That's good. We have you on some pretty strong pain medicine. It should keep the pain where you can manage it, but it also keeps you pretty groggy," Cayson said. He adjusted a knob underneath a drip bag and looked up at Red again. "Are you sleeping alright?"

"I've been having some really weird dreams," Red said. "They aren't nightmares or anything, just weird. Is that bad?"

"No, that's perfectly normal. The medicine often gives people strange dreams." The doctor once again dropped the tablet into his pocket and sat on the edge of Red's bed. "Now, let's talk about your injuries."

Red scooted himself up as best he could in the bed.

"Your right leg is broken, the one in the cast. The left has a hairline fracture. Luckily the dashboard took most of the force of the logs. Several of the bones in your right foot also have hairline fractures. That is why the cast covers your foot as well as your leg. You are going to have to rely on a wheelchair for a little while. You have a compound fracture in your left forearm. That is going to take the longest to heal of all your injuries. You got hit pretty hard in the head as well. You were concussed, but it doesn't seem too major. You have some bruising across your chest, and you'll probably have some bruising crop up almost everywhere over the next couple of days. All-in-all though, you are lucky to be alive, and you should even be able to go home in a day or two after we make sure there are no internal injuries that we haven't noticed yet. Although I think that is unlikely; you are one tough young man," Dr. Cayson said. He smiled.

Red had trouble following the doctor through the litany of injuries, nodding along as he listed each one. Red ran his fingers across the rough cast on his leg. *If I'm this bad, how bad is my dad?*

"So, how is my dad?" Red asked him.

Claire and the doctor shared a quick glance. Claire nodded.

"I can tell him," she said. She turned toward Red and folded his right hand into hers.

"Red," she said. She looked at his hands for a moment, then at the window behind him. "Red, your dad isn't doing real well. He was hurt a lot worse than you were."

"He is going to be alright though isn't he? He has to be okay. He is going to coach the baseball team next year," Red said.

Claire pulled one of her hands away and grabbed a tissue from her lap. She daubed it on the corner of her eyes. Red watched her close her eyes. Her shoulders began to bounce up and down.

"Mom," Red said softly. He brought his left hand over as best he could and laid it on top of her hand that still rested on his. A sharp spasm of pain ran up his left arm, but he ignored it.

"Red, he is in pretty bad shape. The doctors think that there is a good chance he will pull out of it, but they don't know for sure. They said that the best they can do is heal his injuries and that would give him his best chance."

"Pull out of what?" Red asked.

"He is in a coma," she said. She squeezed his hand tightly and looked deep into his eyes, putting on a weak smile. Her eyes glistened as tears welled up inside them.

"So, when the doctors fix everything up, he'll wake up? Right?" Red asked. He turned toward Dr. Cayson. "That is what you are going to do isn't it? You are going to heal him, and then he'll wake back up, right?"

The doctor looked down at Claire who remained silent.

"Will somebody answer me?" Red asked. He could hear the monitoring machines began beeping faster.

"Red, that is the best we can do," Dr. Cayson said. "It is impossible to tell for sure what is going on inside the mind of someone in a coma. Our instruments tell us that his brain isn't dead, but he isn't waking up and not responding to any stimulus. Often people stay that way until their body has a chance to fully recover. Sometimes though, and you need to be prepared for this as a possibility, they don't wake up."

Red looked at his mother and could tell from the very first glance: She not only accepted this as a possibility, but that she fully expected it. *She believes Dad won't wake up.* He knew that if it was the other way around, his dad would never have given up hope. His parents were opposites in almost every respect, this one particularly. Red wasn't sure which way to think. Both world views had always competed in his mind. He was half his mother and half his father. *On one hand, I don't want to give up any hope if there is a chance Dad could pull through. While, on the other hand, why should I risk being hurt even more if he doesn't?*

Dr. Cayson said his goodbyes and left the room, promising to return around lunchtime. For the next few minutes Red and Claire laid and sat silently together, still holding hands. They both looked around the room, or out the window, or stared at the linoleum on the floor, averting their gaze from each other. Each time their eyes accidentally met, they pulled them away quickly. Red came to a decision. While he loved both his mother and father equally, he realized it was the strength and bravery of his father he wanted to emulate. *I will not give up on him. Not as long as there is a single breath inside either of us.*

***

"Everybody awake and decent?" Alexander Lagos asked unnecessarily loudly. He stuck his head around the partially opened hospital door. He opened the door and ushered in Emily, Michael and Sara. Michael swung a canvas tote bag in one hand.

"Alex, Emily. Thanks for coming by," Claire said. "I'm sure Red will be glad to see you two as well," she added to Sara and Michael.

"Hey," Red said. He pushed himself up further in the bed with his right hand. "I'm sorry we messed up the cookout."

Sara and Michael both hesitated. They stood slightly behind their parents. Michael looked up at his mother. Emily put her hand on the back of his shoulder and gently prodded him forward.

"Go ahead," she said.

Red felt awkward, his best friend didn't want to come near him. Michael looked Red up and down, then tentatively walked up beside the bed.

"Don't worry about it. It's no biggie, just hot dogs and hamburgers," Michael said. He wouldn't look Red in the eye. He kept looking at the bandages and casts wrapped around Red. Sara still stood beside her father.

"Not just any hot dogs," Red said, he felt no less nervous than Michael looked. "We were going to have the big thick ones filled with cheese."

"Yeah, those are pretty good," Michael said. He finally managed to look Red in the eyes. "So, you are going to be okay aren't you?"

"Yeah, I'm only going to have to be here a couple of days," Red said. "I get to have a wheelchair for a few weeks though."

"That's pretty cool," Michael said. The longer they talked the more comfortable they each began to feel.

"Geez. You do look awful," Michael said. He wore a sideways smile, the same as his father Alexander often wore when teasing.

"Just wait until the bruising sets in, I'm going to look like a purple dinosaur wearing a red wig," Red said smiling. Having Michael joke around made him feel better than any amount of sympathy or icy pity.

"Don't listen to him, you look fine Red," Sara said. She came up to the bedside, elbowing Michael aside.

"It's okay Sara," Red said.

"No it's not okay," she said to Red, then turned to Michael and gave him a scowl. "You can't just tell someone in the hospital that they look awful, it's just rude."

"Good grief, I was just joking. Grow a sense of humor already," Michael said, he bumped his shoulder against Sara.

"Seriously it's fine," Red said.

"Michael's right though Red, you do look awful," Alexander said. He came up behind his children and pulled them apart.

"Dad!" Sara yelled. She turned and tried to smack her father.

"Well," Alexander said. He laughed and twisted away from Sara. Her slap landed on his shoulder. "There is no sense lying to the boy, he does look bad."

Sara groaned and rolled her eyes. She turned her back on her father as everyone else in the room, including Red and Claire, laughed. It felt good to laugh. The normalcy of it was the best medicine Red could have hoped for. It renewed his hope that everything was going to be alright.

"Seriously though," Alexander said to Red. "You doing okay?"

"Yeah, I'm fine," Red said.

"Here, we brought this for you," Michael said. He handed Red the tote bag and plopped down into a chair near the foot of the bed.

Red opened the bag. Inside was a portable DVD player and nearly a dozen old movies.

"We thought you might get bored lying around all day," Emily said.

"Thanks, this is awesome," Red said. He shuffled through the collection of sci-fi and action movies.

"Are you kids going to be okay for a while?" Claire asked Red. "I'm going to take Alex and Emily to see your dad."

"We'll be fine," Red said. He was already deep in conversation with Sara and Michael.

As soon as their parents left the room Sara threw her arms around Red and burst into tears. A digging pain shot from his neck down his arm.

"Wow, Sara, get a grip. You would think it was our dad in a coma," Michael said before realizing how insensitive such a careless remark might be. "Um, sorry Red."

"No, it's fine. It's good," Red said. Sara's arms around his neck felt better than the narcotic daze he had been in since he woke. He felt cold again the moment she released the embrace. *Does she like me too?* He wondered. *Or is she only being kind?*

"Thanks," he said. He decided to take a chance and grabbed one of her hands as she was pulling away. She didn't pull it away and squeezed his back. Their eyes met and he held his breath. "I really needed that."

Sara pulled her hands away suddenly, and picked up her backpack. Red looked at Michael to see what his reaction was, but he was leaning back in the chair staring at the ceiling.

Sara pulled a board game out of the backpack and set it up on the rolling bed table. They lost themselves in the game, laughing and arguing over the rules.

***

Emily watched Claire's hands shake almost imperceptibly as she shut the hospital door behind them. *What can you say?* She knew she had to come up with words of support or comfort, which was hard enough when the person was an average friend or coworker, but this was Claire, this was Donal. They were more than just friends, they were family. It felt like her own brother was lying in a coma.

She had tried talking it over with Alexander last night as they lay in bed, red and blue lights still flashed through their bedroom window throwing shadows of policemen and investigators on their walls. Their house was only a few hundred yards from the scene of the accident. They talked about the years they spent getting to know the Snyders, in particular the months it took for Claire to open up even the tiniest bit with them. It hadn't been much, Emily knew, but it was enough that she felt she knew Claire better than anyone in the world except, perhaps, for Donal. Claire even asked her to come stay with her one night while Donal was in Chad, covering a conflict, and Red and Michael were at a sleepover.

"I don't think there is too much we have to say," Alexander had said. "We just need to be there for her. I'm having a hard time believing it myself. Of all the dangerous situations he puts himself in, to be nearly killed a few hundred feet from his front door. It's unbelievable."

Emily knew she had to do more than just be there for Claire though. Claire basically defined her entire existence through a Donal tinted lens. Even after all these years it was still hard

51

for Emily to tell where Donal left off and Claire began. *What will she become if Donal passes?*

Back in the hospital hallway, Emily took Claire's trembling hand in hers and put her head on Claire's shoulder.

"There are no words," Emily said. She knew it was true and the right thing to say the moment she said it.

"Thank you," Claire said.

They walked down the cold hospital hallway, Claire's arm in hers. They talked about nothing that really mattered, just vague chit-chat. Alexander, following several steps behind, kept silent. They passed by countless photographs and paintings hanging along the wide hallways. They were always serene, usually rendered in the same muted colors that dominated the color schemes of hospitals and similar institutions worldwide. They were meant to convey calm, quietude and peace. Their purpose so blatantly heavy handed though, that Emily immediately thought despair, death and disease. Their footsteps echoed through corridors that smelled of formaldehyde and industrial cleaner.

"Do you want a minute?" Claire said as they reached Donal's door.

"If you're sure you don't mind," Alexander said. "I wouldn't mind one or two." He slipped past the two women and entered the room.

"How are you really doing?" Emily asked after Alexander was gone.

"I'm doing okay," Claire said. As she spoke, she stared over Emily's shoulder at a large photograph of a waterfall in autumn.

"Really?" Emily said raising her eyebrows. "I would be a basket case."

"I'm just trying to be here for them right now," Claire said. "I don't know what else to do."

"Claire. You know we are always here for you," Emily said. "I love you like my sister. Alex and I are going to be by your side every step of the way."

Claire nodded and the two women stepped into the room. Alexander moved away from the bedside at their approach. Emily noticed his eyes were red, even in the dim light. He had no jokes or quips about Donal's condition.

Emily looked down at Donal. He was barely recognizable. His eyes were closed. His face was swollen and pink.

***

Red, Sara, and Michael had just finished their second game when their parents returned.

"All right Sara, Michael. It's time for us to roll," Alexander said.

"See you tomorrow," Michael said to Red.

"Bye," Sara said. She leaned over and gave Red another hug. The room spun around him, and not just from the pain.

"See ya," he said. *I think she does like me,* he decided. *What is Michael going to think?*

Alexander and Emily waved to Red, and each gave Claire a long hug. As they closed the door, Claire walked over and took the pillows out from behind Red, and fluffed them. She looked a little better and more confident than she had since Red had first awoke.

"There," she said, and placed the pillows behind him. "I think it is high time you got some rest. You've been up for hours."

"Yeah, I'm pretty sleepy," Red said. He scooted down into the warm blanket and rested his cheek against the cool pillows. His brain was full of conflicting ideas and tangled emotions about his father, his mother, and even Sara and Michael. Before he could sort any of them out, he fell asleep.

Smoke and Mirrors

Red woke early the next morning. He lay in the bed with his eyes closed thinking over the last few days. It seemed unreal, like it had happened to somebody else. It felt like a bad movie. If he hadn't been able to hear the machines around him beeping and the people moving about in the hallway outside his room, he would have been able to believe it simply hadn't happened. But he could hear them. Each bleep from the monitors and each squeak of rubber-soled tennis shoes on the floor reinforced the reality.

There was one thing, though, that felt wrong to him. It took him several minutes to finally put his finger on what precisely it was that felt strange. It suddenly hit him. He no longer felt any pain. He felt good.

Red opened his eyes and saw another world.

Each wall, all of the furniture, every piece of equipment was tenuous and wispy like a soft focused and overexposed photograph. Surfaces seemed like flowing liquid or colored smoke shifting underneath glass casings. It was ethereal. It was beautiful.

Red intently examined the chair near the foot of his bed. It somehow managed to look solid and insubstantial at the same time. Smoke-like tendrils flowed underneath the surface. He could see inside the wood frame and gray material inside the cushion. The stuffing was flecked with bits of colored fluff like the lint screen from a clothes dryer. The flowing mass gravitated generally upwards. As it neared the top, the edges of the chair's form became less distinct, showing more and more of the inside, or even through it. The last few tiny wisps that remained lifted off the top and dissipated.

All other thoughts left Red. He forgot about his father, forgot about Sara and Michael, forgot he was in a hospital, and forgot entirely the fact he was in bandages and casts. He sat all the way up and swung his feet over the edge of the bed, and looked around him. The entire room was made of the shifting swirling chaos. Then, he looked down at himself. His casts and bandages were gone.

Unlike the rest of the room, Red's body was not made of the same flowing smoke. His body was whole and unblemished. On top of his skin, a thin layer of blue flame rippled, emitting a slight glow. Red brought his hand up in front of his face and watched as minuscule tongues of blue fire rose off the tips of his fingers.

"Wow," Red said.

He leapt off the bed feeling better than he had ever remembered feeling. He felt like there was nothing he couldn't do, but what he wanted to do at that moment was find a mirror.

He hurried across the room, his bare feet slapping against the floor. Each time his foot made contact with the floor, the blue flames on his skin flowed a short distance across the floor's surface. Where the flames traveled, the floor turned solid, no longer shifting and swirling. When he lifted his foot, the surface returned once again to the fantastic swirling miasma.

Red grabbed the sink in the small bathroom. In his grip the sink turned solid. He looked at the mirror, but couldn't make out his reflection in the insubstantial surface. He reached out with one hand and laid his palm flat against it. Immediately the flames spread out, covering the mirror's surface. It looked, and more importantly worked, like a perfectly ordinary mirror.

"This is so cool," he said laughing.

His entire body was covered in the flames. They swirled across every inch of him, twisting and spinning ever upward. They tapered off to a white-tipped point about a foot over his head. He turned to one side and watched as the flames trailed his movement like the flame of a candle slid along a table. He was a living fireball.

The window, he remembered. *What is it like outside?* Red left the bathroom and walked across the room toward the window on the other side of his bed. As he drew nearer his bed a thought kept trying break through to his subconscious. It bobbed on the surface of his awareness like a fishing float on the surface of a pond. It would be there for a moment, then it would briefly disappear underneath the dark waters only to rise bobbing again to float on the surface of his mind. Suddenly, understanding sprang on him as if the fish had given up on the bait and flew out of the water straight into his arms. *There's something on the bed. A body. There's a body on the bed.*

Red stumbled. He fell forward and caught himself on the edge of the mattress. He stared at the face only a few inches from his. It was beyond familiar. He knew the messy close-cropped red hair. He recognized every freckle dappled across the young face. He knew every eyelash, every crease in that skin. There was the thin scar on its chin. A scar he remembered getting when he fell out of a swing when he had been nine years old. He was staring at himself.

He stood up and examined the body from further back. One arm and one leg were in casts. There were bandages wrapped around the other arm that lay outside the sheet. No blue flames danced on its surface. It glowed, but only the faintest of silver-tinted glows, even fainter than the other things in the hospital room. He reached out his hand to touch it, but as his fingers neared he felt a strange tingling sensation. He drew them quickly away. The glow seemed to be the brightest near its chest. Looking closer he saw that the light was coming from strands as thin as spider silk. They came from all over the body and knitted together, forming a tight silvery cord just below the body's sternum. Red followed the cord. As he did so, it grew fainter and more translucent.

He reached out for the cord with one hand. At his touch the cord grew thicker and brighter. He gave it a slight pull and felt a tug on his own chest. Red looked down and saw that the other end of the cord ended at his chest as well, spreading out just like the other end. He let go quickly and simply stared at his doppelgänger. He looked over every inch of it, in detail and as a whole. *Am I really that short?* he thought. He would have studied it for hours if something hadn't streaked past the outside of his window.

Red left the Red lying on the bed and walked over to the window. He leaned over the shelf at its base, knocking over a get well card, and looked out. His window was on the second floor overlooking a parking lot. The cars and the pavement were of the same nebulous consistency. Just beyond the parking lot, though, was a small park with a few trees, a stream, and a small decorative pond. He thought that he had known beauty before, but he had been mistaken. This was what centuries of artists had failed to recreate. It was Dali and Picasso and Van Gogh all at once, layered on top of each other. This was at least part the deeper truth their art only hinted at.

The trees and the plants shone nearly as brilliantly as he did, but in every shade of green and brown imaginable. Bright flames of yellows and reds were interspersed artfully around the edges of the park and along the walkways. The shrubs were like the burning bush of Moses, a fire that didn't consume. Orange balls of flame, no larger than softballs, darted through the branches and danced up and down tree trunks. Several more fireballs, these a little more yellow, slowly rolled across the emerald lawn near the edge of the pond. One of these took to the air and circled around the water. It made two tight circles before shooting straight toward Red's window. He ducked out of the way, not taking his eyes off it. He was just able to make out that inside the flames was a robin before it flew past his window and landed on the ledge of the room next door. *If the ones by the pond are birds, then the ones in the trees must be squirrels,* he figured.

Red stood mesmerized at the wonder of it all. He watched as cars pulled into and out of the parking lot. Each person that entered or left the hospital was covered in the same blue flames as him, their intensities varied widely. *Why are they so different?*

A car sped into the parking lot and skidded to a halt in front of the emergency room entrance, just a few feet below and to the right of his own window. A man jumped out of the driver's side door, left it wide open, and ran around the car. He threw open the passenger door, reached in and helped a woman out of the car. She was obviously extremely pregnant and in a lot of pain. Both she and the man burned with a slight glow that seemed to be the most common, but from out of her pregnant belly huge, white-tipped blue flames rose in fitful bursts, each flare sending her into another spasm of pain. She bent over, holding one arm around the man and the other underneath her belly. Red could hear her groan even through his permanently sealed hospital window. The man was having trouble keeping the woman from collapsing. Red watched anxiously as a nurse ran to them from inside the hospital and all three disappeared underneath the carport.

He was so caught up in what was happening outside the window that he hadn't realized there were voices coming from inside his room. He turned around and saw a nurse and a doctor trying to wake the other him up.

"Get back inside!" A voice yelled from the doorway.

Red looked around at the door and saw a man standing there. He glowed brighter than any of the other people he had seen. He looked as bright or even brighter than himself.

"Don't just stand there," he said. "You have to get back inside yourself, or you are going to regret it."

Red looked at himself, then his body on the bed, then up at the doctor who was filling a large syringe out of a brown glass vial.

"How? What do I do? I don't know how to get back," Red said frantically.

The monitoring machines buzzed and beeped wildly, filling the whole room with an angry dissonant clamor. The doctor raised the needle over his head and grasped it with both hands. A small bead of liquid glistened at the needle's long tip.

"My lands," the man at the door said frustratedly. "Fine. Just grab the cord, you do know there is a cord connecting you right?"

Red nodded.

"On three," the doctor said.

"Grab it with both hands and pull," the man said urgently. "One."

Red looked down at his chest and gingerly took the cord between his hands.

"Two."

"Now," the man from the door screamed.

Red squeezed the silver cord tightly and yanked. It jerked him forward like he had grabbed onto the side of a speeding train. It pulled him across the room until he slammed back into the body on the bed.

"Three," the doctor said. He brought down the long needle toward Red's chest.

"Stop!" Red yelled. He tried to push himself away from the doctor's stroke. "I'm awake, don't stick that thing in me!"

The startled doctor nearly fell on top of Red. Grabbing the mattress with one hand, he managed to keep himself from following all the way through with his stroke. Red felt the tip of the syringe touch his chest, but barely pierce it. A small drop of warm blood welled up and a cold bead of sweat rolled down his nose. Red looked toward the door for the strange man. There was no one there.

The doctor and the nurse began arguing. Red laid his head back down on the pillow. The sweat was drying and he became chilled. The various monitors slowly calmed down after several minutes of a panic inducing cacophony, returning to their normal pattern of beeps and blips.

The doctor came over and spoke with him while the nurse changed his drip bag and twiddled with the knobs on the monitors. He couldn't follow what the doctor was asking, but he reassured them that he felt fine now. "I think I just need a nap," he said.

"Good idea," the doctor said. "Rest is what your body needs the most right now."

Red nodded. He wasn't sure sleep sounded that great, to be honest. It seemed every time he closed his eyes he had some kind of fevered dream, but a thought niggled in his mind. *If that was a dream, how could I have known what was going on in the room?* He rolled over as far as he could on his side and faced the window. *And who was that man?* The nurse had added more sedative to his IV, it was soon a struggle for him to keep his eyes open. *I'll figure it out later, after I rest my eyes for a minute.*

Before his eyes closed and he drifted off, the robin flew past the window again. For the briefest of moments, Red was sure he could see tiny yellow flames flowing across its bronze chest.

***

Claire sat in the chair beside Red's bed, ostensibly reading the newspaper. The lead article was about the ongoing police search for Laurel Hollows' very own vigilante. She read the article all the way through, twice, and the only thing that managed to stick in her distracted mind was that the vigilante was an African-American male who called himself 'The Brand.'

She reached over and picked up the coffee she bought from the vending machine outside the waiting room near the elevators. She took a sip, and immediately spat it back out into the cup. It was cold and sour. How long ago had she bought it? *Ten minutes? Two hours?* She couldn't remember. She had just returned to Donal's room with the coffee when a nurse came and told her that Red had a difficult time waking up. Everything was fine, they kept telling her, but she felt she needed to be by Red's side for a while to reassure herself.

Claire went into the bathroom and poured the coffee down the sink. A stranger stared back at her from the mirror. It was her face, her eyes, her nose, and her mouth; but the reflection looked like a pale and ghostly version of herself. Her usually smooth hair was frizzled from sleeping in hospital chairs. She had already removed most of her makeup, but there were a couple of spots she missed that showed like dark stains on her pale freckled face, one on the side of her nose, and another at the edge of her lips. A faint gray smudge, like a watercolor painting that bled, surrounded her eyes giving them a sunken look.

She wetted the corner of a hand towel and wiped the imperfections clean before running a damp hand through her hair.

"Ouch!" She yelled, pulling her fingers through a particularly tangled knot. As she tried to work it free she saw Red stirring in his bed.

"Mom?" Red said. He rubbed the sleep out of his eyes with his good hand. "Is that you?"

"Yes, sweetie. It's me," Claire said and did her best to smile at him from the bathroom doorway. "How are you feeling, any better?"

"Yeah, I'm good," he said. He smiled back at her.

To Claire, Red looked so pathetic lying there in the bed, bruised and wrapped in casts and bandages. The moment he smiled, his eyes sparkled and she felt a warmth fill her body. Her forced smile was replaced with a wide genuine one.

She walked across the room and laid one of her hands on his.

"I love you Red. You know that, don't you?" She asked him. His smile had been enough to assure her of his love, but she felt it necessary to make sure he knew of hers.

"Of course. I love you too," Red said. He furrowed his brow. "Is everything okay?"

"Yes, fine," She lied. Since Red and Donal had been admitted to the hospital she had worn a path in the linoleum between their rooms on opposite ends of the hospital. She had hiked back and forth down the corridors, hardly sleeping. At times, she felt that her feet were pulling her along behind them. Each time she felt about to nod off, she would go out to one of the vending machines to get another cup of weak instant coffee that was only palatable as long as it was still piping hot. The trash cans in each room were filled with the wax paper cups and their acrid aroma.

"How is dad?" Red asked. He pushed himself further up in the bed, her hand fell away from his.

"About the same," she said. "The doctors said that his scans seemed more active than they had since he was admitted. They said that it is a good sign, but I don't know."

"Can we go see him soon?" Red asked.

"The doctor said that as soon as you were awake and felt

up to it, we could get a nurse to push you down there in a wheelchair. But first, I want you to at least try and eat some of that cereal and drink some of that juice before we go." She nodded toward the bed tray near his feet.

"Yeah, okay," Red said.

She rolled the tray up to where Red could reach it. He wolfed down the cereal and drained the entire plastic cup of juice in just a couple of drags on the straw.

"You can take your time," she said as Red turned the cereal bowl up to drink the last dregs of milk in the bottom.

"I'm just starving," he said. "I haven't ate anything since Sunday lunch, and it's what? … Tuesday?"

"Tuesday morning," Claire said. "Just don't try to do too much too fast. I'll go ahead and call the nurse." She rolled the tray away and pressed the call button on the bed's rail. *Why did all this have to happen?* She asked herself as the yellow nurse's light began to blink on the wall above Red's bed. *What are we going to do? I don't know how long I can take this.*

***

It took two nurses and his mother to get Red into the wheelchair. One of his feet stuck out in front of him like a battering ram. One nurse pushed his wheelchair down the hallway while Claire rested one hand on his armrest.

Red looked furtively into each room as they rolled past. Most of them were little pockets of warmth, where families and friends laughed and talked with the hospitalized. Those rooms were bright and warm. Flowers and cards lined nearly every available surface. The sick and injured were surrounded by the familiar and the intimate, as if their loved ones knew

65

instinctively the power inherent in objects filled with love and purpose.

As Red neared the long-term care area things began to change. Many of these rooms were cold and dark, despite the muffled sound and blue flicker of television sets. Those that were in these rooms were alone, forgotten. They had been in the hospital so long that their flowers had withered, their cards faded and fallen. Their friends and colleagues first, then their families, came by less frequently, then eventually they stopped coming at all except on special occasions, like birthdays or holidays. A few rooms, sprinkled here and there along the hallway, were filled with life, but those were the exception that proved the rule.

An old man stood outside the door to one of the cold rooms. He wore a hospital robe and hospital slippers. His left hand hung limply on one side, while his right held onto a drip stand on wheels. An oxygen tank was strapped to the side of the stand. A long plastic tube spiraled around the metal shaft out of the tank like one of the grape vines in the woods near Red's home. The other end of the hose ended in a nose plug that hung over one of the man's ears. It dangled near his chin.

Red stared at the man as he was wheeled past. The man seemed familiar, but he couldn't place where he might have known him from. He winked and nodded at Red, giving him a yellow toothed half smile. *It's the man from the room!* Red wanted to stop and talk to the man, but he didn't know what to say, and he definitely didn't want to say anything in front of his mom or the nurse. They would surely have thought that he was losing it. So, Red just nodded back. As he passed the door, he read the name written beside it, 'Tom Clack.'

Since they had left Red's room, none of them had said a

word. Red had been lost in his own thoughts, thinking about the dream or whatever he had experienced the previous night. He had felt sure it had been only a dream, at least pretty sure, until he saw the man standing outside the hospital room door. Now, he was thinking the exact opposite, there was almost no doubt in his mind that the experience really occurred. Red tried to turn around to get another look at the man, but as he did so he felt a flashing pain in his stiff neck.

When I see Dad I'll know, he kept telling himself. *Somehow it will all be clear then. I'll be able to look at him, and I'll be able to tell.*

Red was pushed through the next set of double doors and just a few rooms down, the nurse pulled up to a stop.

"Alright son, here we are," the nurse said. He opened the door and wheeled Red inside.

There were two beds surrounded by curtains in the room. The nurse grabbed the first curtain and walked in a large arc around the room, dragging the curtain along its tracks on the ceiling.

There on the bed was Red's father. His head was shaved. An even greater number of tubes and machines surrounded him than had been around Red at any time since he entered the hospital. Red took one look at his father and knew without the faintest shadow of doubt that it had not been a dream. It was definitely his father's body. Red, however, knew that his father was not really inside it.

***

"I'm telling you it wasn't really a dream," Red said. He was sitting further up in his bed this afternoon than he had yet managed. He felt stronger and less groggy as well.

"But you just called it a dream," Michael said. He sat in the chair beside Red's bed with his feet up on the mattress near Red's knees.

"I know I called it a dream," Red said. "But what I meant was that it seemed like a dream, but it turned out not to be later."

"So, you're telling me that you saw yourself in a dream, but that you were still in the bed," Michael said.

"It wasn't a dream," Red said loudly. He closed his eyes, took a deep breath and rubbed his hand upwards across his forehead.

"Okay, okay. I know," Michael said. I'm just trying to understand what you are trying to say. So, you're telling me that you were in the bed, the doctor was about to give you some kind of shot thinking that you were dying, and then some magical mystery guy tells you to get back into your body, and then you woke up."

"That's it, you got it," Red said. He slapped his hands together, then winced from the sudden pain in his left arm. "Later, I saw the guy again…."

"Hold on a second, I'm still going," Michael interrupted. "Later on when you saw your dad in the ICU, you felt that he wasn't inside his body, that he was somehow able to move outside of it like you can. It was then that you decided it wasn't a dream after all."

"Like I said," Red began. "I saw the guy again in the hallway, his name is Tom Clack, and I didn't decide it wasn't a dream; I realized for sure that it wasn't."

"I don't know, man, it sounds a lot like a dream to me," Michael said. He leaned the chair back on two legs and pulled his phone out of his jeans pocket. He turned it on and was typing something into it with his thumbs. "It sounds like it might be the pain meds they got you on talking."

"Forget it," Red said. He sighed and rested his head against the pillow. "I thought you might not believe me; it does sound kind of ridiculous."

Michael took his feet off the bed and the front two feet of his chair slammed down on the floor. He leaned forward, with the phone in both hands and his elbows on his knees. His thumbs danced over the display.

"Listen to this," he said. "The blue fire around your skin is called an aura."

"A what?" Red said. He leaned forward and slightly sideways again toward Michael.

"An aura. It's like your life energy or something," Michael said. "And they even have a term for leaving your body, astral projection."

"So this is something a lot of people know about?" Red asked. "How come we've never heard of it before?"

Michael scrolled through the article on his phone. "I think the reason is that this sounds like some crazy weird stuff. It looks like most of these folks are all new age weirdos. Some even say there is this kind of magic parallel world where angels, demons and ghosts live. I don't see anything about birds or squirrels looking like little balls of fire at all."

Red laughed. "Great. Maybe I should start stocking up on crystals and dream catchers. Even if there is something true in what they are saying, there is no way to know what parts are real and what parts are plain craziness."

"This stuff," Michael said sliding the phone back into his pocket. "Is a whole ocean of crazy. Dad says that there are more mysteries in this world than there are stars. It's cheesy I know. I think you might be right though, there is probably some drop of truth in there somewhere, but I don't see how you, or anyone, can figure out what is and what isn't."

"So, you believe me?" Red asked. He held his breath as Michael let out a sigh.

"Yeah, I think so," Michael said at last. He brushed his hair back with one hand. "It sounds insane, it sounds stupid, and if anybody but you was trying to sell me this manure there is no way I'd buy it. But I believe you believe it, and that's enough for me."

"Thanks," Red said. He smiled and nearly laughed. "I know I wouldn't buy it if you were the one selling it. It probably would be horse manure."

"So what are you going to do now?" Michael asked laughing.

"I'm going to try and see if I can figure a way back into that other reality tonight after everyone goes home or goes to sleep. I am sure it's real, and I'm going to do everything I can to find Dad in there, whatever it takes."

Exploration

There is a rush of people moving through the hallways in the evenings in a hospital. Friends and family of those in the hospital's care stop by on their way home after work, or before going out to eat dinner. There is an almost constant sound of laughter and warm greetings. The whole place feels warmer and less institutional. As the sun begins to set, however, the hallways empty and all but the most cursory of staff heads home. The fluorescent lights never dim, but the echoing voices in the hallways fade away and any feeling that the hospital is more than just a facility where people are dealt with, rather than truly cared for, disappears.

For Red though, the night could not come quickly enough. His mother had gone home to spend the night in her own bed at the urging of Emily Lagos, Michael and Sara's mother. Along with the absence of his mother, the majority of the machines he was hooked up to the last few days had been removed. Only the IV and a machine that monitored his heart rate remained connected. This also made him happy. He didn't want the doctors rushing back into his room in the middle of the night to stick him with one of those long needles again.

It was nearly ten p.m. when Emily finally dragged his mother out of the room. *It's time,* he thought. He closed his eyes tightly and opened them again, nothing. He tried it repeatedly, each time closing his eyes tighter, and scrunching his face. Each time he failed. He tried imagining he was getting up out of the bed without actually moving his body. Nothing.

What can I do? He couldn't think of anything else to try. He wished Michael had told him more about the article on astral projection, maybe there would have been some clue amidst the nonsense on how to do the actual projecting out of his body. Once he started thinking about the ridiculous, his mind wandered to all the books, movies, and stories he knew that mentioned anything about traveling to other worlds. He remembered secret passageways and old wardrobes. Alice fell down a rabbit hole, and then later she walked through a mirror. There was something he remembered about seeing a soft place in the world out of the corner of your eye and then walking through it sideways, whatever that meant. There was also something about walking widdershins, from a story his grandmother had told him before she passed away, that had been a story about fairies. Apparently, to walk widdershins you had to walk backwards in a circle counterclockwise, and then somehow you would show up in fairy land. *How much, if any, of those old stories have some truth in them?*

Red didn't see any wardrobes or rabbit holes anywhere in the hospital room. Except for the small closet where his mother had put a change of clothes for him to go back home in. He supposed that might count as a wardrobe, but he was pretty sure it didn't. Even though there might have been enough space in the room for him to walk some tight circles in, there was no way he was going to be able to do that in his cast, much less do it backwards. *That knocks out walking sideways as well,* he figured. *And there is no way I'm going to be able to crawl my way into the bathroom, climb up on the sink and push my way through a mirror.*

He remembered that Dorothy clicked her heels together and wished herself home from Oz, but then again, she had been taken there by a tornado to begin with. He might be able to knock his heels together, but it would hurt. However, waiting for a tornado to sweep through the hospital wing was definitely a lost cause. Outside of just randomly waking up there again, the only thing left he could think of was just wishing. Wishing really hard.

Red looked around the room and tried to capture a mental picture of everything. He squeezed his eyes shut as hard as he could, and tried to imagine everything turning into the swirling, liquid smoke. He opened his eyes again. It was just the same boring hospital room. He tried it two more times with the same result.

He decided to give it one more shot. He closed his eyes. *This is the stupidest thing I've ever done. I'm glad Michael and Sara aren't here,* he thought as he clicked his heels together through the cast. He imagined the room melting away, revealing living fractals underneath every surface. Three spasms of sharp pain shot up his leg. He wasn't able to move them well, but he thought the effort might count for something.

Something shifted inside his mind. It felt like a balloon lifting away from your hand, the ribbon sliding between your fingers as it rose. It also felt like he was the balloon as well, being released and slowly rising upwards where you naturally wish to move.

Those old stories might have something to them after all, he thought. It was like a sideways step through reality, falling down out of the world and moving through a mirror all at the same time. He opened his eyes and saw the room swirling like molten glass around him.

***

Red slipped out of the bed, leaving his injured body behind. As his toes touched the linoleum his blue aura spread out across the floor, turning the shifting floor solid. He looked around the room. Everything was again composed of the same amorphous liquid, like the whole world was a giant lava lamp. A wide smile stretched across his face. Looking down at himself, he discovered that he was still wearing his hospital gown, even though the bandages and casts were gone. *I guess it is better than running around naked,* he thought.

He ran out of the room's open door. He navigated his way through the hallways, trying his best to remember the way that the nurse had taken him. Twice he made wrong turns and was forced to retrace his steps. He ran past vacant nurse's stations and empty waiting rooms, his gown fluttering behind him like a pennant. His bare feet squealed against the slick floor as he pulled up to a stop outside a room on the cancer ward.

The name outside the door read 'Tom Clack.' The door was open, but the lights were out. He peered into the room, but he couldn't make anything out in the darkness. Red considered going inside to make sure it was the man he had seen earlier, but he decided it was much more important to get to his father's room as quickly as he could. He squinted his eyes against the darkness one last time. Failing to see anything, he hurried on.

There was only one set of double doors between himself and the ICU. It was the first set of doors he had yet come across that were closed. He stopped in front of them. *Can I open them?* He looked at the doors, they looked thin and insubstantial. Their surface swirled and danced in impossible patterns. He looked at his hands, they were solid and thick in comparison. He reached out toward the metal square on the door to push it open. As he reached forward there was a loud buzzing sound and the doors swung open towards him. Red stepped back near one wall as an orderly wheeled a gurney with a sheet-draped body through the opening. Bright blue flames rippled across the orderly's body. They were some of the largest that Red had seen, nearly as large as his own. There was nothing coming from the body on the bed. The stretcher shuddered as one of the wheels rolled over his toes.

"Ow!" Red yelled involuntarily before clasping both hands over his mouth. He hopped up and down on his other foot.

"What? Who's there?" The orderly said letting go of the gurney. He looked around the empty hallway, his eyes darting back and forth. The gurney careened down the hallway toward the wall at the far end. Red kept his hands over his mouth.

"Oh crap," the orderly said. He took off running down the hallway after the gurney. It slammed against the wall and lilted to one side. He got there just in time to keep it from tipping, a man's arm fell off the side from underneath the sheet. The orderly lifted the arm, tucked it back under the sheet and continued pushing the corpse back down the hallway.

The pain in Red's foot finally subsided. He realized he had been biting down on his index finger. He pulled it out of his mouth and noticed the marks left behind by his teeth, little whites dimples on his skin. *Well, I can obviously still get hurt here.*

Red slipped through the doorway before the doors clicked shut behind him. His father's room was just three doors down on the left. He took a moment to gather his nerves and walked into the room.

Inside, a second orderly was placing new sheets on an empty hospital bed. Red watched as he tucked the sheets under the mattress, then turned and grabbed a plastic bag of street clothes and other personal items that were sitting in a chair beside the bed. The orderly looked around the room once more, then walked out the door. Red stepped out of the man's way just in time to let him pass.

For the second time in just as many minutes, Red put his hand over his mouth. This time, though, it wasn't in pain, but in shock. The bed was empty. *Was that Dad's body in the hallway?*

"Dad?" He said, his voice quavering. He stared at the empty bed, looking for any indication of who had been its most recent occupant. The room was silent except for the monotonous beeping of a heart monitor. Nearly a minute passed as Red stood examining the empty bed. The steady cadence of the monitor divided time into measured units. As he stood there in shock, each beep grew louder and more insistent inside his mind. His vision blurred as tears began filling his eyes. The beeping became the whole of reality.

Beep.

Beep.

B-beep.

There was something he was missing.

The monitor, Red thought. *There is a second bed in this room. Maybe they moved Dad.* Red ran past the first bed and slipped between an opening in the curtains surrounding the second bed.

Donal was stretched out on the bed. His body looked almost exactly as it had when Red had visited earlier. There was no aura around him, only the same slight glow as Red's own empty body lying on his bed at the other end of the hospital. Red ran his fingers over his father's body, they scrambled across his body seeking the faint glowing cord that should be coming out of his chest. *If I could find it, then I could follow it and find my father.* He strained his eyes, but each time he thought he found it, it seemed to slip away, out of his grasp and out of his vision. *Where are you!* He screamed inside his head. Red gave up the fruitless search, the cord wasn't there. He threw himself across his father's body and wept.

"What are you doing here? And who are you anyway?" A voice said harshly from just inside the room. It was the same voice that spoke to him from the doorway the previous evening.

Red didn't respond. He just wrapped his arms tighter around his father.

"You tell me who you are and what you want with this man, and you tell me right now," the man said as he strode into the room.

Red looked at the man, he appeared blurry and indistinct through his tears. It was definitely the same man from before. "He's my dad, okay? Just go away."

The man remained silent, but he didn't leave. Instead, he walked to the foot of the bed. He studied Red and Donal carefully. He looked back and forth between them. His eyes settled on Red's flaming red hair.

"You're his son alright," the old man said. "You want to tell me what happened?"

"Who are you?" Red said. He let go of his father, and turned toward the man.

"My name is Tom—"

"Tom Clack," Red said interrupting him. "I saw your name outside your door. That's your name, but who are you?"

"A friend," Tom said. "You can trust me."

Red examined the man. Tom looked older than Red's dad. His thin white hair was cut short, and it receded halfway back across his scalp. He was heavyset, but stood straight upright, not letting the excess weight pull his shoulders down. He wore a light jacket over a partially unbuttoned white shirt. Bifocal glasses hung between the jacket's zippers at his chest. He looked like a kind grandfather, one that would tell story after story in front of the fire. His blue eyes were the inside of an iceberg. They stared deep into Red's eyes.

"Where are we?" Red asked. "What is this place?"

"You don't know?" Tom asked. He took a step away from the bed.

Red shook his head. He kept one hand on his father, not wanting to let go.

"We are in the spirit world. How exactly do you keep coming here if you don't know?" Tom asked. He crossed his arms across his chest.

"The first time I just sort of woke up here, that was when you saw me. This time I..." Red hesitated, embarrassed to say it out loud. "I clicked my heels together and wished."

"You clicked your heels together!" Tom said. He stared at Red seriously for a moment, then he doubled over laughing. "Like Dorothy? You clicked your heels together, ha-ha? Did you say 'there's no place like home' while you did it?" He managed to finally get out through spurts of red-faced laughter.

"No," Red said, his face also turning red. He let go of his father and crossed his own arms in from of his chest. "Of course I didn't say 'there's no place like home.' I just didn't know how else to get back here."

"What's your name?" Tom asked, his laughter fading away. He wiped a tear from the corner of one eye.

"Red, and this is my dad, Donal."

"Donal Snyder," Tom said and turned toward the bed. "This is not good. This is not good at all. Tell me what happened, tell me everything."

"How did you know our name was Snyder?" Red asked.

"I've known your family for years," Tom said. "I've known your father since he was a little boy, but mostly I knew your grandfather Isaiah. He was kind of like a mentor to me."

"I never knew him," Red said.

"No, you wouldn't have," Tom said. "He died when your father was still a lad."

Red looked up into Tom's eyes. The man looked trustworthy; Red felt he was a good man.

"After Isaiah passed, I kind of lost touch with your family. So, are you going to tell me what happened or not?" Tom asked.

Red told him the story of the accident, he left nothing out that he could recall. Tom asked question after infuriating question, always delving into what Red considered inconsequential details, particularly about the coyote. Had Red ever seen it before? Were there a lot of coyotes around his house?

When Tom was finally satisfied, he sat down on the window sill. He rubbed the stubble on the side of his face with one palm.

"Your father never told you anything about the spirit world?" Tom asked. "He never told you anything at all?"

"No, nothing," Red said. He leaned against the bed, and rested his hand against his father's arm. "Do you think he knew?"

"Yeah, he knew. He knew since before he was even half your age," Tom said.

"How do you know?" Red asked.

"I've seen him in the spirit world," Tom said. "Not recently, mind you. But when he was a boy. Isaiah said that he took to it naturally. It wasn't as difficult for him as it was for me or even Isaiah. He was born to it, you might say."

Red stared at his feet. *How could dad have known, and never told me anything about all this?*

"Listen son, you are in real danger. I can't believe your father never told you anything," Tom said. He waved his hands in the air, dismissing any additional thoughts on the matter. His voice became tinged with urgency. "But that doesn't matter now. What matters is that you need to get up to speed, and quickly."

"Why wouldn't he tell me about it?" Red asked. "And what kind of danger?"

Tom closed his eyes and leaned his head against the window, he spoke without opening his eyes. "Your dad must not have been doing his job. I get it, he probably just wanted to protect you and your mother. I wish I had done something similar myself, but what matters right now is that you are in mortal danger, and you need to learn everything you can about the spirit world, and I'm the only one here that can teach you. The Hermit will be looking for you next, I'll wager, and he'll sacrifice your spirit as surely as he will your father's."

"What are you talking about?" Red asked. He let go of his father, stood up and walked over to Tom until they were nearly toe-to-toe. "Is Dad going to be okay? Who is this hermit?"

"Easy, Red. Your father's spirit can still come back. If it was gone, then his body would have already passed on." Tom said. He gave an appraising glance over Red, looking him up and down. Tom sighed. "I'll tell you about The Hermit when and if you are ready to deal with him."

"Where is he?" Red asked. He looked toward the hospital room door, ready to take off as soon as he learned where he could find his father.

"Whoa, hold on there cowboy. You aren't going to be able to find him until you know how all of this works, and you are going to need to be able to protect yourself if you have to," Tom said. He held both hands up, palms facing Red.

"Can you tell me what I need to know?" Red asked.

"I'll teach you whatever I can," Tom said. "It isn't everything though, and it likely won't be enough in the end. To begin with, clicking your heels together may get you back to Kansas, but is has nothing to do with getting into or out of the spirit world."

***

Red lay in his bed the following morning as the first glow of the coming day began to brighten his window. He tried to empty his mind of all other thoughts. He wasn't sure how much more time he had before his mother or the nurses would come to check on him.

"Traveling back and forth to the spirit world is all about clearing your mind and willing your spirit to shift," Tom had told him. Red's first assignment was to practice going back and forth between the worlds until Red could do it both intentionally and naturally. He had already managed to slip back into the physical world. It just sort of happened, without him really thinking about it. He laid down back on top of his bed on his own body, and suddenly the crazy spinning of the spirit world melted away.

Now he had to get back. He imagined the hospital room as it should be, both solid and normal. He then imagined everything changing, becoming less solid. He tried to hold the image of the whole room in his head, but it was too much information to hold in his mind at one time. *Okay,* he reasoned, *I should try to focus on a single point.*

He opened his eyes and stared at the ceiling tile immediately over his head. He pushed everything else out of his mind, ignoring his peripheral vision and focused all of his awareness at a point where four tiles met. He imagined the point becoming less solid, less a particular spot on the ceiling and more the concept of a spot on the ceiling. He imagined the tiles breaking apart, splitting and becoming insubstantial tendrils of smoke. He squinted his eyes, willing it to change. There was a recognizable shift inside his mind. The intersection became less distinct. An expanding wave emanated from the point, the ceiling, the walls, then the whole room rippled like the disturbed surface of a pond. He shifted fully into the spirit world.

Instead of getting up to explore again, he lay still in his bed, staring up at the same spot on the ceiling. He focused again on the same spot, and willed it to become more solid. This time instead of the change spreading away from that spot, it collapsed in upon it. He was back in the physical world again. Red smiled. He practiced shifting between the two worlds until the Sun breached the window sill and spread its light across his bed. After just a few tries, shifting between them became as easy as changing the focus of his vision from something far away, to something nearer at hand. Once he got the hang of it, it became just as fast as well.

Satisfied that he had the hang of it, he got out of bed in the spirit world and walked over to the window. He tried shifting back to the physical world again, but despite everything around him vibrating, he couldn't manage it. *Tom said I had to be touching my body to shift back,* he remembered.

Red turned away from the window, left the room and headed back through the hospital to Tom's room. The hospital staff was between shifts, changing over from the night to the morning crew. He was careful to avoid any accidental collisions this time. Tom was in the hallway outside his room, looking out the window opposite at the park beyond the parking lot. He turned toward Red as he approached.

"Well now," Tom said. "You seem to have gotten the knack of that pretty quickly."

"It wasn't that hard once I did it a couple of times," Red said. He smiled proudly at his new teacher. "It feels kind of natural now. I still don't understand why I can't just grab the cord again instead of having to go all the way back to my body to shift back into the physical world."

"Think of the cord as a kind of lifeline," Tom said. "It connects your physical body to your spirit, but it is fragile and can be severed. It is actually quite a delicate thing. It will pull you back into your body, but should only be used in an actual emergency. The more you use it, the weaker it will become, and the farther you are from your body, the more likely it is to break. The greater the distance also increases the amount of pain it causes you to use it. It is better to avoid using the cord if at all possible."

Red looked down at where the cord was gathered from the myriad of smaller threads at his chest. He ran his fingers across it and felt it straining to pull him back inside his body.

"Come on, let's go outside. I like to sit beside the pond in the mornings," Tom said. He patted Red on the back, grabbed his shoulder and led him toward the exit.

***

The park surrounding the small pond was a maelstrom of color and movement. Nothing held still very long. The small fireballs that were birds or squirrels flitted and scurried through the trees and bushes. Two fiery squirrels chased each other around a large willow tree that hung over a small stream-fed waterfall at one end of the pond. Hundreds of tiny multicolored sparks flew through the air, insects going through their motions unaware of their inner beauty manifesting itself in the spirit world. The pond glowed diffusely from fish swimming just underneath its surface. Every leaf and stem, every trunk and branch of the plants and trees were more colorful and full of life than anything Red could ever have imagined. It was truly the most beautiful sight he had ever beheld. The hospital room seemed like a child's drawing compared to the masterpiece that was nature.

"It's amazing," he said. He brushed his fingertips across a

cattail sending an emerald dragonfly streaking away across the pond. "It doesn't seem real."

"It's real alright," Tom said. He sat down on a bench. "Whether most folks realize it or not, everything in the physical world has a counterpart here in the spiritual, and vice-versa. The two worlds don't really exist side-by-side like some science fiction parallel world, they overlap and interconnect. They are inseparable."

Tom patted a spot on the bench next to him, and Red sat down beside him.

"Your grandfather told me, and I believe it to be true, that what you see here in the spirit world is a manifestation of a thing's true nature."

"I don't understand," Red said. He looked across the pond, still trying to take it all in.

"Their true nature," Tom said. He raised his arms indicating everything around them.

"What something *really is* is more than just what you can see in the physical world," Tom said. He motioned toward Red and himself. "Take us for example. Have you noticed how little of an aura most people have, and how large yours and mine are?"

Red nodded. "I still don't exactly understand what an aura is, though."

"Our auras," Tom said. He waved his hands in small circles, trying to find the words to explain what seemed obvious to himself. "You know, our auras, how we glow. You've seen how everything that is alive glows, and things that aren't – don't. Some glow brightly, others only dimly. That's our aura, those with stronger spirits have larger and brighter ones. You could say it is sort of an outward sign of an inner spiritual strength."

"That kind of makes sense," Red said. "I just thought they looked like a kind of living fire."

Tom laughed. He slapped his knee with one hand. "You remind me so much of your grandfather, he refused to call them auras. He said it sounded ridiculous. Tell me if this sounds right:

'As for the likeness of the living creatures, their appearance was like burning coals of fire, and like the appearance of torches: And the living creatures ran to and fro in the appearance of flashes of lightning.' I can't remember it exactly, but I think you get the gist of it."

"Whoa. Was that from some book about the spirit world?" Red asked. It was a perfect description of how he saw the birds and squirrels.

"Your grandfather would say so," Tom said chuckling. "It's from the Bible, the book of Ezekiel. Isaiah was very religious; he made me read parts of it. Can't say I bought into it too much, though."

"I thought the Bible was all about being good to each other, and obeying a bunch of commandments," Red said. He knew his grandparents had been very religious, but it wasn't something his parents ever seemed to care much about.

"It's a bit of that, to be sure, but it also has a lot of violence and way too many burning lakes of fire for my taste," Tom said. He leaned forward and rested his elbows on his knees. "Anyway, it seems that only those with really strong auras are able to enter, or even see, the spirit world. Nonliving things, like buildings or manmade objects, are generally less solid here."

"Like the hospital," Red said. He looked over his shoulder back toward the hospital. It looked so much less solid or real than the plants and trees in the park.

"Right. The hospital and most everything in it are still fairly solid here because they have a purpose or reason for being. Things that have lost their purpose fade away quicker here than in the physical world." Tom searched the ground near the bench. He pointed across the path. "See that Styrofoam cup over there? Try and pick it up."

Red stood and walked over to the cup. The cup was there, but as he looked at it closer it seemed almost entirely translucent. The swirling matter of it sometimes faded away almost entirely. He reached down and tried to pick it up. He wasn't able to grasp it, it slipped through his fingers like a handful of water. It took Red several tries and a great deal of concentration to keep the cup from sliding through his fingers. The best he could manage was to get it several inches off the sidewalk before it fell back to the ground.

"It's trash. Unwanted. It has no purpose anymore," Tom said. "It will fade away out of the spirit world, and eventually out of the physical as well. Larger things, and things with more purpose than a Styrofoam cup will last longer."

Red stood back up and headed back toward the bench. Something moved behind a tree on the other side of the nearest stream, catching his eyes for a moment. Convincing himself that it was only a squirrel he sat back down on the bench.

"Now, say you were a baseball player," Tom said.

"I do play baseball," Red said. He glanced back over his shoulder toward the tree.

"Well, take something like your baseball bat, or your glove," Tom said. He was holding his hands in front of him like there was something in his hands. "They probably mean a lot to you. Their purpose is more than just something you need to play the game, they are *your* bat and *your* glove. Those kinds of things would be virtually solid here. You can even bring them with you when you shift back and forth."

"This is all really interesting, Tom, but I don't see how any of this is going to help me find Dad, or how it could protect me if some hermit really is hunting me," Red said. He leaned back against the back of the bench.

"You've got to understand the basics first," Tom said. He sat up straight and rubbed his temples with one hand. "I suppose you're right, though. We don't have months or even weeks for you to get it all down."

Tom stood and walked over to the edge of the pond. He pulled a pocket watch out of his trousers. He flipped it open and ran his thumb across the edge of the opened lid. Flipping it closed, he held it out toward Red and nodded for him to take it.

"Before we can figure out how you can best protect yourself, we first have to figure out what kind of abilities you've been blessed with," Tom said.

"There is more than just being able to shift in and out?" Red asked. He took the watch from Tom. Its long chain slid from Tom's fingers and dangled below Red's like a pendulum.

"For some. Not everyone – and probably not even most people who can shift can do anything else," Tom said turning his back on Red and looking out over the pond. "But there are other things, and they seem to run in families. I figure there might be a pretty good chance you're a maker like your grandfather."

"A maker?"

"It's just a name for what I call it," Tom said. He turned back to Red. "Makers can change things, make ordinary objects into something more than just what they are in the physical world. Isaiah used to take his watch and hang it on a tree or a fence near where he was working. If anyone, or anything, came close, it would set off a whirring alarm. He tried to teach me, but I'm just a visitor. A 'visitor' is what I call someone who can only visit the spirit world, but doesn't have any other abilities."

Red studied the watch in his hand. The lid was carved with what looked like a lighthouse crossed with a trumpet. Underneath it read: Ezekiel 33:6.

"Is this the part you quoted earlier?" Red asked. He ran his thumb across the etching.

"No," Tom said looking at the watch in Red's outstretched hand. "It is from the same book, but this is referring to a watchman blowing his trumpet to let others know the enemy is near at hand."

"I thought you weren't religious," Red said looking up at Tom.

"I'm not. It isn't even really my watch," Tom said. He looked up toward the drifting clouds. "It was your grandfather's. I carry it with me to remind me of him and what he did for me."

"What did he do?"

"He," Tom began. He hesitated and glanced toward the tree across the stream in the direction where Red had seen movement before. "I guess you could say that he saved my life."

Tom took a step toward the tree, then stopped. He shook his head and turned again toward Red. Motioning toward the watch, he spoke quickly.

"Anyway, it doesn't matter right now, I'll tell you all about it later. Right now, let's see what you can do."

"How," Red said. He looked down at the watch held gingerly in his palm.

"The same way you shift," Tom said. "Just focus on what you want it to be, and it will become so."

"What should I try to make it?"

"Whatever you like," Tom said. "I don't know if there are really any rules to it, other that it most likely needs to be something of a similar nature. I'd try something small and mechanical."

Red gathered the chain of the watch and held them away from his body in cupped hands. He stared at the watch. *What should I do? What is the nature of a watch? Time.* Red tried to think of what time means, what time could be. An idea came to him. He unclasped the chain from the watch and dropped it into a pocket on his hospital gown. He put everything out of his mind except the watch in his hand.

It began to move. Red could hear tiny clicks coming from inside the casing. The weight shifted inside it, the cogs and gizmos rearranging themselves according to his desire. The watch rolled onto its edge, the bottom and top covers opened and flexed several times like wings. Suddenly the covers began flapping and with a mechanical whirr the watch rose six inches above his hands.

"Time flies," Red said smiling, his eyes wide in awe.

"I never imagined you could do it on your first try," Tom said. He slapped one hand against his thigh and laughed delightedly. "You might just be the most natural maker I've ever met!"

The sound of someone clearing their voice startled them both. They turned and saw a late teen African-American boy standing near the tree on a rock where the two streams met. He was dressed in all leather. It was darkly tanned with streaks of glowing red and yellow that reminded Red of burning coals. His foot-long hair was in twists and was tied behind his head by a strap of leather. He wore sunglasses over the splotchy beard of someone trying to grow one out before they reached full adulthood. In his left hand he held a black policeman style billy club.

"If he is a maker," the young man said leaping over the stream and walking confidently toward Tom and Red. "Then what am I?"

Red froze. The watch fell back into his still outstretched hand, the lid still open, but a normal watch again.

8

The Brand

Three years earlier...

Large, heavy snowflakes had fallen slowly but steadily throughout the evening, continuing late into the still night. There was sure to be another six or seven inches on top of the ten already covering the ground by morning. The snow on the ground sparkled in the light of street lamps and Christmas decorations. Colored shadows were flung across front yards and into the gray slush of streets and lanes, a brilliant tapestry no one in the neighborhood was awake to see.

The Timber Ridge's main street, Oak Street, wound up a valley between two ridges, a wide flat river of asphalt. Narrow streets, like rivulets with cul-de-sac springs, fed into it from higher up the steep ridges. The long course of Oak Street ended after a sweeping bend that led to a cul-de-sac of its own near the ridge crest at the edge of the forest. Halfway around the cul-de-sac stood a modest split-level brick house.

The house was smaller than Celia and Charles Lewis would have preferred for their three children. The house had no rooms to spare and only a smallish basement, but the moment Celia stepped into it the first time, she knew it was going to be their home. She had always been able to see the world in a way others could not. It was difficult for her, normally, but here in this house it came to her as naturally as falling asleep in the hammock beneath the cool shade of their twin elms. It wasn't until several months after they unpacked the last of the boxes from their old apartment that she began seeing things even when she didn't want to, particularly at the forest's edge. It felt like the forest, or at least the animals in it, were spying on her. She put the strange notions behind her, though, imagining it to be her own mind playing tricks. She did take some precautions, nevertheless. She fashioned amulets in the shape of anchors, and made all three of her children and her husband wear them as a form of protection.

The snow eventually began to pile up on the window ledge outside the room of Chase, their oldest child. The drift grew higher and higher against the panes until one too many flakes landed and a miniature avalanche sent the drift falling to the ground ten feet below.

Fourteen-year-old Chase lay restlessly in his bed, reliving the bout that had won him the state's mixed martial arts championship earlier that afternoon. On a hook on the bed's headboard hung the gold-chained anchor pendant from his mother. Every inch of his body ached. It was the good kind of ache, though, the kind that comes from mastering your body, harnessing the full potential of your muscles' ability to the point of exhaustion. He was the youngest male, and the only African American to ever win the state's fly weight title.

Outside his window at the rear of the house, unseen by any human eye, dark forms slipped out from the shadows underneath the forest's snow laden branches. One large shadow differentiated itself from the darkness. An old man leaning on a crooked staff stepped forward and approached the French doors.

"I need the woman," The Hermit said. "I don't care about the rest, do with them what you will." He placed the tip of his staff against the door. It began to vibrate. The pins shook free of their hinges and fell onto the white tile inside the Lewis' dining room. The door fell inward with a crash and tinkle of breaking glass.

Chase heard the noise below, but instead of getting out of his bed to investigate, he pulled a pillow over his head. *Good grief, will Caleb and Charice ever sleep through the night?* The ten-year old twins were notorious for their nocturnal hijinks. They fed off of each other, growing more and more daring by the week. Their night time adventures were the reason Chase took to not only locking his bedroom door at night, but to putting his computer chair against the handle as well. He figured his mom and dad would take care of it.

None of the investigators had ever been able to explain precisely how the fire had started. They thought it might have been from the gas stove, or it might have been from the gas fireplace, but within minutes of the door crashing on to the dining room tiles, the entire house was engulfed in hungry flames. From miles around, the house at the far end of Timber Ridge glowed in the otherwise dim night. Flecks of ash still smoldering orange around the edges fell on top of the glistening snow.

Chase leapt out of bed at the sound of his mother's scream, but it was too late for him to be of any help. His bedroom door was already beginning to char. The wood at the bottom was black. Smoke seeped into the room between the door and its frame. He kicked the chair out of the way, and reached out to grab the handle. The doorknob seared his fingers at the first touch, he jerked his hand back.

Celia screamed again. This time the sound came from behind Chase, outside the window in the backyard. Smoke poured into the room, not only from the door, but now from gaps in the hardwood floor. Chase ran to the window. Outside, through falling snow and ash, he saw his mother being dragged into the woods by what looked like dozens of animals. He saw an old man with a cane or staff walking behind them. Fire shot up from the downstairs window directly below his. He stepped back, shielding his face with one arm.

The smoke in the room grew thicker and blacker, forcing Chase to his knees. He hacked and coughed, and tried to regain his breath. For some reason he thought of the necklace his mother had made him. *The amulet, I need Mom's amulet.* Chase crawled across the floor of his bedroom to the bed. Orange tongues of fire lapped away at the floor beneath his bed. He reached up and grasped the anchor from the headboard in his right hand. It burned. It burned horribly; he could smell the flesh of his palm roasting. He held onto it as long as he could, hoping it would cool down in his hand. When he couldn't hold it any longer he flung it across the room. Holding up his hand, he saw a raw pink burn, blackened around the edges, on his hand. It was already beginning to swell where the anchor symbol was now branded into his palm. The floor gave way and he fell through the gap into the den below. He landed on the couch, his head bouncing on the armrest. He blacked out.

The sound of distant sirens growing nearer was the first thing Chase was aware of when he woke. The burning pain in his hand followed closely after. From out of the black sky, white snow and gray ash fell around him. He lay on the floor of his den, the top floor of his house was gone. Around him nothing in his vision would hold still. There was smoke everywhere and everything seemed to be melting like an abstract painting. *It must be from the heat,* he thought. He got to his feet and brushed the ash off his night shirt. He climbed out of the den onto the slushy and ashy grass behind the house. He saw his father and the twins standing near the bottom of their driveway. Caleb had buried his face into his father's right leg, while Charice had buried hers into his left. Even from where he stood, Chase could see the reflective streaks of tears running down his father's face, and even though he couldn't hear the words, he could tell his father was screaming out plaintively for both him and his mother. Chase shook his head, trying to clear his mind. It looked to him like the three of them were covered in blue flames.

Flashing lights and wailing sirens came around the curve in the road. Chase looked at his family, then at the forest. Nothing held still in his vision, it was all constant motion and swirling chaos. He knew that the decision he was about to make was one that could never be unmade. *No one will ever believe me if I tell them what happened,* he thought. *I have to find that old man who took my mother and make him pay.* He took one last look at what remained of his family. Without a tear, the heat had sucked all the moisture out of his body, he turned his back on his family and sprinted into the woods in the direction he thought they had taken his mother.

Chase rubbed his eyes. Ever since he had woken from his fall his vision was wrong. The constant movement made him both nauseous and scared. He stumbled through the dark trees, running almost blindly and becoming increasingly sick from the swirling vision and lack of oxygen. The smoke he had breathed in was still not clear of his lungs. He leaned against a tree and closed his eyes. In the cold air his nausea began to subside. As his queasiness left, the pain in his hand grew more intense. He fell to his knees and stuck his hand into a snow drift. It felt so good on his burning palm. He closed his eyes and leaned forward, resting his head on the snow covered ground. The cold calmed him and he took long greedy gulps of the cool air. He was hot and sweaty. Steam rolled off his bent form, even through his blackened pajamas. It wasn't long before he grew cold.

He had lost the trail of those who had taken his mother hours ago. He knew that if he kept running blindly he would only get further lost himself. *Where can I go?* He thought. *I can't go home, until I find who did this.* Chase stood up and looked around the forest. Thankfully there were no leaves on the trees, and he could see a fair distance through them. The glow from Laurel Hollows was visible in the sky just over the next ridge. He took off at a jog to keep himself warm, but his core body temperature kept plummeting in the freezing night.

Finding somewhere warm was all that he could think of when he stumbled into the glow of a campfire at the edge of town. He was so cold he gave no notice of how the residents of the homeless camp were covered in blue flames. His hands and feet were numb, and he was pretty sure he was delirious.

"Help me," he said to the surprised men and women before collapsing in a heap beside the fire.

The first few weeks following the fire had been the most difficult days of Chase's young life. He stayed with the homeless group only the one night, but their kindness in keeping him warm, feeding him and providing him with warm clothes was something that he would never forget. He returned there often since, bringing food and camping supplies.

He found a basement in an abandoned warehouse at the edge of downtown that still inexplicably had electricity. He made that basement his home, and eventually his base. To his shame, those first days he stole what he needed to survive. He stole food and clothes. He stole a heater on display outside a hardware store, an electric griddle from a window display and a laptop from a man at a cafe who left it untended at his table when he went inside for a coffee refill.

It was the computer that let him end his career as a petty thief. He set up an online bank account and began programming mobile phone utilities and apps to sell. They were nothing fancy, and he didn't charge much, but they sold well. He didn't have many actual expenses either. The day when his new debit card arrived at his rented post-office box was the day that his life really began to turn around. That first day he went around and left money at all the places he had stolen from. If he could have found the man whose computer he had stolen, he would have paid him back as well.

The nauseating way he had begun to see the world since the fire had not gone away. He had learned to live with it. Over the months that passed slowly, he eventually took a kind of pride in being able to see the world differently, and what he felt was more fully real than everyone else. He remembered his mother had said that she saw things more fully, and he wondered if this is what she meant. She had said that she could see how the world *really* was, and that it was far stranger and more beautiful than anyone imagined. She had seen it only in glimpses, though. Chase saw it all the time. The vision wasn't the only change in him either. His whole body glowed in fiery blue, like everyone else he saw, but his more so than almost anyone he had seen. His hand though, the one that now bore a branded scar, glowed white constantly. The brand was a near perfect replica of a ship's anchor.

He spent his nights writing code and his days trying to find out anything he could about the man he had seen outside his house that night. The homeless friends he had made while staggering through the woods had refused to talk to him about it, saying only that he was called The Hermit and that he was very old. According to them, he was usually accompanied by a menagerie of wild animals or birds everywhere he went. No one knew where he lived, or wouldn't tell him if they did. They were terrified of him and told tales of even stranger creatures that The Hermit controlled.

He began to feel that his searching was pointless and considered returning home. The police and the newspapers had concluded that both he and his mother had died in the fire, despite the fact that their bodies had never been recovered. He regretted the added pain he inflicted on his father and the twins, but he didn't know how he could go home again while The Hermit was still out there. He knew that they had moved into another house in the same neighborhood, but it wasn't his home anymore, and it wasn't his mother's home. It was just a place his family lived. Home was where they were all together.

He attended his own funeral. It was a double affair. He hid behind trees and cars well behind the crowd, straining to hear what they said about him and his mother. He was too far away to understand much of what they said, but he could hear them crying. He understood that. After the crowd dispersed, he watched as workers lowered the caskets into the ground. It wasn't until the flowers atop his mother's casket disappeared beneath the ground into the grave that he actually believed she was dead. They were empty caskets, he knew, but it removed a gnawing sense of urgency from his chest. It was too late to rescue her. He knew in his heart that she was already dead, but there was still plenty of time ahead for him to have his vengeance.

***

Two months after the funeral, Chase walked down the alley two blocks from his hideout. Water spewed out of the mouths of downspouts from the buildings on either side. The heavy winter rain had stopped as abruptly as it had begun just twenty minutes earlier. The running water met in the center of the concave alley and pooled six-inches deep around a metal-grated and partially clogged drain. The sun neared the horizon, casting long shadows that stretched down the alley.

"No, let go!" A child's high-pitched voice echoed down the canyon-like brick walls. Chase turned around quickly and looked back down the alley. He shielded his eyes from the direct sunlight with his arm. He could just make out a small girl running into the alley, her blonde hair billowing behind her. She looked right at Chase, but said nothing and threw herself against a grimy wall behind a dumpster. Chase stepped sideways into the shadow of a doorway and watched.

"C'mere. You can't get away from me!" A voice growled.

A creature, no larger than a child itself stepped around the corner. Instead of having the usual blue aura he had grown used to seeing, it glowed a sickly yellow. Its light brown skin was covered in sparse green hair. Its arms and legs were as thin as bone, while its knees and elbows were knobby and large, like the joints of diseased tree branches. Large hands ended with long thin fingers that stretched out wide, ready to wrap around the girl when he finally found her. Each slinking step brought the creature closer to her hiding place.

Chase looked around him, searching for anything he could use as a weapon. A piece of rusted wrought iron about three-feet long lay on the wet ground just a couple of feet away.

The creature took its time making his way up the alleyway. It examined, each possible hiding place. The sun came from behind it, making it difficult for Chase to make out any details in the face, but he could see that its eyes were several times larger than they should be and its mouth stretched from just underneath one elongated and pointed ear to the other. The creature cast no shadow in front of it as it advanced toward the girl cowering behind the dumpster. It was just a few feet from the dumpsters edge when the girl let out an inadvertent sniffle.

The creature turned sharply toward the noise. In silhouette now, Chase saw its long crooked nose was several inches long and its horrendously wide mouth was filled with pointed, canine-like teeth.

"I can hear you," the creature said in a high pitched sing-song voice. It took another step closer to the corner of the dumpster. It was almost upon the frightened girl. "There is no need to keep silent any longer, you can scream all you want. No one can hear us or see us here."

Chase stepped out of the doorway. He grabbed the iron rod

in his left hand and walked, more confidently than he felt, into the sun's light. He bent his knees and got into one of his fighting stances. He held the rod over his shoulder with one hand. He held out his other hand, palm toward the creature and stretched out fingers still sore from grasping the amulet.

"I can see you," Chase said. He tried to make his voice sound as deep and confident as he could. He was terrified of the disgusting creature, but he didn't want it to know that. "You need to leave her alone."

"Ah, another one. It looks like I'm going to get two for one tonight," the creature spat out between his teeth, spittle flying in front of him. "You should know better than to get in the way of a kobold and his prey." The kobold grabbed the edge of the dumpster, and using it to push itself forward, came rushing up the alley at Chase.

Chase stood his ground, refusing to budge as the creature advanced on him. *Use your opponent's strength and speed against him*, he reminded himself from his years of training. The kobold took long strides as it ran, then lunged six feet into the air in front of Chase. It came down at Chase – arms wide and teeth first. *Wait for it.* At the last possible moment, the sharp teeth mere inches from his face, Chase took a half step sideways. He leaned back as the kobold narrowly missed him. He brought the iron rod down and whacked the back of the kobold. It landed, splayed across the asphalt, just beyond Chase.

Chase said nothing, he just spun around to face the downed kobold and reset himself in a new stance. He held the makeshift weapon over his head like a fencing sword, his right hand still held out protectively in front of him. He was balanced on the balls of his feet, ready to move in any direction.

The kobold scrambled back to its feet much faster than Chase imagined possible.

"How did you do that?" The creature sneered, narrowing his eyes at Chase.

Chase didn't respond. He took a half step to the side, putting himself directly between the kobold and the setting sun, taking any advantage he could against the unknown foe.

"You didn't shift when you picked up that iron. That's not possible," the kobold spat.

Chase made the mistake of taking his eyes off the kobold for a split second to look up at the rod in his hand. The kobold seized the opportunity and threw himself onto Chase. Its long arms pinned Chase's against his sides. The two fell down into the edge of the water gathered around the drain. Chase tried to free his arms as the foul water splashed into his mouth and his eyes. The kobold was too strong, its fingers curled around the back of Chase's neck. Chase wormed his arms between his body and the kobold's chest. They rolled, fighting for leverage, through the murky water.

The kobold loosened its embrace momentarily to be able to wrap its fingers tighter around Chase's windpipe. The extra few centimeters this afforded was enough for Chase to get his right hand between their bodies, but it also allowed the kobold to completely wrap its fingers around Chase's neck. Chase, now gasping for air, could not push hard enough to get the deceptively strong kobold off him. They rolled over again, the kobold straddling Chase. It slammed Chase's head into the metal grate in the center of the alley. The water completely covered his face now. Chase let go of the iron rod and brought his left hand between their bodies and on top of his right, he pushed against the leathery chest of the creature as hard as he could.

The palm of his right hand glowed brighter than ever before as he focused on pushing the kobold away. The light escaped from between his fingers and the side of his palm. The kobold loosened its grip and looked down at the light coming from its chest.

"What is the meaning of this?" the kobold said before a thunderous crack echoed down the alleyway. Light poured out of Chase's palm. The kobold was flung off of Chase and slammed against one of the walls like a wet rag. It fell down in a heap. It feebly tried to push itself up, before crumbling back to the ground.

Chase sat up and took a long gasping breath of air. He held his hand out in front of him and stared at it. The white glow diminished until only the outline of the anchor on his hand glowed white and pulsated. He unsteadily got to his feet and walked over to the kobold. He held his hand out between himself and the strange creature. The kobold didn't move. Its pale yellow aura began to fade, then as if by some unseen wind, the yellow flames were extinguished like a candle blown out by a breeze. Chase nudged one of the kobold's arms with his foot. Where his boot touched the body it crumbled to ash. He did it again to the kobold's side. Again, where his boot touched, the body turned to ash. Chase lowered his hand and kicked the lifeless thing until only a thin layer of ash on the asphalt remained.

"What did you do to that thing?" The girl asked, coming up beside Chase.

Chase looked at the girl, she couldn't be any older than six or seven. He ignored her for the moment, and turned his right hand over and looked at the anchor brand again. It had faded to the same level of brightness as it had been since the fire.

"I don't know. It just sort of happened," he said looking at the girl. "How old are you anyway, and why was that thing after you?"

"I'm eight," she said. "Eight and a half actually." She stood up as straight as she could. She held her chin high. "That thing was after me because it caught me following it."

"Why in the world would an eight-year-old girl be following that thing?" Chase said, nodding toward the ash.

"I didn't know what it was. I hadn't seen anything like it before. I was tracking it, then I came around a corner and it was there waiting for me. I ran away as fast as I could and it came after me," she said looking up at Chase. "What I want to know is how you are able to even see either of us."

"What do you mean?" Chase asked. "You're small, but you ain't so small that I couldn't see you."

"I mean, how did you see me when I'm invisible like this?" the girl said.

"I hate to tell you kid, but you're not invisible," Chase said. He looked the girl up and down, noticing that her aura was larger and brighter than anyone he had met. "You look as real as anything else."

"I am too invisible," she said. She threw her arms down straight by her sides. She spun, sending her hair flying around her face. She took three stomping steps toward the light underneath a streetlamp that just lit for the night, and spun in a circle. "See, not even a shadow." She stopped and crossed her arms across her chest. "Invisible."

Chase walked over to her. She was right, there was no shadow. He shrugged.

"You're right. No shadow," he said. "I guess I can see the invisible now."

"You shouldn't be able to see me unless you are invisible too," the girl said. "Are you?"

"No, everyone else can see me," Chase said. "But I can see the way things really are, even when I don't want to."

"You mean you can see the invisible stuff all the time," the girl asked. Her eyes were wide as she walked up to him.

"I guess so."

"That is so cool," she said rocking from her heels to her toes, a wide smile on her innocent face. "I'm Wendy. Wendy Wright."

"I'm Chase."

"Pleased to meet you Chase," Wendy said and gave a slight curtsy. "Will you be my friend?"

"What?" Chase said. He took a step backward. "Your friend?"

"Yeah, I don't know anybody else that can see the invisible stuff besides you and me," she said. "Besides. You saved my life just now. We kind of have to be friends."

"I don't think so, kid," Chase said and began to turn away. "I've got too much going on to be friends with a little girl."

Wendy looked at the ground. She held her hands clasped together in front of her. Her shoulders sagged and she idly nudged a small rock with one of her feet.

Chase turned back to her. She was the most pathetic thing Chase had ever seen. He could tell she knew how she looked and was playing him. It worked, though.

"Okay, okay. Let me think about it," he said.

"Woohoo!" Wendy shouted. She ran over to Chase and threw her arms around him in a big hug. "We are going to have so much fun. I'll be at the zoo all day tomorrow, come find me."

She took off skipping down the alleyway. She stopped at the end and turned around. "Oh, and thanks again for saving me. That was so awesome, you're like a superhero! See ya' tomorrow, Chase."

Chase watched her turn and disappear around the building. *Maybe Wendy can help me figure out what happened to my mom, or at least show me how she was tracking that creature, that kobold. How can something like that even exist?* Chase walked out of the lamplight and turned down the next alley. He felt particularly proud of himself for saving the girl, it felt good. As he slipped through the metal double doors of the warehouse, he was thinking about how he had knocked the creature away. It was like magic, or some kind of superhuman power. *Is that what I am now? Some kind of superhero.* He closed the door behind him and placed a wood plank through the handles for extra security.

"The Brand," he said to the empty shadows. *That sounds like a superhero kind of name. If I've got some kind of superpowers, I should have a name.*

"I am The Brand." His pronouncement echoed as he repeated it, each time growing louder until the echoes merged into a multitudinous voice like a chorus, reaffirming him.

9

Leaving the Hospital

"**A**fter that night, I started calling myself 'The Brand,'" Chase said. He sat on the park bench with his elbows on his knees and facing the ground in an apologetic posture. Red and Tom stood several feet away on the sidewalk.

"I have literally been prowling the streets at night as a vigilante. I fight crime whenever I see it, but in reality it has all been about finding this Hermit," Chase said. He looked up at Tom and Red. "That's it really. That's my story."

Red and Tom exchanged glances.

"Chase, can I see your hand?" Tom asked.

Chase held out his hand, palm up, for Tom to examine. Tom took it in one hand and traced his index finger across the anchor shaped scar.

"Well," Tom said, letting go of Chase's hand. "It's a real anchor."

"Yeah, I know it's an anchor," Chase said. "It was from my mother's pendant."

"No," Tom said. He spun his hands in front of him trying to find the words to explain. "I mean, of course the symbol is an anchor, but it serves as a literal anchor as well. In the sense that it *anchors* your spirit to your physical body. It prevents your spirit and your body from separating. Symbols have a lot of power in the spirit world, and the anchor is a very old and very powerful symbol."

"So, back to my original question," Chase said. He turned his branded hand over and ran his fingers across the raised scar. "If he is a 'maker,' what am I?"

"What you are is a reckless teenage boy who has more power than he knows what to do with," Tom said shaking his head. "But to answer your question, I'd call someone with your ability a 'walker.' You're the only one I've ever actually met. Walkers are able to see and affect both the physical and the spirit world at the same time. Your ability is rare and powerful."

"Hold on, back up a second," Red said stepping between Tom and Chase. "Are you the vigilante they keep talking about on TV? The one the police can't find?"

"The one and only," Chase said. He stood and smiled. "The Brand at your service."

"That is so cool," Red said. "You are like the coolest thing ever to happen in this town."

"He's the luckiest guy in town," Tom said. "Without the anchor he would have been killed by that kobold. He is playing a dangerous game, one which he's ignorant of the rules."

"Listen here, old man," Chase said. He walked up to Tom and put his index finger in his chest. "I'm just trying to figure out who this Hermit is and where he lives so I can make him pay for what he did to my mom and my family."

Tom didn't flinch. He put his finger in Chase's face. "No, you listen to me. You don't understand what is really going on here. It's much bigger than your mother or Red's father, and you aren't the only ones who've lost someone to The Hermit. I know how it feels to want revenge. He killed my wife and tried to kill my daughter. The Hermit is too powerful. If you do manage to find him, he will kill you! Moreover, if he finds out what you are, and what you can do, you won't have to find him; he will hunt you down and kill you!"

"Stop it!" Red yelled. He reached between Tom and Chase, pulling them apart.

Chase took a step backward and held his branded hand up defensively toward Tom. He looked at Red.

"Both of you, calm down," Red said. He stood firm between them, looking back and forth. "We are all friends here."

"Ack! It's useless," Tom said. He waved his hand dismissively at Chase, and turned his back on the two boys. "You don't understand."

"He killed your wife?" Red said. He put his hand on Tom's shoulder. "What happened?"

"We were camping. It was a mistake," Tom said. He stared out over the pond at the trees on the other side. "I thought we were far enough away from where The Hermit lived. I was wrong. In the middle of the night we heard animals nearby. I got out of the tent to try and frighten them off, but there were dozens of them, even a bear. I realized what was going on even before The Hermit stepped out of the trees.

"I tried. I tried to fight them off, but there were just too many. They took Nancy, my wife, and Heather. Heather was so little, so young. She was only seven. They took them and left me. I…" Tom's voice began to crack as he told the story. "I was knocked unconscious and fell down a ravine trying to stop them. They must not have been able to find me."

"I thought you said it was just your wife," Red said. He looked up at Tom.

Tom shook his head, he was holding back tears.

"We got Heather back," Tom continued, "Isaiah and I. But first I went to the police. They investigated it and decided it was just a wild animal attack. I went to Isaiah. Together we went into the woods in the spirit world. Isaiah knew where The Hermit's cave was. We were too late to save Nancy, but we found Heather huddled in a cell. We thought we were going to be able to sneak back out, but we were attacked."

Tom looked down at Red, and put his hand on his shoulder.

"Your grandfather," Tom said. "Your grandfather sacrificed himself to save me and my daughter."

"I always thought he died in his sleep," Red said. He sat down in the grass at the edge of the walkway.

"Your grandfather fought The Hermit?" Chase said to Red. "How old is this man?"

"He's old. Very old," Tom said sitting back down on the bench. "Listen Red, your grandfather was a great man, and he took protecting this world seriously."

"What do you mean 'protecting this world?'" Chase asked.

"You didn't invent trying to take down the bad guys, kid," Tom said. "Isaiah's parents moved here from Ireland and built their farm where they did for a reason. They knew there was an interstice somewhere nearby in the forest. They came to make sure it didn't open up."

"What's an interstice?" Red asked. He stood from his place in the grass and sat down beside Tom.

"It's a kind of soft spot," Tom said. He moved his hands in a circle again. "A thin place where the spiritual and physical worlds sort of touch, so to speak. It can even allow a person to move from one side to the other, or for a djinn or other spiritual creature like a kobold, to come through to the physical world."

"Wait, what's a djinn?" Chase asked. He was beginning to realize how little he actually understood.

"I told you there was a lot you didn't understand," Tom said. "The djinn are malevolent beings of pure spirit. You've heard stories of genies trapped in magical lamps. Djinn are where those stories come from. They don't have the power to grant wishes or anything like that, though they are powerful in their own right. What they want is to destroy the barrier between the two worlds. That can only be done from this side. So they have to come through one of the interstices. Living in the physical world is difficult for them. They have to have a physical body, a person's or an animal's, to go into. For each one to come to this side, a person with a strong spirit must be sacrificed in exchange."

"So, that's what The Hermit is trying to do?" Red asked. "Bring more djinn through the interstice?"

"In part," Tom said. "His ultimate goal is to turn it into a kind of permanent gateway where djinn and other evil spirits can freely enter the physical world. Each time a sacrifice is made, the barrier becomes weaker."

The three looked at each other in silence, not sure what to say next. A flurry of questions piled in heaps like fallen snow inside Red's and Chase's minds. Red idly watched the cars entering and leaving the hospital's parking lot.

"So, you know where The Hermit's cave is?" Chase asked. He squeezed the handle of the billy club hanging at his waist. He still wanted to head off as soon as he learned which way to go.

"I don't remember, and even if I did, I wouldn't tell you," Tom said. "You would just run off half-cocked and get yourselves killed."

"Do you think that is where my father's spirit is?" Red asked. He was trying to look at Tom while still keeping one eye on the parking lot in case he saw his mother's car drive in. "Is he going to sacrifice my dad to try and open up the interstice?"

"Listen," Tom said. He put one hand on Red's shoulder. "There is nothing we can do. It isn't worth the risk to try and go after your father. It's best to move on before anybody else gets hurt or killed. It's for your own good."

"My own good?" Red said. He dropped his shoulder so Tom's hand would slide off. "'My own good' is rescuing my father before his spirit is sacrificed by The Hermit. I'm not going to just stand around learning about how my father is going to be killed, and do nothing about it."

"Red, you don't understand -" Tom began.

"I understand enough to know that Dad is going to be killed if somebody doesn't stop The Hermit. What I don't understand is why my dad is still alive at all if his spirit is going to be sacrificed anyway. Why hasn't The Hermit killed him already? If you won't help me rescue him, can't you at least tell me that?" Red said. He spoke faster and louder with each sentence. He glanced at the parking lot again and saw his mother's car pulling into a parking space.

"There is a ceremony The Hermit has to perform; I guess you could say some kind of rite," Tom said. He took a deep breath and rubbed his temples with one hand. "It seems like he prefers having several spirits, or even regular people if he has to, before he goes through with it. He keeps them in cages inside the cave near the interstice. That's where he was keeping my daughter."

Tom stepped in front of Red, blocking his view of his mother as she struggled toward the hospital with a coffee cup in one hand, a backpack in the other and her purse hung over one shoulder.

"Please," Tom said. He put both hands on Red's shoulders. "I beg you, for my sake and for your grandfather's. Please don't try and do this, not on your own. You are so young and still have so much to learn before you have a chance to remain alive."

"He won't be alone," Chase said, stepping up beside Red. He looked Red in the eye. "I mean, if you'll let me come with you. We can do it together. Wendy, the girl I saved in the alley from that kobold, will want to come too."

Tom looked at Chase who stood confidently beside Red. He lowered his head to the ground and patted one of Red's shoulders before turning aside. "This is a really bad idea, Red," he said. "Think this through before you go through with it. At least let me teach you what I can before you do anything rash."

"Help us go after my dad," Red said. "We don't have a lot of time and I need your help. Why else are you bothering to train me at all then?"

"No," Tom said firmly. "And if you had any sense you wouldn't do it either. I don't want to see anyone else hurt by that mad man. I'm training you to protect yourself, nothing else."

"I don't understand," Red said. Frustration and anger welled up inside him. "What's the matter with you? Are you really just going to sit here by the pond and keep letting people be sacrificed?"

"He's a coward," Chase said with a look of disgust on his

face.

Tom glared at the vigilante. "I am not a coward," he said. "My reasons are my own. It's complicated, you wouldn't understand."

"Try us and see," Red said.

"Forget him," Chase said and flicked his wrist at Tom like he was swatting away an annoying fly. "We can do it without him."

"Red," Tom said turning back to him. "You know where to find me. Whenever you calm down and come to your senses, I'll teach you everything I can. Until then."

Tom turned and walked slowly back up the path toward the parking lot.

"You have to help us," Red yelled to his back. "You owe it to my grandfather at least!"

Tom paused. He stood still for a moment, but didn't turn around. Just when Red thought he was about to speak, he started walking away again. The only sound was the warm static of tumbling water falling into the pond.

Chase walked up beside Red and together they watched Tom weave his way between the cars.

"Thank you, Chase," Red said. "I can really use your help, if you and Wendy are really willing." He didn't say how terrified he was of actually going through with it, or how worried he was about panicking and freezing up if they were caught.

"I want nothing more than to get rid of The Hermit," Chase said. "I'm in."

"Hey, can we talk later?" Red asked, realizing that his mother was probably already nearing his hospital room by now. "My mom just got to the hospital. How can I get hold of you? Do you have some kind of bat signal or something?"

"Yeah, something like that," Chase said laughing. "It's called a cell phone."

Chase gave Red his number and left. He headed off around the pond toward the other side of the park. Red watched the orange and yellow fireballs scatter out of Chase's way. Over the last several days, everything he thought he had known about the world had been turned inside out. Everything was more beautiful, complex and ultimately more dangerous than he could ever have imagined, and he felt things were about to get worse.

As he walked back to the hospital his legs began to burn. He stopped and looked down. There was nothing there. He felt a tug at his chest. It felt like when he touched the silver cord that connect his spiritual body to his physical body. He felt another slight pull, then it jerked him into the air.

It felt like his chest was tied to the back of a speeding train. His arms, legs and head were thrown back as he was pulled toward the hospital. The cord glowed brightly as it pulled him along. It was more painful than he thought possible. He was pulled faster and faster through the air toward the hospital. His feet hit the top of a van, flipping him head over heels. He was heading straight toward a second floor window. It was coming up fast. He managed to roll himself into some semblance of the fetal position with his hands covering his face right as he crashed through the window.

***

Claire held a Styrofoam coffee cup in one hand. With the other she dragged a chair from the wall to Red's bedside. She was still groggy from a combination of a poor night's rest and the sedative she had taken to get what little sleep she did manage. She had lain in the bed watching the slowly rotating blades of the fan above her bed. They circled around and around like her thoughts. She thought of Donal lying in his coma, then Red – looking so pathetic in his bandages and casts, she thought about the accident, what she was going to do now, and then her thoughts drifted back to Donal, starting the whole cycle over.

A leg of the chair she was dragging caught on the edge of a misaligned tile. Her coffee slipped out of her hand and overturned on the bed. It poured out of the plastic lid in pulsating spurts, spilling onto Red's legs. She grabbed the cup and ran over to the sink, throwing it into the basin and pulled paper towels frantically from the dispenser. She ran back over to the bed and daubed the paper towels at the spill. Her initial worry that the hot coffee would burn Red's legs was overwhelmed by her growing anxiety that it hadn't even woken him up.

She was about to call out for a nurse when the window on the other side of the bed shattered inward. Glass fell onto the window sill and onto the floor. Several thick shards landed on Red's blanket.

Claire screamed.

"The window!" Red yelled. He sat bold upright in the bed, his eyes wide.

Claire stood with the soaked paper towels clutched in her shaking hands.

"Mom, are you okay?" Red asked. His voice broke her out of her sudden shock.

"I'm fine," she said, her voice unsteady. "I spilled my coffee, and then, the window it…"

"What happened in here?" A tall nurse said running into the room. She stopped just inside the doorway examining the scene. Several more nurses and orderlies spilled into the room behind him.

"I don't know," Claire said. "It must have been a large bird or something. The window just seemed to explode."

"Here," the tall nurse said. "Let me take a look at you both." She walked over to Red and turned his face from side to side.

"Did any of it hit you?" she asked Red as she picked up his arm and examined it.

"No, I don't think so," Red said. A breeze fluttered the thick curtains on their rail.

"Sherri, can you find them another room?" The nurse said to one of the people still standing by the door. A small woman with frizzy hair nodded and hurried out the door. The rest busied themselves with checking both Claire and Red and picking glass off the bed.

"Check his legs too," Claire said. "I spilled my coffee just before the window blew."

The nurse pulled off the blanket. The leg that wasn't in a cast was red, but not seriously burned.

"It's not bad, it should be fine," she said. "Does it hurt at all?"

"No, it's fine," Red said looking down at his leg. He could feel some burning, but it didn't feel any worse than a slight scald.

I did that, Red thought looking at the shattered glass strewn around the room. *It must have been when Mom spilled the coffee on me. Apparently it forced me back inside my body.*

"Wow, it really is a mess in here," Dr. Cayson said as he

came into the room. "Fortunately, the room right next door is empty, so we are going to move you into there as soon as it is ready. But don't get too comfortable, Red. I think we are getting ready to discharge you. You can go home this afternoon if everything comes back looking good from the lab, which I fully expect."

"I can't go home," Red said leaning on one elbow. "What about Dad? Mom needs to be here."

"Don't worry about that Red," Claire said. She was still clutching the coffee soaked towels in one hand. "I talked to Emily and she said you can come and stay at their house with Michael and Sara for a few days. Would that be okay?"

"Yeah, that would be great, but … You sure you're okay here by yourself?" Red asked lowering himself back into the pillows.

"I'm fine," Claire said. "I'm sure there will be plenty of visitors to keep me company, and you'll be much more comfortable somewhere familiar."

"How is my dad?" Red asked the doctor.

"You know I'm not his primary physician. I don't know too many details, but to the best of my knowledge not much has changed," Dr. Cayson said as Red nodded solemnly.

"Which is actually not bad news," the doctor added quickly. "If he was getting worse, or falling deeper into the coma, we would have cause to be more concerned."

After the doctor left, Red pulled out the portable DVD player the Lagoses had lent him. He had just finished watching his second sci-fi movie of the morning as lunch arrived. With the steamed vegetables that all tasted exactly the same and the still crunchy macaroni and cheese, came the confirmation that he would indeed be going home as soon as all the paperwork was finished.

Red decided to eat just enough to keep his stomach from growling. He hoped he could stop on the way to Michael's house for some fast food, or at least something that resembled actual food. Just before two in the afternoon, Alexander and Michael arrived.

"I can't believe they're letting you out of here," Michael said. He sat down in the chair next to the bed, leaned back on two legs and put his feet up on the mattress. "You still look like you had a fight with a deranged gorilla and lost."

Red threw his pillow at Michael, the seat fell backwards dumping Michael onto the floor. They both laughed. They had only talked for a few more minutes about Michael's new video games when a nurse arrived with discharge papers and a wheelchair.

Claire, Alexander, and the nurse helped Red out of the bed into the chair. Claire bent over and put her arms around Red's neck. "I love you honey. I'll come by whenever I can get away from here."

"I love you too, Mom," Red said. Their hug lingered for several moments, neither wanting to be the first to let go.

"Alright, here we go," Alexander said as Claire and Red finally pulled apart. He leaned the wheelchair back into a wheelie and pushed it out the door.

"Think we can stop for some real food on the way home?" Red asked once they reached the hallway.

10

The Ringmaster's Plan

The sun, still high in the air, made the yellowed and trampled grass brittle underfoot in the deserted midway of the Circus Paenultimus. The air was still and heavy. It was several hours before the performers would put on their costumes and the ticketing stands would open for the evening performance. A tent flap was thrown open from inside one of the sideshow's small tents. A cloud of thick blue-gray smoke drifted lazily out. Synesteria emerged from the cloud. She glided smoothly across the grass, pulling a trail of the smoke behind in her wake. Her long serpentine body stretched out behind her in graceful arcs. The only sound in the midway was the sound her body made as it propelled her toward the big top, the sound of sand sliding across the stretched head of a drum.

The half-snake, half-woman slithered her way through the big top and out the rear entrance. Outside a temporary neighborhood had been erected. Caravans and campers were clustered in small circles like the sideshow tents in the midway, but with little space between the groupings. In the center of most circles was a fire pit rimmed with stones or bricks. Paths, worn down through the grass in just the few days the circus had been in town, wound between the aluminum homes. They all led from the campsites to either the big top or the dining tent. Synesteria moved down the most trampled one and ducked underneath a flap into the dining tent.

Inside the otherwise empty tent were the acrobats, Luca and Nadya Hibbard, and the ringmaster, Rinthim Straub. Synesteria slinked up beside the ringmaster, and coiled her body underneath herself like the lounge in her tent and reclined her upper body against it.

"It seems we have a problem with the local harbinger," Straub said. He was wearing a dirty white button-up shirt, unbuttoned halfway down. The sleeves were rolled up beyond his elbows. Every inch of his exposed skin was covered in hundreds of tattoos. The symbols and sigils were all in the same blue-black of faded India ink.

"This one calls himself 'The Hermit,'" Luca said in flawless English.

"Why do they always give themselves such ridiculous names?" Nadya asked.

"Anyway," Luca continued. "The Hermit is far behind where he should be in opening up the interstice. It seems he has forgotten that his duty isn't to himself, but to the Kindred."

"How many ssspiritss iss it then? How far iss he behind?" Synesteria asked, dragging out her esses in her otherwise sonorous deep voice.

"It's hundreds," Luca said wincing. The voice of the half-snake was deep, but it still shook his nerves. It was like fingernails scraping across a chalk board. "Nadya and I examined the interstice for ourselves last night."

"I know thiss iss a sssmall town, but that iss unacceptable."
Synesteria's thin forked tongue flicked out of her mouth, its
tip wiping one of her eyeballs. "What are we going to do to
him? Or should I ssay *with* him afterwardsss. It would be
sssuch a sshame to wassste hiss body."

"You know how I love to indulge you Synesteria, but we
don't have time to install another harbinger here," Straub said
petting Synesteria's scaly form. "We need all the interstices
to open at the same time if we are going to permanently
destroy the barrier. My plan is going to be more to your
liking anyway."

"Oh, do tell," Synesteria said. She flicked her tongue
against Straub's earlobe.

"We are going to have to an accident. A horrible, unforeseen
tragedy." Straub held his pinky finger to the corner of his
eye and mimed wiping away tears. He continued in falsetto:
"It will all be just so unfortunate. All of those people killed
when the tent's rigging unexpectedly fails, and the entire
thing falls down on the crowd. Oh, the humanity. Oh, the
horror."

"Are you sure that's the best plan?" Nadya asked. Luca
caught his wife's eye, and raising his eyebrows, he shook his
head at her in an effort to get her to remain silent.

"I think," Luca said quickly. "What my wife is trying to
say, is that, isn't it a little dangerous to put ourselves at risk?
What if they suspect us of setting it up, especially if none of
us are caught in the ... *accident.*"

"There is a risk," Straub said, smiling thinly. "I imagine a
few of us, perhaps even the least of us, you might say, will
have to make the ultimate sacrifice for the Kindred."

Nadya and Luca were both thinking of their daughter

Esmerelda. Esmerelda, whom they feared might be just beginning to get an inkling about the true purpose of the circus. They were both fairly sure that Straub also knew she was beginning to figure things out for herself. She had begun asking uncomfortable questions that neither of them wanted to answer.

"What do you want us to do?" Luca asked.

"Go back to The Hermit's little cave," the ringmaster said. "Tell him that Synestcria and I will be paying him a visit tomorrow afternoon. Don't tell him our plans yet; I'll fill him in on the details when it suits me."

Straub turned to Synesteria. "You don't mind accompanying me for a stroll through the forests of these beautiful mountains do you? They are supposed to be some of the oldest in the world."

"It will be my pleasssure," she said. She uncoiled her long body, closed her eyes and gave a hiss that sounded like a contented purr.

As the four of them went their separate ways, an unseen watcher moved away from a crack between flaps of the tent.

11

SARA'S GHOST

Michael stood in the center of his den. Playing cards seemed to magically rise off the table and fling themselves toward him. One bounced off his forehead and he burst out laughing, falling to his knees.

"This is the coolest thing I've ever seen," Michael said.

Red opened his eyes. He was lying on the Lagoses' couch, his feet resting on one of its arms. Covering almost every wall of the wood-paneled room were concert flyers for Grateful Dead and Phish. One whole wall was their massive record collection, while another was covered in framed LPs. Michael's parents had been big into the concert scene when they were younger.

"I think I'm really beginning to get the hang of it," Red said as he pushed himself up on the couch.

Michael sat on the floor, the cards were scattered all around him.

"I can't believe you actually met The Brand," Michael said.

"Yeah, The Brand, Chase I mean, is actually a pretty cool guy, even if he is a bit intimidating," Red said.

"I'm still having trouble believing all this. It just doesn't seem possible," Michael said. He gathered the cards into a pile, then looked up at Red straight faced. "Are you really going to try and go after your dad?"

"I have to try," Red said. He put two more pillows behind his back. "I can't just sit by and let him get killed."

"How are you going to do it?" Michael asked as he tossed the cards back on the table.

"I called Chase," Red said. "He is coming over tomorrow with his friend. I think we are going to try and find out where The Hermit's cave is and see if there is any way to rescue Dad without anyone knowing we were there. Apparently Wendy, Chase's friend, can track down anything in the spirit world. You're sure nobody else will be home tomorrow?"

"Yeah, one hundred percent," Michael said. He sat back down cross-legged on the floor. "Mom and Dad are going with Sara to her soccer regionals in Morristown. They are leaving right after breakfast and won't be back until late."

"Good," Red said. "I think that will give us enough time."

"What can I do?" Michael asked. "I don't think I'd be much use. Oh, I could be your lookout or something. I could keep an eye out while you all try and sneak in."

"You can stay here, and I don't know if we'll be ready to sneak in just yet."

"But I want to help," Michael said. "I don't want to just sit here while you guys risk your lives. There has to be something I can do."

"Seriously," Red said while scratching underneath his leg cast with a pencil at a particularly annoying itch. "Staying here will be a big help. We need somebody to make sure nothing happens to mine or Wendy's bodies while we are in the spirit world."

"Yeah, I can do that," Michael said. His shoulders slumped

as he idly picked lint out of the rug on the floor. "I guess it's better than nothing. I just wish there was more I could do than just sit here alone."

Red didn't want to risk the life of his best friend. "Look, I don't know what is going to happen out there," he said. "It is going to be dangerous, and at least me, Chase, and Wendy have a chance to defend ourselves."

They heard the low hum of the garage door as it opened, followed by the sound of car doors shutting. Michael's parents and Sara clomped up the stairs from the garage and into the kitchen.

"We'll talk about it in the morning," Red said hurriedly. "I don't want Sara to find out."

"Michael. Red. We're home," Michael's mom shouted down the stairs. "I'm going to get dinner going, is everybody doing alright?"

"We're fine, Mom. We've just been playing cards," Michael shouted back.

Overhead they heard Emily banging pots and pans as she pulled them out from underneath the oven. Michael rolled onto his back laughing.

"What is it?" Red asked.

"Oh, this is going to be so awesome," Michael said through his snickering. "You need practice doing stuff in the spirit world right?"

"Yeah," Red said drawing out the word, unsure of what kind of plan Michael was hatching this time. *It's probably going to be another of his ridiculous pranks.*

"Well, I got a great idea. I'll fill you in on it later," Michael said as they heard someone coming into the den.

Sara hopped down the stairs, jumping down the last couple

of steps.

***

Tom Clack sat alone in his hospital room. The green tinted light from a streetlamp fell across his face as he stared out the window. The only sound was the faint wheezing of his breath and the harsh rasp as he sucked air through the hose from his oxygen tank. He kept his silent vigil, unmoving even when the door cracked open and shut, apparently by itself. He knew something else was in the room with him.

"It's been a while," he said. He pulled the plug out of his nose, sighed and shifted into the spirit world.

A kobold stood at his feet. Its head no higher than his chest.

"You know why I'm here," the kobold said.

It always surprised Tom at just how repulsive the vile creatures were each time he saw one. Their mouths were the worst. They stretched so far around that it looked to him like their heads were hinged at the spine on the back of their necks.

"Surely I've done enough," Tom said. He stood, still in the spirit world, and walked to the window so he wouldn't have to look directly at the kobold. His physical body slumped slightly in the chair. "Tell The Hermit I'm done with all this. I've been repaying him for over twenty years."

"And you'll do it twenty more," the kobold said. He leapt up on the window sill. His face was even with Tom's. It's long, twisted nose touched his. "That is if you have that many years left in your pink, diseased body."

Tom turned his face away. The kobold laughed and with one bony finger caressed the side of Tom's face, and turned it

130

back facing his own.

"Do I need to remind you of the arrangement," it asked. Shiny streaks of saliva led from the corners of the kobold's mouth down to its chin. Its lips rimmed white with the drying drool.

"I know the arrangement," Tom said. "I find spirits for you, and The Hermit lets my daughter live. It's been three years since you came, I was hoping he had forgotten about me, or that she had been the final one."

"He never forgets," the kobold said tapping its finger on the tip of Tom's nose. It jumped off the window sill and landed on Tom's physical body in the chair. It sat down on one of his legs like a child on Santa's lap. The kobold put one arm around the body's neck.

"Get off me," Tom said and kicked at the kobold. It dodged his kick and clambered onto the bed. "Heather's moved away. The Hermit has nothing to hold over me now."

"How does she like her new house?" The kobold said. It smiled wide, the sharp teeth reflecting the sickly fluorescent light.

"What?" Tom said spinning toward the bed. "What do you know about it?"

"Me," the kobold said. It somehow managed to broaden its smile at Tom's distress. "I know nothing personally, but The Hermit wants you to know that she must be awfully lonely all by herself in that little brick cottage in Asheville. We can send some friends to keep her company."

"You disgusting little vermin," Tom spat. He dove at the kobold, but it was too fast. It jumped over Tom's grasping arms, swung off the curtain rod over his bed and landed in the middle of the room.

"Now, now," it said. "All you have to do is give us some names and where to find them, and your little Heather will be right as rain."

Tom slammed his fist into the mattress. *Why won't this end?*

Tom had never been able to remove from his mind the look Isaiah had given him when they had snuck into The Hermit's cave. They had come in through the lower entrance. They were just a few feet in when they were surrounded by The Hermit and his djinn.

"Why?" Isaiah had asked turning to Tom; he had known immediately that it was a setup. He looked at Tom, confused and hurt, pain evident in his eyes. It was then that Heather stepped out from behind The Hermit. Little, tiny, innocent Heather.

"Daddy," she yelled and ran into his arms.

"I see," Isaiah said. His countenance changed to one of pity and understanding. He dropped the short sword in his hand without any protest. It clinked on the rock floor and morphed back into a garden hoe.

"Promise me you'll protect my family," Isaiah said to Tom as he was dragged away.

Tom only nodded in reply. He could find no words to justify this betrayal. He picked up his daughter and ran out of the cave.

I can't tell The Hermit about Red. I'll never break that promise. It's too late for Donal, but I can keep Red a secret. He lay with his face down on the mattress for several breaths. Finally, he pushed himself up and turned again toward the kobold. *Isaiah, I pray your God will have mercy on my soul.*

"I only know of one you'd be interested in right now," Tom said. He looked at a point just over the kobold's bulbous eyes.

"He's powerful, and still young."

"Only one?" The kobold spat. "In three years, you've only found one more."

"Look at me," Tom said pointing toward the figure wasting away on the chair by the window. "I'm old, sick, and dying; stuck in this hospital day after day."

"Fine, just tell me where to find him."

"I don't know for sure," Tom said. He couldn't believe he was being forced to sentence another person to death. "His name is Chase. He lives somewhere near downtown, in a warehouse."

"What are you trying to pull on me?" the kobold asked. He pointed one yellow-nailed finger at Tom. "Why would he live in a warehouse?"

"His last name is Lewis. He's the oldest son of the last woman I told you about," Tom said. He spoke flatly, trying to block any emotion inside him. *I didn't see any way out of it all those years ago, and I don't see any way out now,* he thought. *I can't let anything happen to my daughter.*

"Can't be," the kobold said. "Her oldest brat died in the fire."

"No one ever found his body," Tom said. "He's been living secretly as the vigilante in town. He calls himself 'The Brand.' He says he won't stop at anything until he hunts The Hermit down and kills him."

"You say he's powerful?" The kobold asked. "Is his spirit stronger than his mother's?"

Tom nodded.

"And you don't know of any others?" The kobold asked. It turned its head slightly sideways and peered at Tom as if trying to see into his eyes.

"No, nobody else," Tom said. He continued staring at a

point just above the kobold's brow ridge.

"Look me in the eyes," the kobold said.

Tom reluctantly obeyed.

"What about the Snyders? The offspring of the one you traded for your daughter to seal the bargain," The kobold said.

"You've already got Isaiah's son," Tom said trying to keep his eyes from betraying Red. "His grandson is just a regular boy, there's no more to his spirit than the average person."

Tom stared into the kobold's eyes not blinking.

"Fine," the kobold said breaking his gaze.

Tom felt like a weight was lifted off his shoulders.

"The Hermit is speeding up the sacrifices, the Kindred are growing restless," The creature said walking toward the door. "I'll be back in a few days, you better have found me some more."

"What do you expect me to do? I can't very well travel far from the hospital," Tom said he raised his arms in an exaggerated shrug.

"A lot of people work in this hospital, and even more come through it," the kobold said over his shoulder. "Find more."

The kobold slipped out of the door and disappeared into the hallway.

Tom leaned against the wall and slid down to the floor.

"It's for Heather. She'll be safe for a while now," Tom said as he sobbed in the dark room.

***

"I don't know, man, it just seems mean," Red said. The thought of sneaking in to Sara's room and pretending to be a ghost didn't seem right to him, especially considering everything else that was going on.

Sara had finally gone to bed just before midnight, leaving Red and Michael in the den alone for the first time since she had gotten home.

"C'mon, it will be hilarious. Sara will pee her pants," Michael said as he filled up an air mattress with a bicycle pump. "We play pranks on each other all the time, and I still haven't got her back for the itching powder."

"What?" Red said laughing. "You never told me about the itching powder."

"Yeah, well. It was embarrassing," Michael said plopping the filled mattress down on the floor beside the couch. "Remember that game a couple of weeks ago when I kept running to the bathroom every time we came in to bat?"

"You said you ate something that gave you the runs, the whole team placed bets on which inning you would finally crap your pants," Red said. He laughed until his side ached.

"Yeah, I didn't want anyone to know, that was the first thing I could think of," Michael said laughing too.

"Your lie was worse than the truth!"

"Yeah, by the time I realized what I said it was too late," Michael said. He threw himself down on the mattress. "Anyway, she put the itching powder in my jock strap. I didn't even notice until the game started. It was all I could do to keep from sticking my hands down my pants and scratching while I was on the field. I kept trying to wipe whatever it was off with toilet paper in the bathroom, but that only spread it around more. You can't even see that stuff, it's virtually invisible."

"Stop, stop," Red said. He imagined Michael dancing

around the disgusting bathroom with his pants around his knees. He couldn't catch his breath he was laughing so hard. His face was bright red and he waved one hand plaintively at Michael. "It hurts too much."

"I didn't even know what was going on at first," Michael continued. He mimed scratching himself furiously. "It kept getting worse and worse. It wasn't until I was running out of the dugout in the eighth inning and saw Sara busting up laughing from the stands that I figured it out."

"Okay, okay. Enough," Red said. He slowed his breathing down and finally stopped laughing. "I'll do this prank for you as long as you promise never to tell her it was me."

"I'll never tell," Michael said. He ran his fingers across his lips like a zipper. "Besides, no one is ever going to believe you have this magical ability to turn yourself into some kind of ghost anyway."

"Good point," Red said.

Ten minutes later Red lay all the way down on the couch and shifted into the spirit world. The now familiar world rippled into reality spreading across the den's ceiling and down the walls.

"Have you shifted?" Michael asked looking around the room.

Instead of answering, which would have been pointless anyway, Red knocked a coaster off an end table.

"I really wish I could see her face," Michael said. He wore a mischievous grin.

Red walked up the stairs into the kitchen, turned and went up the second set into the upstairs hallway. He stood outside of Sara's door. It was covered with posters of her soccer heroes: Hope Solo, Mia Hamm and Alex Morgan.

Red focused on his hand as he grabbed the door knob. His aura flowed from his fingers across the brass turning the knob solid. He turned it slowly, trying to be as quiet as possible. It stopped turning. *Sara must have locked the door.* Red released the knob and stepped back, thinking of giving up. He stared at the slowly swirling mass of the door. It looked so insubstantial, no more solid than a sheet of falling water. He remembered trying to pick up the piece of trash in the park. It had slipped through his fingers like water, but it had gone *through* his fingers. *What if I could walk through the door?*

It seemed like a ridiculous idea as soon as he thought of it, but it would really be something if he could.

Red placed one hand over Mia Hamm's face. The blue flame of his aura spread out across the poster. It turned solid. He focused on the rippling blue flame and imagined it drawing back from the poster's surface, back to his body. It was similar to the way he shifted between worlds. His aura responded. It pulled itself back to his hand, the poster no longer solid. His hand sank several centimeters into the wood. He pushed his hand tentatively forward. It passed the rest of the way through as if the door wasn't there. He took a step forward and walked straight through the door.

He went through the door twice more, the last time he hardly had to think about it at all. *This is going to be useful,* he thought.

Red stood in Sara's room just looking around. Nearly every inch of the walls and ceiling was covered with more soccer posters. Clothes and soccer equipment were piled in heaps around the floor. Dozens of medals hung on the posts on each side of a large dresser mirror. A reading lamp on the bed's headboard shone a small pool of light on Sara's face. She had fallen asleep with a notebook and pen in her hand.

Red felt a surge of guilt and nervousness come over him. It was the first time he had actually been inside Sara's room, and here he was – alone with her, in her locked bedroom. Somehow the fact that the door was locked made him even more uncomfortable. Before doing anything else, he turned and unlocked the door.

He walked over to the bedside, not sure of what a ghost would do. He looked at Sara under the halo of light and admired her long curly brown hair splayed across the pillow. Her eyes, with their long eyelashes, were closed. She was asleep. The notebook in her hand turned out to be her diary. He told himself not to, but Red leaned over her shoulder and read it anyway.

Today was absolutely unbelievable!

To begin with, we had our last practice before regionals this afternoon. I know we are going to win tomorrow night and go to the state tournament next week.

But the most exciting thing is that Red came to stay at our house today. I don't know how long he is going to be here, but his dad is in the hospital, so it will probably be at least until he gets out. He is in a coma, but I'm sure he is going to be fine. He has probably been in worse situations before.

Red looks so cute in his casts! I hope he can stay here at least until the tournament is over, maybe he'll even be able to come.

Red stopped reading and stood straight up. His head reeled with the idea that Sara really did like him too, and that she thought he was 'cute.' He steadied himself by putting one of his hands on the bedside table, accidentally knocking over a glass of water that spilled its contents before falling to the floor. Sara mumbled something in her sleep and rolled over on her side.

He was afraid that the falling glass might have woken her up until he remembered that she had to be awake for the prank to work. He couldn't believe he let Michael talk him into this. Not only did he feel bad about doing it in the first place, but now that he knew Sara liked him too, it just seemed cruel, but he was determined to go through with it. It was just a prank after all.

He walked over to the dresser and cracked open up a drawer. He looked in with only one eye, worried that it might be filled with Sara's underwear, but when he saw it full of socks, he relaxed and opened it the rest of the way. Thoughts of the prank being mean or not passed from his mind as he picked up a pair of rolled socks and tossed them at Sara's head.

Sara woke to a pair of knee high socks bouncing off her forehead. "Michael, quit it. How did you get in here anyway? I know I locked the door."

She sat up in bed. Several pair of socks fell to the floor near her dresser. She threw her covers off and slid out of bed knocking her diary to the floor. She pushed it under the bed with her foot, hoping Michael didn't get a chance to see what it was. "Where are you, I know you're in here."

She looked around the room, but didn't see anyone. She stomped over to the closet and opened the accordion doors wide. The inside of the closet was piled with clothes, shoes and soccer balls, two of which rolled out into the bedroom. A jangling sound made her spin around.

Her various award medals were bouncing and shaking on their lanyards beside her mirror. One of them levitated from the top of the post and dangled in the air by itself for a moment before flying toward her and landing at her feet. She watched stunned as several more came off the posts and sailed through the air, one hit her bedside lamp and knocked it over.

Sara walked toward the dresser. She hoped somehow Michael had put together some kind of contraption out of fishing line. As she neared the medals, they stopped moving. She had to stand on her tiptoes to reach the top of the post, but she didn't feel wires anywhere. In the mirror she saw a depression move across her bed, upsetting the blankets. She managed to duck as a pillow flew off her bed and came hurtling toward the back of her head. It hit the mirror behind her and fell onto the dresser. *This isn't Michael, it's some kind of ghost.*

Red slid off the side of the bed nearest the closet. Despite his thinking the trick was mean, he still stifled back laughter at the look on Sara's face. He accidentally kicked one of the soccer balls as he hurried away from the bed. It bounced loudly off the door. Red stumbled and fell down.

"Mom, Dad!" Sara screamed. She threw open the door and ran out of the room and down the hall toward her parent's room.

Red snuck out of the room after her, and went back downstairs to the den. Michael was lying on the floor looking at the ceiling and laughing so hard tears streamed down his face.

12

RECONNAISSANCE

Wendy Wright wrapped her arms tightly around Chase's waist as the four wheeler she 'borrowed' from her parents bounced along the winding country road.

"Everywhere I've traveled in the spirit world the last few days there have been all sorts of new tracks," Wendy said, speaking loudly over the wind and the growling motor. "I haven't been able to even identify them all. Nor have I discovered a meaningful pattern. There is more activity than I've seen before."

"What do you think it means?" Chase asked over his shoulder as they sped around a corner, momentarily tipping onto two wheels.

"I'm not sure," she said, pulling a lock of hair out of her mouth. "But it is unsettling."

Chase dropped down into a lower gear and coaxed the four wheeler up a steep incline. The paved road continued down the hill another four hundred yards before ending at a driveway, a dirt road headed off at a right angle to the left toward the forest.

At the bottom of the next hill near the driveway to the last house there was an overturned logging truck and logs scattered on both sides of the road. The road was covered with a crisscrossing pattern of neon orange lines.

"That must be where the accident was," Chase said nodding toward the markings the police used when they recreated the accident. "Michael's house should be just before that."

Chase turned into the driveway and pulled the four wheeler to a stop behind a shed out of view from the road. Chase and Wendy climbed off the ATV and went to the back door. Chase knocked once on the glass door, then four times more rapidly.

"Why did you knock like that?" Wendy asked. She took off her glasses and let them dangle on their cord.

"It's 'A Shave and a Haircut,'" Chase said with a shrug.

"I know what it is," Wendy said, rolling her eyes. "but why did you do it? If anybody else is here, they'll answer the door anyway. This isn't some kind of secret society."

They heard two knocks from the other side of the door in response.

"Two bits," she said. She threw her hands into the air. "Unbelievable."

Michael opened the door.

"Whoa. You must be The Brand." He looked up at seventeen-year-old Chase's imposing figure standing in the doorway. He then looked down at Wendy. The eleven-year-old was as thin as a pencil and wore a maroon cardigan that hung down almost to her knees, even though the temperature was creeping into the nineties. She reminded Michael of his librarian from elementary school, even her blonde hair was pulled back into a tight bun. Underneath a particularly hideous plaid skirt was the pink plastic of an artificial leg.

"It's prosthetic, I lost it in a boating accident," Wendy said.

She held out her hand. "My name is Wendy Wright. Pleased to meet you. And you are..."

"Oh, uh, Michael. Michael Lagos. Come on in, Red's downstairs." He shook her hand before the three of them went through the kitchen and down the stairs into the den.

Chase introduced Red and Wendy to each other and they all sat down.

"So, how are we going to do this?" Red asked. He rubbed his hands together.

"I think Wendy already has a plan," Chase said and nodded toward the slight girl.

Red and Michael looked at her. Michael raised his eyebrows and gave a shrug.

"It isn't so much a plan as a first step," she said. She put her glasses back on. "I think the first thing we have to do is go to where the accident happened and see if we can find any clues or tracks."

"But I thought we were going to go and try and rescue my dad," Red said looking back at Chase.

"That is definitely the end goal of this entire enterprise," Wendy said looking at Red over the top of her glasses. "But to begin with, we don't know where your father is, we don't know how he is being held, and we don't know how much resistance we are likely to encounter. Until we have adequate answers to those questions, I firmly believe any attempt at a rescue operation is premature."

"How old are you?" Michael asked.

Chase laughed.

"I am eleven," Wendy said. "But that is irrelevant to our current situation. What matters is coming up with a set of parameters we can follow to safely execute an extraction while limiting the danger to our persons, both spiritual and physical. That is paramount."

"I thought I was pretty smart until I met Wendy," Chase said. "She is really the brains behind The Brand. I sometimes think I'm just her puppet."

Wendy blushed.

"Okay," Red said. He slapped his hands together. A sliver of pain ran up his broken arm. "So what do we do first?"

***

Red looked at the logs that had been cleared off the road and the wreck of the logging truck for the first time. He had been lying down in the back of the Lagoses' minivan when they brought him to their house from the hospital. He stood at the same point in the road where their car was when the logs came flying off the truck. He closed his eyes and immediately recalled the image of the coyote leaping onto the hood, and the logs tumbling through the air toward him, bouncing off the asphalt. He was worried that there was nothing left to find, despite Chase's insistence that Wendy could track anything through the spirit world.

"I've never seen anything like this before," Wendy said. Both she and Red came to the accident site through the spirit world. Their physical bodies still in the den at the Lagoses' house. She stood higher than the road surface in the field opposite the forest looking down on the whole scene. "It's true that the tracks are fading, just like I feared, but there were so many of them that it is unmistakable."

"What do you mean?" Chase asked. He turned away from examining the overturned truck's cab.

"Who are you talking to?" Michael said as he looked around confused.

"Wendy," Chase said. "Hold on a second." He turned back toward Wendy. "What is unmistakable?"

"The chances of this being an accident are minuscule," she said. "It looks to me like a large canine of some sort was on this hill for quite a long time. It was probably waiting for Red and his father to pass by."

"It was a coyote," Red said, and walked to the edge of the road nearest to where Wendy stood.

"A coyote?" Chase asked, jogging up the incline to get a better look.

"Why are you talking about a coyote?" Michael asked Chase. He hopped up on one of the logs and began walking across it like a tight rope. "We all saw the logging truck turn over. That's what caused the accident."

"This is getting old real fast," Chase said to no one in particular. "Look Michael, Wendy is telling us what she is seeing, she said there was some kind of large dog. Red is the one that said it was a coyote. Let Wendy finish what she has to say, then I'll tell you what she said."

"Okay, sorry. I just feel left out. I don't know what the rest of you guys are saying or doing," Michael said, throwing his arms into the air and jumping off the log. "I feel kind of useless here."

"He is kind of useless," Wendy said.

"Michael's my best friend," Red said. "He's not useless."

"I don't mean he is useless in general," she said. She put her glasses back on, seemed to think better of it, then took them off. "I mean that there is nothing useful he can do here. I mean no disrespect, I'm sure he is a fine and attentive friend otherwise."

"Tell him I'll explain everything back at the house once we are done here," Red said.

"Red says he'll explain everything to you later," Chase told Michael. "Now, give us a few minutes to let Wendy tell us what happened."

"It's fine," Michael said, throwing one hand into the air. "Don't worry about it. Tell Red I'm going to go on back up to the house."

"He'll be fine," Red said. He watched as Michael walked up the driveway toward his house. "I don't think anything ever really bothers him, at least not for long."

"To be honest, I have no idea what precisely occurred here," Wendy said, shaking her head. "Everything is too confusing and too faded for me to tell for sure, but I can see the path of several spirits leading into the forest. They are clear enough that I'm sure I can follow them."

"Let's go," Red said and turned toward the forest. He was anxious, but if it had to be done, he wanted to do it and get it over with.

"No," Wendy said. She jumped down off the embankment landing in the road beside Red. "I'm going to reconnoiter alone. I'm quick and silent; you two maladroit oafs stamping through the trees would only hinder me and increase the likelihood of our being spotted."

"Recon-what?" Red asked.

"She's going to go spy it out first," Chase said, coming back down the hill. "She likes to impress everyone with her vocabulary."

Wendy stuck her tongue out at Chase. "I'll be back as quick as I am able." She took off without waiting for them to respond and sprinted across the field toward the forest.

"She is fast," Red said as she disappeared under the trees. "And a bit of a know it all."

Chase shrugged. "You get used to it. Let's go check on your friend. I think he really is upset with us."

***

Wendy rushed headlong into the forest's embrace. Every traveler, whether pure spirit or in a physical body, left behind traces in the spirit world that she could detect. These traces were like dust motes in a shaft of light to her. If something stood still long enough, and she got there soon enough, she could even make out the shape of what had been there, in the same way that sparkling dust can define the shape of light.

It had been too long for her to tell with precision what anything on the roadside had been, the traces were muddled together and beginning to fade and flow away down the valley. She was still able to follow them, though she had no idea what to expect when she finally found whomever or whatever made them. She was only able to tell that one had been doglike because of the long hours it had sat motionless on the hill.

Wendy's silent strides slowed as she delved deeper into the forest. The light grew dim, and the shadows long, even though the sun wasn't yet halfway across the sky. It seemed colder to Wendy as well, though she knew hot and cold had no real meaning in the spirit world. Slowly but insistently, dread crept upon her. She slowed to a jog, then a walk, and finally she stopped completely. The traces she had been following became too hard to distinguish from the plethora of others in the dark woods. If she had not been confident she could follow her own trail out, she would have despaired and given herself up as lost.

If I take my time, I can figure this out, she thought. She sat on a boulder overlooking the narrow hollow between two ridges. Traces of past spiritual visitors crisscrossed the valley, even up the trees and through the intertwined branches. She traced one path after another from the crest of the surrounding ridges until they disappeared, either further down the valley, or across another ridge. One by one, she eliminated them from the group she was following. Either they were too fresh, or too old. They were made by too many spirits, or too few. She threw out any that went up a tree or traversed through the branches. Concentrating on the complicated task relaxed her mind and her spirit. Each trail she was able to cross off her mental map of the valley brought order and calmness to her. The forest grew a little less intimidating, the task a little less daunting.

"That's the one," she said and jumped off the rock. She headed down the valley following one of the many paths.

The original trail she had been following had been overtaken by a much newer one. It was so fresh that the remnants of the older one had been obscured by the new. She figured that it must have been created in the last few hours. She could tell that the new group included three or four adults and what she thought was a bear or another large animal. Something else really threw her off. If she hadn't known it was impossible, she would have sworn it was a twenty-foot long snake with a diameter of at least two-and-a-half feet. Whatever had left the illusory form in its passage was something she hoped to never see in real life.

As she followed the intertwined trails, she realized that there were other, even older paths here as well. It was a well-traveled trail, both in the spirit and the physical worlds. The mossy ground she followed had been worn down to a furrowed dirt path.

She set off down the trail. The path in front of her seemed illuminated by the passage of other spirits before her. The way became obvious and she hurried quietly down it as through a tunnel of soft light overhung by darkness. She was unaware of another that followed behind her. The other figure, also silent, stayed off the paths between the trees, choosing instead to make its way through the interlacing branches in the forest's canopy overhead.

Wendy heard voices not far ahead, just over the next rise. She stepped behind the trunk of a large oak tree and listened. She couldn't make out the words, but there was obviously a heated argument going on. Darkness had descended around her since she had left the path, like lights dimming before the start of a movie.

She made her way from tree trunk to tree trunk, drawing nearer to the voices with each move. At last she was able to see the large mouth of a cave at the bottom of a cliff directly in front of her. The opening had been obscured by the trees. It was there that the voices were coming from. Underneath the overhanging rocks at the entrance, a bear and a large coyote looked out toward the forest across a small grassy clearing. *That must be the coyote,* she thought.

A small creek tumbled out of a smaller entrance to the cave. The second entrance was to the left of the larger one and further down the ridge that the cliff extended out of. Hundreds of birds had made the craggy rocks on the cliff wall their home. They darted back and forth between the forest and their nests. It looked to Wendy that there might be just enough room between the creek's edge and the wall of the cave for her to slip inside.

She carefully made her way toward the creek, staying out of sight of the two dangerous and deadly creatures. It mattered little whether they were true animals or the djinn that Chase had described. Either way, drawing their attention would be a very bad idea. A pile of rocks that had fallen from the cliff blocked the view from the main entrance to the smaller one. She hurried past the rocks and slipped into the cave.

She was not quite able to make out the words in the bickering conversation, so she slipped further into the cave. Behind her, something swung out of the trees and landed on a small ledge just above the entrance. Wendy hadn't heard a sound.

"I assure you, Straub, I have not forgotten my duty," a gravelly and aged voice said. It echoed through the cave. "I have maintained the interstice. I've been waiting to open it further until I received word that it was time."

"Hermit, don't take me for the fool you are. You surely know that the time is already at hand," a second voice said. Its oily tones slid along the stone walls instead of echoing like the first speaker's voice. "You are far behind the other harbingers. You must drastically escalate your contributions to the Kindred's cause."

Wendy cautiously crept further into the cave. As her eyes adjusted to the darkness, she realized that the room around her was a small dome. One large stalactite, like the Sword of Damocles, hung in the very center over a pond surrounded by tumbled down stones. From a small crack in the wall ahead of her came a flickering light and the sound of the voices. She made her way to the crack and peered through it, hoping that the glint of her eyes wouldn't be visible.

Two figures stood in silhouette against a small fire. The man nearest her wore a large and tattered coat over a ragged shirt and torn pants. *That one must be The Hermit.* The other figure, the one The Hermit called Straub, was tall and thin. He wore a top hat and a coat with two long tails that trailed behind him as he paced in front of the fire. He waved a long baton around as he spoke, punctuating his words with swipes and jabs.

"I already have one powerful spirit ready to sacrifice, and a second one my djinn should be bringing in anytime now," The Hermit said. He stood still, resting his weight on a long stave. "I can't act too boldly, Straub. There are only so many I can take in a small town and still go unnoticed."

"The time for stealth is over, Hermit. I don't care if you are caught, skinned, and hung out to dry," Straub said. He swung his baton through the air, only inches from The Hermit's face, miming slicing him in pieces. "I thought you were supposed to be one of the most powerful harbingers in the colonies. All I see is a pathetic old man who clings to a pedestrian idea of power, instead of reaching out to take real power in his hands."

The Hermit didn't move.

A movement on the opposite side of the fire caught Wendy's attention. There were several prison-like cells on the far wall. She had never seen anything like the cells before. The cage doors looked like they were made of steel. Purple sparks of energy, like electricity, ran between the metal bars, crackling and leaping between them. Between two of the cell doors a wide purple arc of energy rose repeatedly toward the ceiling. As it reached the top of the steel, it crackled loudly and vanished, only to start the cycle again from the bottom. *That must be how they keep the spirits caged.*

Straub walked away from The Hermit and out of Wendy's view.

"That power is mine," The Hermit said. He pounded his staff against the stone floor. The same purple energy flowed down The Hermits arm and danced around his staff. "I will not let anyone take this power away from me."

"Yes!" Straub yelled. He came back into Wendy's view and stood near the fire.

The Hermit stood up straight and slammed the staff into the ground again. The energy began swirling furiously around the staff.

"All who face me, face the gathered strength of the Kindred," The Hermit said as if it was a mantra. "I am their right arm, I am their sword!"

Wendy took a step back from the opening, but she couldn't pull her eyes away - her curiosity overpowering her nervousness. Over the last few days she had learned more about the spirit world than she had in the previous three years since she discovered the spirit world. She was eager to lap up any stray morsels from their conversation.

"That's good," Straub said. His voice was less harsh than before. He held his hands in front of him at his waist as he took a half-step back.

"I am the harbinger of doom. I am the one who opens, the one who rends the veil between worlds!" The Hermit chanted, each new phrase growing in volume and voracity. He struck the stones with each pronouncement. Each time, the energy encircling his staff grew brighter and wilder. At his final stroke, the energy jumped between the cells and his staff. Wendy felt the little hairs on the back of her neck stand up. He held the staff in the air and took a step toward Straub.

Straub took two full steps away from The Hermit, his hands held out in front of him.

"You are only one of many harbingers," Straub said. His voice was firm, but faltering. "Don't think too highly of yourself. We can always find others who would be more than willing to sacrifice everything for even a portion of your power."

Wendy watched in horror as a giant snake with the upper body of a woman glided into the fire's light. *That must have been what I saw in the spirit traces. She's a nāginī.* The creature's body reared eight feet into the air, like a cobra prepared to strike. Straub laid one hand on her coiled flank.

"Easy Synesteria," he said.

"You're only a djinni yourself, Straub," The Hermit said pointing his staff toward Straub's chest. "You wear that skin like a costume. Until the interstices are all opened, your kind can never wield the same level of power in the physical world as someone born here."

"I have enough power to put you in your place if I have to," Straub said. He lowered his hands and stood up straight. "We both know that no matter which one of us is stronger, the Kindred are even more powerful. They will make us both suffer if our bickering derails their plans."

The Hermit lowered his staff, and the energy swirling around it dissolved. He waved one hand dismissively in the air toward Synesteria. "Call off your serpent, Straub. I have nothing to prove to you."

"It's alright," Straub said to Synesteria patting her side.

She lowered her body down to human height and glided away from the fire near to the crack Wendy was watching from.

Wendy jumped back, fearing that Synesteria, had seen her. In her haste, she kicked a small pebble. It bounced down the embankment. The echoes seemed to go on forever. The pebble finally fell into the still water below.

KERPLUNK

KerPlunk

kerplunk

The sound echoed off the rock walls. Wendy clenched her eyes shut and leaned back against the wall, hoping beyond hope that nobody heard the sound.

It sssoundss like it came from down there!" Synesteria said.

Wendy heard the serpentine body rasping against the stone as it moved through the upper chamber. Something moved between the crack and the fire, blocking the light. There was a crash outside, and she heard the coyote release a loud, long howl.

"It's outside!" Straub yelled. Wendy heard him run toward the entrance.

Whoever was blocking the light from the crack moved away, and the firelight showed through it once again. *If I stay here, they'll definitely catch me. My best option is to run.* She ran down the embankment and out of the cave, picking up speed as she left the rock strewn cavern floor and headed down the path that ran alongside the creek.

"There," The Hermit shouted. "It looks like a little girl." He raised his staff into the air. The purple energy flowed, twisting around his arm and onto his staff. He pointed it at Wendy's retreating figure.

A softball sized stone bounced off the back of his shoulder, sending him stumbling forward and dropping the staff. He spun around, but didn't see anyone. Passing through the trees overhead was a second figure, unseen by all. It headed away from the cave, following Wendy.

"After her," Straub said. "Follow her, but remain hidden. She may lead us to others."

Synesteria and the bear took off through the forest. Synesteria slithered gracefully through the forest, her long body sliding smoothly over the mossy ground, avoiding tree trunks and the sparse undergrowth. Elsa the Dancing Bear tore through everything, sometimes bouncing off the trees and charging full speed through brambles. Her pink tutu turning to shreds from the snagging thorns of blackberry vines.

The Hermit nodded at the coyote. It took off behind Synesteria and the bear.

Wendy heard the bear crashing through the woods behind her. Branches snapped and its footfalls thumped. She ran as fast as she could manage while still trying to stay relatively silent. Trees flitted past her. Gigantic ancient trees were initially spread far apart, but the longer she ran, the thinner the tree trunks became, and the closer together they grew. The darkness diminished, and sooner than she expected she ran out from underneath the last overhanging branches of the trees and out into an open field. She picked up speed again and ran straight toward Michael's house.

As she reached the road, she chanced a look over her shoulder to see if she was still being followed. She didn't see anyone - or anything - behind her. She kept running full speed up Michael's driveway.

I really hope this works. She had tried to pass through solid objects before, but had only intermittent success. She ran up the front porch steps and threw herself at the front door. There was a moment of panic as her head neared the wooden door, but she passed through it unscathed and fell to the carpeted floor, relief surging through every inch of her body.

At the edge of the forest, Synesteria, the bear, and the coyote turned back toward the cave after following Wendy's frantic race across the fields. For several minutes nothing moved. Then, the unseen pursuer dropped silently to the ground and made its way toward the Lagos house.

IDENTITY

Claire Snyder's eyes were pink and bloodshot as she leaned over her husband's body. She rearranged his hands so they overlapped at his waist. Her thin fingers trembled. She held one hand on Donal's. The other she held out in front of her, trying to force the shaking to stop. But the harder she tried, the more violently her fingers shook. She squeezed his hands tightly one more time and sat back down in the hospital chair.

She wanted nothing more than to just sit by Donal's side. Being near him was the only time she felt capable of going on. Her mind kept returning to Emily's visit on Monday afternoon. She was the only friend Claire felt she truly had in the world. *Why do I have to always keep the walls up? Why can't I just let someone, anyone, know how much I'm hurting? Would it really be so horrible?*

During the conversation, she had changed the subject to immaterial things like the weather or the news every time Emily tried to probe Claire's feelings. Claire hoped that she hadn't been rude, but she was fairly sure that Emily had picked up on it, especially on the unconvincing lie that she was 'doing okay.' She knew anybody could take one look at her and realize that wasn't true, especially her closest friend.

More than any time in her life since she had run away from home, she felt the emotions inside her needed a release. She remembered the first night in her tiny apartment after leaving home. She had cried all through that night. The tears had come from an overabundance of long swallowed and varied emotions. There was relief that she had finally escaped, but fear of what might happen next. There was even a kind of distorted sadness at leaving her family behind. She hated to admit that to herself, even now. She had lain on the cool bathroom floor crying as silently as she could manage, hoping her neighbors couldn't hear her through the paper-thin walls. Long after her tear ducts had dried up, her body still shook from the never-ending sobs.

At some point during that long night she had begun laughing. She had laughed in joy about her new life - and its new possibilities. She had laughed at herself for crying so much.

That had been almost exactly half her life ago. She had released eighteen years of pent up emotion in a single night. Since then, another nineteen years had passed by without another significant release. There had been a couple of times when things had become too much for her, and she had locked herself in the bathroom for fifteen minutes - pretending to take a shower. The hot steam coming from the shower had fogged the mirror. It helped hide her tears, even from herself. She allowed herself those brief outbursts only rarely, and never outside her own home. That was, until the accident. Now she felt that she could barely go fifteen minutes without breaking into another heart-wracking cry.

She had first met Donal after living in the apartment for only a couple of months. Claire immediately became completely subsumed by his dominant personality, like an empty cask that desperately needed to be filled. The few drops of her newfound personality that swirled around inside her turned out to be enough for Donal to fall in love with her. But instead of continuing to develop her own identity, she allowed Donal to develop it for her. As they grew closer and began talking of marriage, she realized that she was exactly who Donal wanted and needed her to be, and because of that, Donal was exactly the man she needed. In a way, Donal had inadvertently created her. She had let it happen; it had been far simpler than finding her own identity. *Who am I if Donal doesn't wake up?* she wondered for the hundredth time in less than five days.

Claire leaned back in her chair and closed her eyes. She massaged her temple with trembling fingers. She knew that Emily only wanted to help, to be there for her hurting friend. She imagined how good it would feel to let it all out, not only the stress and horror of the past few days, but every emotion she bottled up and hid away inside her for her entire adult life. She knew she needed the loving support of a friend. She knew she needed to open up, to become vulnerable and to let someone else inside her self-erected fortress of perfection.

She looked down at her hands and was surprised to see that her cell phone was clutched there. She turned the phone on and dialed Emily's number. She paused, her thumb over the green send icon, not sure what to say if she answered. *I'll just say 'Come. I need someone to talk to.'* She pressed dial.

There was a polite knock at the door, and one of Donal's nurses stepped into the room to change a drip bag on the IV. Claire cancelled the call, dropped the phone back in her purse, and smiled at the nurse.

***

"The name Straub sounds familiar," Red said. He sat up on the couch, his feet resting on a pair of pillows piled on the den's coffee table. "I know I've heard the name recently, I just can't remember where."

Red, Chase, and Wendy were all back in their physical bodies and sat with Michael in a circle on the chairs, couch, and floor. Wendy sipped hot chocolate that Chase had made for her. He hadn't bothered asking Michael's permission before rummaging through their kitchen cabinets.

"Anyway," Wendy said. She wanted to get the story out as quickly as she could while all the details were still fresh in her mind. She knew she didn't have a photographic memory, even though her retention was incredibly high. "After The Hermit started threatening Straub, this nāginī comes in and…"

"Wait, a what?" Michael said. He sat on the couch next to Red holding a pillow on his lap.

"You know, a nāginī, half snake and half woman," Wendy explained.

"Synesteria!" Red and Michael shouted together.

"You know this … monster?" Wendy asked, looking at the two friends over her steaming mug.

"Yeah, she was one of the sideshow freaks we saw at the circus," Red said.

"And Straub was the ringmaster," Michael said, butting in. He tossed the pillow in the air over his head like a basketball. "He shoots, he scores!"

"The Hermit has been around for years," Chase said, ignoring Michael. "How can the circus coming to town have anything to do with that?"

"The interstice," Wendy said, snapping her fingers. "It all has to do with opening the interstice. Apparently, there are others like The Hermit, each one trying to open an interstice. They all appear to be accountable in some manner to the ringmaster."

A frantic knocking on the back door made them all jump. None of them realized how on edge they were until the sound jolted them.

"Do you think that's your mom?" Michael asked Red.

"No, she would have called first," Red said looking up the stairs toward the kitchen door.

The knocking came again, this time even louder.

"You better go check," Red said to Michael, who didn't look to Red like he was in any hurry to go.

Michael stood and headed toward the stairs.

"I'm coming with you," Chase said. He pulled his billy club out of a loop on his belt and followed the visibly relieved Michael up the stairs.

Chase stood with his back to the wall next to the door. He held the club in his left hand and bent his knees. He was prepared to attack if the need arose. He nodded to Michael who turned the doorknob and opened the door.

"It's you," Michael said incredulously to the teenage girl standing just outside.

She looked nervously over her shoulder. She wore a tight black canvas crop top. Instead of buttons, the front was held together with an assortment of straps and buckles. A long purple sash was tied around her waist, the ends of which hung well below her short black skirt edged with purple lace.

The same lace topped her tall black leather boots and her elbow-length gloves. Her thick dreadlocks were tied back behind her head, leaving her slender neck bare.

"It's you," Esmerelda Hibbard said. They stared unblinking at each other.

Esmerelda pushed the door open just enough to slide in, forcing Michael to stumble back. She slammed the door closed behind her. Michael's gaze remained unbroken

"I'm sorry about that," she said. "But I just wanted to make sure nobody sees me."

"Who is this?" Chase asked. He stepped away from the wall and stood near Esmerelda's side.

"She's," Michael stammered. "She's from the circus."

Chase pounced on Esmerelda. She tried to evade his attack, but she acted too late. In one swift motion he wrapped his arms around her, pressed her face against the kitchen floor, and wrenched her arms painfully behind her back.

Chase put his mouth next to her ear. "What are you doing here? How did you find us?"

She squirmed, trying to free her arms.

"I followed some girl," she said, her mouth pressed against the tile floor. "She was spying on Straub."

"So they sent you here?" Chase asked. He wrenched her arms up a few inches.

"Ow," Esmerelda screamed. "No, I helped her escape. I don't have anything to do with his plans."

"I'll be the judge of that," Chase said. He grabbed a kitchen towel from the counter and wrapped it around her arms. "I am The Brand."

"Is that seriously how you introduce yourself when you are out there fighting crime?" Wendy said, stepping into the kitchen. She was wearing her glasses again. "Without any context, out of the blue, you just attack someone and say 'I am The Brand?'"

Esmerelda moaned and Chase loosened his grip slightly, but not enough for her to work herself free.

"So what if I do? What's wrong with that?" Chase asked. He knelt on his knees beside Esmerelda. "We don't know who she is working for, and I want her to know who she is dealing with."

"Look, I don't know who she is or what she is doing here either," Wendy said. She took her glasses off and let them fall against her cardigan. "But if The Hermit or Straub wanted to attack us, they would not have had the courtesy to knock on the door; they would have busted it down. They also would not have sent a solitary, scrawny, and unarmed teenage girl. "No offense," Wendy said looking down at Esmerelda lying face down on the floor.

"You're one to talk, pip-squeak," Esmerelda said. She lifted her face an inch off the floor. "And I'm lithe, not scrawny."

"Are you saying I should let her go?" Chase asked.

"Yeah, let her go, but keep an eye on her," Wendy said. Chase released Esmerelda's wrists and stood up.

Michael reached down to help her up. He still had not taken his wide eyes off her.

"Are you okay?" he asked as she stood.

"Yeah, I'm fine," Esmerelda said. She wiped the dust from the floor off her clothing.

"What do you think you are doing here?" Chase asked her. Despite Wendy's reassurance, he was still loath to trust her.

"I followed you," Esmerelda said to Wendy. She rubbed her wrists where Chase had wrapped the towel around them. "I decided to escape, to run away from the circus. Then I saw you spying on The Hermit and Straub. I thought you might be able to help me. I refuse be a part of it anymore, now that I know what their true purpose is."

"What happened to your accent?" Michael asked her. "I thought you were supposed to be some kind of European gypsy or something."

"It's all part of my act. I think you might actually be the first person to be fooled by my horrible accent," Esmerelda said smiling. "That is so cute. My grandparents really did come from Romania, though; and we prefer Roma, not gypsy."

Michael blushed and averted his eyes.

"Is anyone going to tell me what is going on?" Red shouted up the stairs.

"Sorry," Michael called back from the top of the stairs. "It's the girl from the circus, the magician."

"I'm Esmé."

"I'm Michael," he said hoping his cheeks weren't red.

"Yeah, I remember," Esmé said. She put her hands in the back pocket of her skirt and bounced on her heels. "You were so nervous during the performance the other day. How could I forget?"

"Come downstairs," Wendy said after she and Chase introduced themselves to Esmé as well. "If you can adequately convince us of your trustworthiness, we'll be able to provide mutual assistance."

"What's their deal?" Esmé asked Michael, nodding toward Chase and Wendy, as they walked down the stairs.

"Don't ask," he said.

Chase cautiously watched every move Esmé made. He was

ready to take her down if she made one move toward anybody else. *She is kind of cute, though,* he thought as he looked out the door to make sure no one was outside waiting to ambush them. Satisfied there was no one there, he locked the deadbolt and followed the others down to the den.

Wendy made Esmé tell her story after she and Red were introduced.

"I started getting suspicious about what was really going on with the Circus Paenultimus a couple of years ago," Esmé said. She stood in the center of the circle. "It never made sense to me why we would pass up larger cities and perform in small towns like this one."

"Is it always small towns?" Red asked. He kept rearranging the pillows behind and around him trying to find a position that wasn't uncomfortable.

"Not always, but it usually is," Esmé said. "Every place we stopped, Straub, the director and ringmaster, would send my parents, or sometimes Synesteria, out to talk to strange people. My parents would never tell me what it was about. They always tried to change the subject when I asked. They even told me it was better if I didn't know, and that I shouldn't ask any more questions about it."

"Did you ever find out what they were doing?" Wendy asked. She was taking notes in a reporter's pocket notebook.

"Yesterday," Esmé said. "I eavesdropped on my parents talking with Synesteria and Straub. I knew whatever was going on wasn't good, but I had no idea how evil it really was."

"I would think the nāginī would have given you adequate indication that something wasn't normal," Wendy said.

"I guess I was used to her," Esmé said shrugging. "I grew up in the circus and she had always been there. A lot of us there can go into the spirit world; she's not the strangest thing I've ever seen."

"Really?" Michael said sitting forward on the couch. "What's the weirdest thing you've ever personally seen?"

"Let her finish, Michael," Red said. He shook his head at Michael and mimed slapping his forehead.

"Anyway," Esmé said, squirming under the scrutiny. "I think each place we stopped at has its own interstice, like the one in The Hermit's cave, and its own harbinger, like The Hermit. We must have stopped in a hundred places over the last few years.

"There is something else," Esmé continued and looked around the room at each of the young faces. "Your town is in a lot of danger."

"What kind of danger are we talking about?" Chase said.

"Straub plans to kill everyone in the crowd during a circus performance," Esmé said. The sentence hung in the air like a partially deflated helium balloon. No one said anything.

"Apparently, The Hermit hasn't done enough to open the interstice, and Straub is going to force an accident during the show. He is going to rig it so that the entire big top will fall on top of the crowd. It has something to do with needing spirits to open the interstice. I'm sorry, but I don't know what that means exactly."

"The interstice is a soft spot between the spirit and physical worlds," Red said. He rested his head back on a pillow and closed his eyes. Two days with Tom and he was already beginning to sound new age. "There is this group of spirits, djinn, kobolds, or something, I'm not exactly sure, called the Kindred. The Kindred are trying to destroy the veil between the two worlds so that they can take over this one."

"How do you know all this?" Esmé said eyeing his casts and bandages. "Does it have something to do with your injuries?"

"I think it does, actually. I'll tell you about it later.

"Tom, a man that knew my grandfather, has been explaining a lot of what is going on to me. I don't know a lot; this is still very new to me," Red said opening his eyes and looking at Esmé.

"Has Straub done anything like this before?" Chase asked. His arms resting on his knees.

"No," Esmé said shaking her head. "Nothing like this."

"The problem for them though," Red continued, "is that right now the only way to bring a creature of pure spirit into the physical word is to exchange it with the spirit of someone or something from the physical world, and that can only be done by someone born in the physical world. That is what The Hermit is doing. It's the job of the harbinger to sacrifice spirits from this side, to bring others over. Each time he does so, the barrier between the worlds grows weaker."

"So The Hermit intends to exchange hundreds of spirits through the interstice from those attending the circus?" Wendy asked Red and Esmé.

"I think it is even worse than that," Esmé said turning toward Wendy.

"Much worse," Red said. "I think he is trying to open up all the interstices he can find at the same time. It would be the end of everything; the Kindred would be able to take over the world."

"We have to stop it," Esmé said. "I've spent my whole life helping in a plot to destroy the world and I didn't even know it. We have to figure out a way to stop Straub's plan."

"Do you know the intended time and means of Straub's

stratagem?" Wendy asked Esmé. She was already trying to come up with a plan of her own. Her notebook was filled with ideas that she had already began to cross out as impossible or simply too dangerous.

"I have no idea how to answer that. I don't even understand half the words you keep spouting out," Esmé said. "Education isn't exactly one of the perks of being raised in the circus."

"She means 'do you know when and how Straub is going to do it?'" Chase said, then turned to Wendy. "We all know how smart you are Wendy, but let's take the vocab quiz down a couple of grade levels."

Wendy rolled her eyes, and Chase smiled at her to soften what she might otherwise have taken as a scold.

"I don't know for sure, but I think tomorrow night," Esmé said. She looked around the room again at the strange group. Each one was a different age; except for being aware of this danger, they probably had little else in common. "Let's figure out a way to stop it. I'm assuming everyone here is adept in some way?"

"Adept?" Chase asked.

"You know, adept. Being adept means you're aware of the spirit world and can either go there, or manipulate something there, or even just see it," Esmé said.

Michael now sat cross legged on the couch beside Red. He sighed.

"Everybody but me," he said. "How is it I'm the weird one here?"

"That's fine," Esmé said. "There's nothing wrong with that. Some have it, some don't. What about the rest of you? What kind of abilities do you have?"

"Hold on a second before anyone else answers her," Chase

said. He stood up in the center of the room beside Esmé. "I don't think we should go telling her everything about ourselves unless we all agree to trust her."

"I trust her," Michael said.

"Me too," Red said.

"What about you, Wendy?" Chase asked. It was really her opinion he wanted most of all. She had a good nose for telling who could be believed - and who couldn't.

"I believe her," Wendy finally said after a long pause. She nodded to Esmé. "She's got my vote."

"That makes it unanimous," Chase said. "If everybody else is sure, I'll trust your judgment."

"Okay," Esmé said. She sat down on the floor between Michael and Wendy. "If it makes any difference, I trust you all as well. I'll even tell you my ability first. I'm a true shifter."

"What does that mean?" Wendy asked. Her pencil was in her hand just over her notebook.

"I can shift back and forth between the worlds anytime as fast as an eye blink," Esmé said. She smiled, she was proud of her ability. "What makes me a 'true' shifter though is that when I'm in one world I don't have a counterpart in the other. I don't leave a body behind when I'm in the spirit world, and my spirit doesn't exist in the spirit world when I'm in the physical."

"I can just travel to the spirit world," Wendy said. "My physical body stays behind. But I'm also an excellent tracker. I can see wherever anyone has moved through the spirit world."

"I wondered how you found The Hermit's cave," Esmé said. "I would never have been able to find it if I hadn't been following you.

"I'm in both worlds at the same time," Chase said. "All day, every day, twenty-four seven."

"That's just like The Hermit," Esmé said.

"I'm like Wendy," Red said. "I can't track, but I do have the ability to change one object into another."

"You're a transmuter?" Esmé said, sounding impressed. "That is so cool."

Red shrugged.

"I don't know what that means," he said. "But Tom, the guy who told me all the stuff about the interstices, called me a 'maker.'"

"You can't really make things, though, can you? You change the nature of things, right?" Esmé asked him.

Red nodded.

"You *transmute* them," Esmé said. "That is really impressive. Have you always been able to do this?"

Michael laughed. "He's only known about the spirit world for two days!"

"Seriously?" Esmé said, looking at Red.

"It's true," Red said. He pushed himself all the way up into a sitting position. "Esmé, we didn't know anything about Straub or the circus having anything to do with all this when Wendy went out to spy on The Hermit. All we knew was that The Hermit had kidnapped my father's spirit. We think he is holding him in a prison cell in the cave. We were planning a rescue mission when you came to the door."

"I'm sorry," Esmé said. "I mean, about your dad."

"Thanks," Red said. He took a deep breath and looked around the room, making eye contact with each person. "I think we should all work together to rescue my father and anyone else The Hermit is planning to sacrifice, and then find a way to stop Straub from murdering all those people. Does everyone agree?"

"I'm in," Chase said without hesitation. "For the last three years, the only thing I've wanted to do was take down The Hermit."

"We have to do it," Wendy said. "Saving all those lives is a moral imperative. I'm in."

"Me too," Esmé said. "I have to find a way to undo some of the wrongs of the circus."

"I think we are all crazy to think a bunch of teenagers, no matter what kind of weird powers we have, can take down The Hermit or this Straub guy," Michael said.

Red looked at Michael, surprised by his reaction.

"Somebody had to say it," Michael said. "It is the most insane thing I've heard in my entire life, but you can count me in as well. I would never turn my back on my best friend when he needed help the most."

Michael punched Red in the shoulder.

"Ouch," Red said and punched him back harder. "That really hurt."

After several hours talking and planning, they finally decided that they would meet back up in the morning after Michael's parents left. They were just beginning to discuss about how they might be able to sneak into The Hermit's cave, when Michael's cell phone rang. He walked up the stairs before answering it.

A moment later Michael ended the call and jammed the phone back in his pocket, and returned to the den. "Party's over. That was my parents, they'll be here in less than twenty minutes."

"I'll see you all in the morning," Red said. "Chase, Wendy, are you two sure borrowing the four wheeler again is no problem."

"They hardly use it," Wendy said. She got up to head out the door with Chase. "It might take them weeks before they even noticed it was gone. They aren't the most observant creatures on the planet."

"Good, I think we'll have to use it," Red said.

Esmé was still sitting in a recliner even though Chase and Wendy were already up the stairs and heading across the kitchen. She slowly rose out of the chair.

"I guess I'll see you tomorrow," she said to Red and Michael.

"Yeah, it was good to see you again," Michael said.

"Hey," Red said as she was leaving. "Do you have someplace to stay tonight?"

"I'm thinking of trying to sneak back into my caravan," she said. "It is pretty near to the edge of the camp, I have some camping supplies and other stuff there I'd like to get."

"Don't you think it's too dangerous?" Red asked. "What if they saw you at the cave? Even if they didn't, won't missing the performance tonight be suspicious?"

"I guess you're right," Esmé said. "I don't know where else to go. I'm too old to pretend to be Wendy's friend, and there is no way I'm going to go stay with Chase. He freaked me out a little bit with that whole 'I am The Brand' thing."

"You can stay here," Michael said. His eyes gleamed with the possibility.

"I appreciate it, but I don't know," Esmé said. She stared at the floor between Michael and Red.

"Michael, you know that's a bad idea. This house is already full enough," Red said. "I've got a better idea. My house is just down the road, and nobody is going to be there.

My mom is staying at the hospital with Dad. You can stay there."

"Are you sure that's okay?" She asked.

"Yeah, it's no problem," Red said. "As long as you don't make a mess; my mom is a real neat freak. And there are also a couple of things I'd like you to bring over in the morning if you could."

14

DOUBTS AND DREAMS

THE VIGILANTE

Later that night...

The Brand ran silently along the raised edge of a three story downtown rooftop. He leapt across an alley down to the neighboring building one story lower. If either of the two men breaking into the car below would have looked upwards, they would have seen his silhouette fleeting across the white cloud of the Milky Way. No one ever looked up. He landed on the graveled rooftop, absorbing the impact with bent knees before dropping his shoulder and rolling forward to a crouching stop near the edge. He felt alive. His muscles, used to rigorous training, strained to exert their pent up energy. He had spent almost the entire day cooped up inside Michael's den. He peered over the edge at the thieves below.

If Chase had looked up, he would have seen a large black bird passing between him and the collected stars of the galaxy. No one ever looks up. The djinni coasted over the town toward its home on the cliff above The Hermit's cave in the forest beyond. It had delivered its message to Straub. One line. *We will have the girl tonight.* There had been no reply. The bird looked down at the strange figure on the rooftop. The figure leaned over the roof's edge. It was in both the spirit world and the physical world at the same time. The bird dipped one wing and spiraled down toward the city below. It landed on a nearby streetlight, one of hundreds in the town that no longer lighted the night. *Is this the one The Hermit is searching for?* Black eyes focused on Chase. It waited to see what happened.

The Brand lowered himself from the building's rooftop onto the top of a portico, dropping the last few feet. He had hoped the exertion and coming confrontation would clear his mind, but he couldn't stop thinking about The Hermit and the opportunity to avenge his mother. These last few years of fruitless searching were finally, and hopefully, coming to an end. He crawled to the edge of the angled roof. Underneath him he heard the car's door click unlocked. He had not given any thoughts before tonight on what he would do after his vengeance was complete. *Is this all I am now? Am I just The Brand?* It had always been about finding The Hermit, defeating him, and avenging his mother. Without that as the underlying motive, he questioned his future. *After that what do I have to fight for?* His feet touched down on the sidewalk just as one of the car thieves opened the door.

The second thief was much larger than the greasy haired man who had jimmied open the lock. He wore a tank top and cut off cargo pants. He turned around at the sound of Chase's boots on the brick sidewalk. The man looked out of tiny dark eyes no larger than glass marbles. He scanned The Brand's costume and smiled.

"What are you supposed to be? Some kind of superhero?"

he said.

"I am The Brand," Chase said. He took a step forward and hit the man in the chest with an open palm.

The man gave only a slight grunt and swung a right hook at Chase. Chase ducked underneath it and landed four quick jabs in the man's side. *What is the point of risking my life like this night-after-night to keep ham-fisted idiots like this from stealing some rich person's car?*

Chase dodged another sweeping punch from the big man. The other thief grabbed the door to pull himself out. He was smaller than the other man, his wiry muscles rippled like piano strings under his skin. He wore a sleeveless jacket over a ratty gray T-shirt. Chase kicked his fingers where they wrapped around the door. The man yelled and let loose. Chase again kicked the door. It hit the man in the face, knocking him back into the car seat. The big man grabbed his shoulder, bent him over, and kneed him in the chest. The blow knocked the wind out of Chase, but he was able to stumble out of the man's grasp before falling to the ground.

Chase thought about the fight with the kobold in the alley. *Is this really my purpose in life that I was given from that night?* He rolled over onto his back, spinning like a break dancer on his shoulders. He kicked the large man in the back of the knees. His legs buckled and he fell to the ground.

Chase put his hands behind his head and pushed himself up off the brick. He landed on his feet. The wiry man with the greasy hair was getting out of the car again. This time Chase grabbed the door and jerked it forward. As soon as he felt resistance from the man, he threw his weight against it. The door slammed against the man's face again. Chase heard the man's nose break. It crunched like a handful of dry spaghetti.

Through a smear of blood on the window he saw the man fall unconscious to the ground.

The larger man was beginning to stand up behind him. Chase turned back to him. Since the night in the alley with Wendy, he often felt a hole inside him that yearned for purpose – for meaning. There had been only a handful of situations that he felt that need was being met. *What was different in those times?*

He kicked the big man in the jaw. The kick knocked the man's head back. His eyes rolled backward and he too fell unconscious on the dark sidewalk. Chase knelt down and searched the man's pockets for his cell phone. *It was when I was helping or saving people.* He decided that was what made those moments different. It was the man he rescued from an overturned car, the woman in the liquor store parking lot with three attackers and a knife to her throat. It was the times when his actions had directly saved or aided a person that he felt The Brand mattered. That truthfully, he felt *he* mattered. Because of what he had done, those people could go back to their homes and their families. They could go on with their lives again, more joyful in their second chances than Chase had ever felt. He found the man's phone in one of the large pockets of his cargo pants. He flipped the phone open and punched in 911.

Chase felt a hard kick on his side. It knocked him against the car just behind the front tire well. One of the unconscious men lay face down next to him in the gutter. The phone fell out of his hand and clattered on the sidewalk. Chase looked up at a tall man with grease stained jeans and a faded blue mechanic's shirt. The man pulled a pistol out of the back of his pants. He cocked the sliding barrel and pointed it at

Chase's face. The man smiled and stomped on the cell phone with his tall motorcycle boot, just as the connection was made. He ground the plastic into the brick.

"Hands up," he said, spitting a toothpick out of his mouth.

Chase put his hands over his head. The tips of his fingers touched the underside of the car's mirror, cursing himself that he had been so distracted. He had never let anyone sneak up behind him before.

"Boy, you've cost me a whole lot of money," the man said. He took a step closer to Chase. "Seems every time one o' my boys tries to jack a car, you show up."

"Who are you?" Chase said. He wiped away a trickle of blood off his lip. He had bitten it when the man bowled him over.

"It don't matter who I am," the man said conversationally. "Let's just say I'm the guy you screwed over one too many times. My plan tonight was just to warn you to stay off my turf. I had reckoned you was just some upstart that wanted to make a move on this town. Looks like I got it all wrong, you think you're some kind of hero that calls himself 'The Brand,' heh heh. You're that guy the police is searching for, ain't ya?"

Chase pushed himself more upright against the car with his feet. He didn't answer, just tried to figure out a way out of this mess.

"Uh, uh," the man said shaking his pistol side to side. "You don't want to be doin' that."

"So, are you going to shoot me or not?" Chase said. He scowled and stared the man in the eyes.

"Yeah, I'm gonna kill ya. I just wanted you to know it weren't personal, you just got in the way of me and my business," the man said. He pushed the gun forward and turned his body to

179

the side preparing to shoot.

Chase turned his branded hand toward the man. He felt the energy gathering in his palm. It gathered there like a balloon about to burst. It surged out of his hand forming a shield. He pulled himself up off the ground by the car's mirror and advanced on the gunman.

The man pulled the trigger. The streets echoed with the report. The bullet hit the shield, ricocheting off with a sound like a shattered gong. Chase pulled the billy club out of his belt as a second shot bounced off his shield. He swung the club at the pistol in the man's hand. There was a scream of pain as the gun went flying, skittering across the sidewalk. The man's trigger finger was broken and bent at a ninety-degree angle to one side.

"What are you?" The man asked. He fell to his knees clutching his hand.

"You said it yourself," Chase said standing over him. His shield gone, though it was at the ready in a moment's notice. "I am a superhero, and Laurel Hollows is *my 'turf.'*" He kicked the tall man in the chest, knocking him to the ground against a building. Chase was still deciding what to do with him when he heard police sirens in the distance.

"Why do you do this?" The man said. He pushed himself up on his knees with one hand. "What's the point of it?"

Chase was caught off guard by the question. He paused for a moment with his club in the air. "I'm still trying to figure that out." He brought the club around, hitting the man in the back of the head. He fell back down on the ground, unconscious. Chase took off down the alley, wondering if there could ever be a joyful second chance to return home to his father and the twins, or if he had thrown it away in his selfish quest for vengeance.

The black bird watched Chase disappear into the dark alley as the first police cars arrived at the scene. It spread its wings and dropped off the pole. It followed Chase, staying well above the buildings until he had ducked into a warehouse near the railroad tracks. It had an interesting tale for its master. The vigilante was found.

THE CYNIC

While Chase ran down the dark alley, Wendy Wright laid down the book she just finished on the nightstand and stared at the ceiling. Books were stacked on every available surface in her small bedroom. There was even a row of books running two high along the entire length of one wall. Her parents had never understood why she would waste her time reading when she could be doing something else, *anything else.* Her father said it was no wonder she didn't have any friends since she locked herself in her room everyday reading the ramblings of dead people. "It don't do you no good to know more'n everybody else," he slurred late one night after returning home from a card game with his buddies. "'Specially if you're a girl."

The real reason she shut and locked her door was so that she didn't have to listen to the sound of her parent's constant arguing, and in the hope that they would just leave her alone. *At least,* she thought, *as long as I stay out of sight, they do pretty much pretend I don't exist.*

Reading about science, theology, and philosophy was, for her, another kind of door. The thoughts of Plato, Origen, and

Hawking were doorways into new and fascinating ways of understanding the universe, doorways she used to shut out her dysfunctional family. When she read, she was caught up in a myriad of possibilities and ideas. But it was the time spent after reading a particularly interesting or novel idea that really helped block out the external world. She passed countless hours lying in her bed, staring at the ceiling, trying to mesh those new ideas into what she already understood about the world. In particular, she was trying to comprehend the observable fact that there is actually a spirit world, and the meaning of its existence.

She had just finished reading Plato's 'The Allegory of the Cave.' Wendy closed her eyes, and emptied her mind. She let the images of the allegory fill the darkness in her mind. There were prisoners inside a cave.

She imagined herself as one of those prisoners. Everything was dark. Around her she could hear or sense the rustling of others. The flapping sound of the threadbare confederate flag her father had secured with zip-ties to the guttering just outside her window distracted her for a moment. Shaking her head, she once again dropped into the cave.

Now a fire lit up behind the prisoners, out of their sight. Shadows, cast by the fire's light, began dancing and flittering on the wall in front of her. The shapes of people moved back and forth from one side to another. Wendy remembered from the story that there is a pathway between the fire and the backs of the prisoners that people traversed, but for the sake of understanding she tried to forget the explanation of the two-dimensional shapes. From her perspective as one of the prisoners, the whole of reality was the wall and the dark shapes that moved across it. She knew nothing of the real people living in the three-dimensional world who cast those flattened shadows.

Wendy closed her eyes and shifted into the spirit world. Opening her eyes again, the room moved like smoke, or like shadows dancing on a cave wall. The shifting colors were brilliant and fleeting. It gave her something to focus part of her mind on, while the rest of it wrestled with the deeper meaning behind Plato's allegory. So much of what she had read denied even the possibility of any supernatural or spiritual reality. Those philosophers and scientists proclaimed that the entire observable universe was all that existed. The universe doesn't need supernatural agents to make it work, therefore – none exist.

She looked around the room and disagreed. Her *observable universe* did include the spiritual. "How could they see anything but the shadows if they were never allowed to turn their heads?" Plato wrote. She struggled with the concept that since there was no need for anything supernatural to make the universe operate, then obviously the supernatural didn't exist. A cuckoo clock chimed twice from the wall behind her bed. She looked up at the tiny mechanical bird and the cartoonish numerals that circled the clock's face.

A sudden understanding came upon her at that moment. She realized that the concept wasn't completely fleshed out, but it was a starting point for her to work from. The numbers. They were painted on the clock's face, but the clock itself didn't need them to operate. If the numbers were changed to some random symbols, the cuckoo would still come out every hour, the two hands would continue in their same circuits. But the numbers were important too, she realized. The numbers gave meaning and purpose to the clock. What the numbers stood for, the allotted hours, minutes, and seconds of the day, was the entire reason the clock even existed in the first place.

She shifted back from the spirit world. Her room returned back to what she was accustomed to as normal. It was strange to her that over time the spirit world was beginning to seem more and more like the "real" world to her. Real, not in means of tangibility, but of something more than her normal senses could grasp. It possessed a substance and vitality that didn't seem to exist in the physical world.

The day had been filled with danger and intrigue. Despite that, there had also been a plethora of, new friends, and a chance to do something that really mattered.

It had been one of the best days of her entire life.

THE GYPSY THREAD

Esmé Hibbard sat on the edge of Red's bed. The large farmhouse, silent and empty, made her skin crawl. She couldn't remember ever sleeping inside an actual house before. Red's room alone was almost twice the size of her small trailer, and only recently had she gotten a trailer of her own. It had been a gift from her parents on her sixteenth birthday. Until that day she had shared a caravan with them. The trailer was a symbol of her budding independence. Her parents had told her that it was more than just a place for her to sleep; it could also be an escape from the world. During the long rides between shows, and the too short nights between performances, the small trailer had become the refuge her parents had hoped it would be. Its aluminum skin might be cool to the touch, but to Esmé it became the warmest of bosoms. It was more her safety net than any of the real-life nets stretched out beneath her trapeze wires.

In her hands was a long strand of thread she had untied from her hair. Repeatedly she stretched the thread out and made a half dozen loops that hung limp beneath her left hand. She cut the loops with a tiny dagger that she also kept hidden inside the thickest dread of her hair. She wadded the cut thread into a ball between the index finger and thumb of her left hand. She then grabbed one of the ends with her right hand and pulled. The thread was restored, as if by magic, to its full length between her outstretched hands. The trick called 'The Gypsy Thread' was one she sometimes did in her magic act. She was in the habit of practicing routine tricks until they became rote whenever she felt nervous or lonely. Tonight she felt both keenly.

From the fingers of her left hand, short pieces of thread fell slowly downward, landing on a small pile already on the floor beside her. The secret of the magic trick was that she had a separate piece of full length thread already hidden in her other hand. It was that piece that is stretched out for the final reveal, making it look like she had restored the cut strands to whole again. She hid the cut pieces scrunched in a tight ball between her fingers until the trick was over and she could discard them out of view of her audience. She watched as the threads fell lazily out of her fingers and drifted to the floor.

She had been inside her trailer when the threads of her own life began unraveling and falling away. It was an overheard conversation between the ringmaster, Rinthim Straub, and Synesteria. The two had been right outside Esmé's cracked window. They were discussing how the local harbinger was right on schedule. "Everything," Synesteria had said. "Isss moving exactly as planned. The Interssticess will all open at the ssame time." Esmé had not known what the words meant at the time. She had asked her parent's later that day, but they had refused to talk to her about it. They dismissed her and told her to tell no one else of what she had overheard.

Over the next several months she had sought out opportunities to spy on Straub, Synesteria, and even her own parents. The small threads of conversations she eavesdropped on had eventually began to form a solid strand, and the sinister secret of the circus became as obvious to her as a flash in a poorly performed illusion.

Esmé retied the remainder of the thread in her hair and secreted the dagger back into its accustomed dread. She picked up the discarded threads and dropped them into a small wastebasket underneath Red's nightstand. The thought of sleeping under the covers in a real bed was too strange for her, so she curled herself up on top of Red's blanket and covered herself with one of his baseball jackets.

Spying on Straub and Synesteria at The Hermit's cave had been her boldest move to date. The conversation at the circus dining tent had terrified her. She had to know more. She had known that whatever Straub and the rest had planned was bad, and that people would get hurt, but it wasn't until she heard Straub and her parents calmly discussing the deaths of hundreds, many of them innocent children, that she realized just how truly evil their intentions were. *I can't believe Mom and Dad are okay with this,* she thought. She felt she had to do something about it. *I'm responsible too. My whole life I've been working with the Circus Paenultimus. I've been helping them.*

It didn't matter to her that it had been unknowingly; somehow she had to atone for it. So, she had followed Wendy back to her friends and hoped that by helping them keep the disaster from happening she might balance out some of the bad to which she had unwittingly been an accomplice.

Red's jacket smelled freshly laundered as she pulled it up around her shoulders, but underneath the chemical cleanliness there was still the natural aroma of grass and dirt embedded between the fibers. The smell of the outside world was a comfort to her as she closed her eyes. She thought about how life is like a high wire, one must always keep a balance.

Today, she ran away from the only life she had ever known. She left her parents behind as well as her tiny trailer, the only place she had ever felt at home. She left behind all the tiny pieces that made her who she was. She knew she would have to reform herself from the scattered pieces that remained. As sleep mercifully began to overtake her, she wondered if there was any way she could ever be whole again.

It had been the worst day of her entire life.

THE ABANDONED

Just a few hundred yards away from where Esmé slept, Michael kicked his legs in his sleep. In his dream he rounded the second corner of the high school track. Ahead of him on the back straight of the track were the hurdles. Dense fog hid the stands and all but the first hurdle. He leapt over it, alone on the silent oval. As his right foot touched the rubberized surface of the track, the next hurdle emerged from the fog. Again and again he leaped over hurdles. Each time the next one came into view just as his forward foot touched the ground. It seemed to go on forever.

He heard a wolf howl behind him. He kept running. A second wolf howled, then a third. Michael, not breaking his stride, looked over his shoulder. He saw nothing but the thick wall of fog. When he turned his head back around Red was running in the lane beside him.

"The wolves are coming," Red said. "They are going to eat us if we don't run faster."

Michael didn't say anything. Coming out of the fog now were not just the hurdles, but tall trees as well. The tree tops disappeared into the fog high overhead before the first branches reached out. Michael and Red now had to dodge the trees as well as jump over the hurdles. They were forced out of their lanes. They weaved around each other between the trees. He looked over his shoulder again; he could now see dark shapes dimly through the fog. As he faced forward again his right shoulder clipped a tree. He stumbled forward toward the ground. The track was covered with moss, dead leaves and a few scattered branches. The lanes were painted on top of the debris. The hurdles were gone, replaced with fallen logs and large tree roots. Red grabbed him by the arm and pulled him upright.

"Where are we?" Michael asked as they took off at full speed again. Behind them the wolves began howling louder. He thought he could hear them growling. It sounded like they were right behind them.

"We're in the forest," Red said. "The Hermit sent the wolves after us."

"No, that can't be right," Michael said. "I was in a race. The 400 meter hurdles." Beneath his feet the ground grew still more uneven. Still, the lines were marked on the ground, disappearing into the fog ahead of them. Small patches of the track's surface were visible in only a few scattered places.

Red ignored him. "We need to get off the path. Our only hope is to lose them in the forest."

It was then that Michael heard the panting behind him – the sound of the wolves closing in. He refused to turn around. "I have to finish the race."

"There's no time," Red said. "Come on, everyone is waiting for us."

"Everyone?" Michael said. He looked beyond Red. Three figures were running together where the football field should be inside the track's infield. As they neared the figures became more distinct, and he saw that it was Esmé, Chase, and Wendy.

"Come," Red said. He reached out and grabbed Michael's shirt sleeve.

"I can't," Michael said. "I have to finish the race. The wolves are catching up. If we finish before them, they can't hurt us."

"Red," Esmé yelled. "Get Michael and let's get out of here."

"He won't come," Red said to the others. He turned back toward Michael. "That doesn't make any sense. They aren't running a race, Michael. Come with us, we need you."

Michael stumbled again and Red helped him back to his feet.

"No, I can't go. I need you here," Michael said. "I need you to help me. I don't know why I keep tripping." He heard the soft padding of the wolves' paws on the mossy ground behind them.

"Red!" Chase yelled. "We have to go now."

"But Michael," Red pleaded.

"There is no more time," Wendy said. "Come with us. It is now or never."

"Michael, come," Red said urgently, turning away from the group back toward Michael.

"No, the race," Michael said. He felt sweat beading on his forehead and running down his back in little icy rivulets. He leapt over a fallen tree. "I want you to stay."

Michael stumbled forward again and Red pulled him back to his feet - the wolves gaining each time they paused.

"Red," Esmé said. "Leave him, we have to go."

Red watched as the others began to drift off to one side in the fog. He turned again to Michael "I'm sorry." He veered off to the left and joined the others.

"No!" Michael screamed. He could feel the breath of the wolves on the back of his legs now. He watched as Red and the others slowly dissolved into dark shapes in the fog. Tears began to blur his vision. He dodged another tree and tripped over a tree root. He stumbled to one side and banged his shins against the branches of a fallen tree. He spun and fell backwards over the log onto the leaf littered ground. He saw the blackened dead branches stretching across and through the white fog of the sky. His feet rested on the log he had fallen over. He pushed himself up on his elbows and looked up at his feet. A wolf was standing on top of the log looking down at him and snarling. Three more leapt onto the log and joined the first.

"Red, why did you have to leave me? I needed you."

As one, the four wolves crouched and leapt off the log at Michael. He felt the impact of the paws as the first wolf landed on his chest.

Michael sat upright in a snap. A pillow fell off his chest,

landing in his lap. He was in his den on the air mattress beside the couch where Red had been since he arrived at their house.

"Did you hear something?" Red asked in a harsh whisper.

THE COWARD

While Michael dreamed of running through the forest, Red's own dream took place in the forest as well, but in his dream there was no fog, only the silvery darkness of moonlight filtering through the branches above. It was no place in the woods that he had ever visited before, but an amalgam of places he knew, mixed in with Wendy and Esmé's description of the area around the cave.

"This way," Wendy said. She was sitting in her wheelchair. One of her legs was missing. She wheeled herself down an embankment toward a creek at the bottom of a cliff. Chase, Esmé, and Michael followed behind her.

Red looked up at the imposing cliff face before them. It rose up impossibly high above the trees. It looked like a fortress, the turrets lost in the darkness above. Red turned back, the group was already at the cliff wall. The creek flowed out of a small opening at the bottom of the cliff near where they stood. He hurried after them.

As Red approached the cave mouth he heard the muffled sound of voices within.

"Your dad is in there," Esmé said. She pointed into the darkness.

"Why would he be in there?" Red asked. "He is in the hospital."

"His spirit is in there," Chase said. He pointed with his billy club into the darkness as well. "You have to go rescue him."

Red took a tentative step toward the entrance. The voices were louder now, echoing off the walls and the small pond immediately inside the entrance. The ponds surface rippled with reflected moonlight.

"In there," Wendy said and nodded toward the cave's gaping mouth.

"Go," Michael said. He pointed ahead.

Red took a first tentative step into the dark. The air around him seemed stale and heavy. Claustrophobia overtook him. It felt like the very air was being compacted around him, like the walls were closing in. He turned back toward the group wanting nothing more than to run away. They stood silently in a row at the entrance, still pointing behind him into the darkness.

"Won't any of you come with me?" he asked. He could hear his voice faltering even as he spoke.

They continued pointing silently onward.

"How can I see?" He asked. "I don't have a light or a weapon. What if I see The Hermit?"

"You don't need a light," Michael said.

"If you had a light they would see you," Esmé said.

"You have your bat," Wendy said. She lowered her hand and pointed toward Red's knees.

Red looked down, he was holding his baseball bat in his right hand. He felt sure it wasn't in his hand before that moment. He was also wearing his catching vest and knee pads. He reached up and felt his catcher's mask over his face. He searched his mind for another excuse not to go into the cave alone, but couldn't find one. He turned toward the darkness.

After just a couple of steps he spun around again. "What are you all going to do?" He asked. Deep in the cave he heard the sound of metal scraping against metal. Then a loud squeaking like rusty hinges echoed through the rock walled chambers.

"Get him!" A voice yelled. "He is escaping."

Red peered into the black, but couldn't see anything. A large form melted out of the shadows between himself and his companions.

"Now what do we have here," the shadow said.

Wendy wheeled her chair back a couple of feet. The rest of the group stepped backward as the shadow advanced toward them. It held a large staff in one hand. The moon dropped below the roof of the cave, shining into Red's eyes. He felt suddenly exposed and took a sideways step to hide in the shadows.

"It's The Hermit," Esmé said. She picked a stone up out of the creek and hurled it at the shadowed figure.

The Hermit raised one hand and flicked his wrist. The stone was sent hurtling back. It hit Chase in the chest and he fell to the ground. The rest of the group all began throwing rocks as well. The Hermit flicked his wrist at each one, sending them back like ping-pong balls.

Red started to take a step forward, but he couldn't move. One of his feet was wedged between two rocks.

The Hermit laughed. "Is that all you've got? You think a few pebbles can harm me?"

He slammed the bottom of his staff against the rocks. The ground rumbled. Rocks and stalactites fell around Red. A section of the cave wall behind him crumbled, revealing a lighted chamber beyond.

The group got to their feet after being knocked down by the tremor. Chase helped Wendy back into her chair. They stood together defiantly.

"Red, is that you?" a quiet voice said behind him.

Red immediately recognized it. It was his father's voice. "Dad?"

"Yes, son. I'm free, but they are right behind me." He stood only about ten feet from Red.

Red heard something scrambling over rocks in the lighted chamber beyond.

"He went through here," a voice said.

"I can't move," Red said. He twisted his foot back and forth, unable to get it free. "My foot is stuck."

"I want to thank you all for your sacrifice," The Hermit said. He raised the staff above his head.

Donal reached forward toward Red, but was grabbed from behind by the tail of a giant snake. It wrapped him up like a boa constrictor. The tip of the tail covered his mouth. Synesteria's upper body came into view, she flicked her long forked tongue out. It caressed the side of Red's face.

"Mmmm. You tassste good," she said. "I'll be back for you." She whipped around and headed back toward the crevice in the wall.

"No!" Red screamed at her retreating figure.

"Remember," Donal said, pulling Synesteria's coils from around his throat.

"Remember what?" Red yelled back.

"It's okay," his father said, struggling to keep the coil from wrapping around his neck again. "It's okay... remember ... remember what is fear, and what is bravery."

As his father disappeared through to the chamber beyond,

Red was thrown back to when he was still learning to ride a bicycle. *How,* he wondered, *have I forgotten the memory for so long?*

"But I'm scared," seven-year-old Red had said, standing beside his bicycle. The training wheels taken off for the first time.

"That's okay," Donal told him. He rested his hand on Red's shoulder. "You just have to be brave."

"I'm not brave. I'm scared," Red said. "I'm not like you."

"Red," Donal said softly. He knelt down beside Red, and looked him straight in the eye. "I get scared sometimes too."

"No you don't. You go all over, even to where there is fighting and everything," Red had said between sobs. "Nothing scares you."

Donal laughed.

"Are you laughing at me?" Red asked indignantly.

"I'm not laughing at you," his dad had told him. "I'm laughing because I hear people say that kind of thing all the time." He sighed. "I'll be honest with you, son. I'm scared all the time."

"You really get scared?" Red said, looking deep into his father's eyes.

"All the time. Being scared and being brave aren't opposites like most people think. Bravery isn't about not being afraid; bravery is going ahead and doing what needs to be done even when you're scared, especially when you're scared."

Red nodded. "I can be brave," he said. He wrapped his fingers around the feathered rubber handle grips and threw his leg over the bike.

His dad slapped him on the shoulder. "I know you can."

"Red, help us!" Esmé said, bringing him back to the present. She, along with the rest of the group outside the cave's mouth, was lying on the ground. They shielded their eyes from a bright light emanating from The Hermit's staff.

"No one is coming for you," The Hermit said. He spun the staff in circles over his head, building up speed.

Red wedged his bat between his foot and the cave floor. He pushed down on the handle and it pulled his foot free of both the shoe and the rocks.

"Hurry Red!" Wendy pleaded.

Red raced toward The Hermit, still a dark shape at the cave's mouth. He raised his bat over his shoulder. He was just a few feet away. His other foot slipped between another pair of rocks and was again caught. He nearly fell forward.

"All you have to do is hit him," Michael said. "It's just like batting practice."

The Hermit looked over his shoulder at Red who was struggling, trying to pull his foot free. "Coward," The Hermit said and turned back toward the others. "He's never going to be able to help anybody."

The Hermit grabbed his spinning staff with both hands and brought it down on the ground in front of him like a lumberjack splitting wood. The ground exploded where it struck. Rocks and dirt flew out away from him. Everyone was thrown through the air. They slammed into trees and boulders and fell crumpled and lifeless to the ground.

Red screamed. His foot came free and he took two steps backward. He tripped and fell back into the cold water of the pond. He took a deep gasping breath as he went under, then he sat bolt upright on the couch at Michael's house.

"It was just a dream," he said quietly to himself as he gasped again for air. As his breathing slowed he began to become aware of noises coming from upstairs. Between trying to catch his breath and coming back to reality from his nightmare, he couldn't make out what was going on. He heard what sounded like a window or door slamming shut, then all was quiet. He listened for another minute or two, but didn't hear anything else. He grabbed one of the pillows from behind his head and threw it at Michael on the floor.

Michael sat up, apparently startled.

"Did you hear something?" Red whispered.

Michael moved the pillow off his lap. "No, I didn't hear anything."

"It sounded like somebody was running or something upstairs."

"It was probably just Sara," Michael said. He laughed. "I'll bet she can't go to sleep after that scare last night."

Red lay back down on the couch. He felt guilty about scaring her. He considered shifting into the spirit world to go check on her, but decided that the noise must have just been his imagination.

THE SUFFERER

Sara sat on her bed with her knees drawn up under her chin. She had suffered all through the day, unable to get the idea out of her head that her room was haunted. A cool night breeze blew through the open window, fluttering the curtains. She had almost convinced herself earlier in that day that it had all been a bad dream like her parents told her when she ran terrified into their room the night before. Almost, but not quite. She had lain awake all night, and she planned to do the same tonight. She would just sit here and wait for the morning. She did not think she could ever sleep soundly again.

Sleep, however, did not make the same vow. It overpowered her will in small increments. She began blinking her dry, tired eyes. The blinks grew more frequent, each time her eyes stayed closed a tiny bit longer. The cool air crept up past her ankles into her pajama pants, and blew down the gapped back of her shirt, so she slipped between the sheets – not to sleep, but just to keep herself warm. The wind felt good on her face, she decided to close her eyes completely, just to give them a chance to rest. Her body fell naturally into the slight depression where she curled up each night. The bed's warm embrace, familiar and comforting, teased the last strands of wakefulness from her, and sleep overtook her.

A large black bird lit on her window sill. It looked around the room with beady black eyes before spreading its wings and hopping gracefully down to the carpet. It turned over a sock with its beak, shook its head as if at the smell, then with a brief flurry of its wings, jumped onto the foot of the bed. The bird studied Sara for a moment, then flew back out the window. It flew to the waiting figure of The Hermit below and landed on his outstretched arm.

"It is the girl's room," he said to the animals and kobolds around him. He looked down at the coyote at his side. "Are you sure this is the same girl who was at the cave?"

The coyote looked up at The Hermit, and threw her head back once.

"This house is where you followed her?"

The coyote made the same motion again.

The Hermit held out his staff, and motioned toward the window. "Bring her to me." A hand-rolled cigarette dangled from his lips. It was stuck to his bottom lip with dried saliva and bounced up and down with each syllable. He took a long drag and an orange glow illuminated his face from below, turning his ghastly visage even more hideous. "I will wait for her at the cave." The bird fluttered off his arm as he spun around and strode off into the forest.

The bird flew back through the window and perched on Sara's dresser beneath the hanging medals that draped the mirror. Two kobolds placed a ladder made of branches tied together with grape vines against the side of the house. They climbed into the room through the window followed by a raccoon, a fox, and two more kobolds carrying rope.

The kobolds approached Sara's bed. The raccoon and fox dug through a pile of clothes and pulled out a t-shirt. The two animals wrestled for it - rolling over each other. The raccoon finally pulled it free of the fox's mouth and took it to one of the kobolds.

Sara awoke with a start. She felt something thrown over her head. Her arms and legs were held tightly. Long fingers wrapped around her upper arm and her thighs. She tried to scream for help, but at the first sound something was stuffed into her mouth through the covering that surrounded her head and secured with a rope. She shook as violently as she could manage and kicked wildly. The fingers slipped free of one of her legs.

She kicked where she imagined one of her attackers to be and landed a hard blow with the ball of her heel. She heard one of them fall to floor with a grunt and a thud. Immediately, another took its place and grabbed her legs. She was lifted off the bed. She kept kicking and flailing, but without the bed to push off of, she no longer had leverage. She could feel the cool air of the night as she was pushed head first out of the window. She was upside down as the kobold carried her down the ladder. One of her kicks managed to make contact with the bottom of the window. It crashed down on the sill.

Sara struggled as she was carried off across their back yard toward the edge of the forest. She never stopped fighting and squirming until she was thrown down hard on a stone floor. As she lay there motionless, she heard a shuffling of feet moving away from her and the slamming of an iron gate.

15

MISSING

Red and Michael both woke up to the aroma of fresh-ly brewed coffee and the gurgling of the percolator as it spurted out the last few drops of water into the coffee grounds. In the kitchen, Michael's parents, Emily and Alexander, talked in hushed voices.

"I don't think we should bother them," Emily said. "Just go look in on Red and Michael and make sure they are okay."

"What about Sara?" Alexander said.

"I don't want to risk waking her up. She didn't sleep at all night before last," Emily said through a yawn. She shook her head, trying to wake up.

"What do you think made her believe her room is haunt-ed?" Alexander said.

"I don't know," Emily said. She took the coffee pot off the warmer and filled her travel mug.

"I'm sure she'll be fine," Alexander said. He handed his own travel mug to Emily to fill up. "Listen. I've been thinking a lot about it, and I think we are really going to have to help Claire through all this. Whether she likes it or not."

"When you say 'we,' you really mean 'me,'" Emily said. With a smile, she bumped Alexander with her hip as she walked past him on her way to retrieve her purse. Coffee splashed out of his mug onto his hand.

"Ouch," he said and chuckled. "Seriously, though."

"You're right," she said. "I may have to just pull her along kicking and screaming."

Emily grabbed the car keys out of her purse. "C'mon then. We need to get going."

"I'll go check on the boys first," he said heading toward the den.

Red and Michael were stretching and rubbing their eyes when Alexander came down the stairs.

"Morning Mr. L.," Red said.

"Good morning, Red. How is camping out on the sofa treating you?"

"Fine," Red said. "I'd give anything to be able to get up and run around a bit though."

"I'm sure you would," Alexander said.

"Hey, what's for breakfast?" Michael asked.

"Today we have a very special breakfast planned," Alexander said. He clapped his hands together. "Today, you two and Sara, are going to have something prepared for you in a manner never before seen in this house."

"Uh, okay," Michael said hesitantly. "So, what is it?"

Alexander shrugged and flashed his trademark smirk. "I have absolutely no idea."

"What?" Michael said.

"I have absolutely no idea what breakfast is going to be, because you are the ones preparing it for yourselves," Alexander said.

"Aww, come on. Seriously."

"I am, like, so serious," Alexander said, doing what he

seemed to believe was a spot on impression of a teenage girl before returning to his normal speech. "Your mother and I slept in after getting back so late from Sara's game. We have to run."

"How did it go? Did Sara win?" Red asked. He reached behind his head and turned on the lamp beside the sofa.

"No," Alexander said. "They lost two to one. Sara had three shots on goal, but she missed all three. But don't tease her about it. She's beaten herself up about it enough already."

"That sucks," Red said. He wondered if she would have done better if he hadn't scared her so badly the night before.

"She'll get over it," Michael said. "Nothing keeps a Lagos down long."

"Red, did you have a good night?" Emily asked coming down into the room.

"Yeah, it was fine."

"Good, I'm glad. There is cereal in the cupboard, milk, eggs, and bacon in the fridge," she said. "And let Sara sleep in if she wants to. So breakfast is up to you."

"Yeah, Dad already told us that," Michael said sullenly.

"Well, we'll see you this evening," Alexander said. He and Emily, satisfied that everyone was taken care of, left the den and headed off to work.

"What are we going to do about Sara?" Red asked after Michael's parents were gone.

"Let her sleep all day if she wants," Michael said.

"No, I mean everyone else is coming over here soon. We are going to have to tell her."

"We can't tell her."

"We can't *not* tell her," Red said. "How can we keep it secret when everyone gets here? She'll recognize Esmé at the very least."

"Esmé," Michael said in a reverent tone.

"She is cute, but I don't think you have a chance with her," Red said.

"What?" Michael asked as he was pulled back to reality.

"Esmé is *way* out of your league," Red said. "And she is older than you."

"She is not out of my league, Michael said. "Who says I like her anyway?"

"Aww, come on. You can't even form a coherent sentence when you're around her."

"I can too," Michael said. He slid out of his sleeping bag and tried to hide his blushing face from Red.

Red laughed. "Seriously, though, what are we going to do about Sara? Everyone else could get here any minute."

Michael groaned. "Okay, you're right. We have to tell her something."

"Should we wake her up?"

"I'll get her up after I fix breakfast," Michael said. "Does cereal work for you?"

"Your mom said you have bacon," Red said.

Michael threw one of his pillows at Red. He caught it and threw it back. It bounced off Michael's shoulder.

"Fine," Michael said. "I'll make his highness a plate of bacon, will there be anything else?"

"I'll have scrambled eggs and toast as well, if you please, kind sir."

"Shall I send the maid out for fresh milk as well?"

"That will not be necessary. The milk you have will be fine," Red said.

Michael clomped up the stairs, he spun around on the top

step and bowed. "As you wish, your gimpness."

***

Red held the last bite of bacon between his greasy fingers. He closed his eyes and taking the bite, he savored its mixture of salt and sweetness. Despite Michael's best effort to burn the bacon, it still tasted wonderful.

"She's not there," Michael said. He bounded down the six stairs leading into the den in only two steps. "Sara is gone."

"What do you mean?" Red asked.

"I mean she's gone. She's not in her room, she's not in the bathroom, or anywhere else in the house," Michael said through heavy breaths. "She's gone."

"I'm going to go look," Red said.

"You can't walk. How are you going to-" Michael started to ask. He watched as Red stared off into the distance and fell back down onto the couch, crumpled like a rag doll. "Oh yeah. You mean *that* way. I don't know if you can still hear me or not, but that was incredibly creepy."

Red ignored him. In the spirit world he got off the couch, and ran out of the room, up the stairs and down the hallway to Sara's room. Michael had left the door open, and inside it was a mess. Of course it had also been a mess the other night when Red was there as well, but before it had looked more intentional. This time there seemed no sense to the disarray. Red tore through the house. He didn't bother with trying to go back into the hallway between rooms, he ran through one wall after another until he finished searching the entire house. He went back down into the den and shifted back into his body.

"She's not in the house," he said.

"Yeah, that's what I said," Michael said. A knock on the back door startled them. They looked at each other.

"Go get it, it might be Sara," Red said. "Maybe she went outside, and just got locked out."

Michael ran up the stairs to the back door. Without even looking to see what was on the other side, he threw it open. Esmé was standing outside the door with a large duffel bag thrown over one shoulder.

"Hey," Michael said.

"Hey." She was still wearing the same skirt from the night before, but she now wore one of Red's baseball uniforms as a top. She had cut the arms and back off the jersey, and had used shoe laces to tie the shirt around her back. She stood still waiting for him to invite her in. Seconds past. She bounced on her heels. "So, can I come in?"

"Sorry, yeah. Come in," Michael said. They brushed shoulders as she slipped past him. A ripple of excitement went through his body, and he nearly forgot about Sara's disappearance. "Listen, we've got a problem."

"What is it?" She asked. She sat the duffel bag down on the kitchen floor.

"It's my sister, Sara. She doesn't know what's going on, and she is missing."

"Do you know what happened?" Esmé asked.

"No, I just went to check on her. I figured we had to tell her something before everyone got here, but when I went to her room she was gone."

"Who is it?" Red yelled up the stairs from the den.

"It's Esmé," Michael said. Outside he heard the rumble of a four wheeler coming up the driveway. He turned back to

Esmé. "Go on down, I think Chase and Wendy just pulled up."

Esmé grabbed the duffel bag again and headed down the stairs. Michael held the door open for Chase and Wendy as they made their way from the back of the shed toward the house. He could hear Red yelling from the den.

"That's *my* shirt," Red said as Esmé came into the den.

"I hope it's okay," she said. "It looked old and worn out. I didn't think you would mind."

Red closed his eyes and swallowed his frustration. *There are more important things going on than my favorite uniform getting sliced to bits,* he told himself. "No, it's fine."

Chase, Michael, and Wendy came down the stairs.

"Michael says his sister is missing," Chase said. "That doesn't sound good."

"I'm going to go take a look in the spirit world and see if I can see anything," Wendy said. She sat down on one of the recliners and shifted over.

Red and Esmé shifted as well. Together the three of them headed off to Sara's room.

"So I guess it's just the two of us then." Michael said to Chase.

"I'm going too," Chase said. He took the stairs in two long strides.

Michael looked around at the limp bodies of Red and Wendy, sighed, then walked up the stairs behind them.

"Kobolds," Wendy said. She stood just inside the doorway to Sara's room. She could see the forms of the creatures from the spiritual residue they left behind. "There were at least three or four of them, and some smaller animals too."

"What do we do?" Red asked. He tried to keep from panicking. Even though he was no longer in his physical body, it still felt like his heart was racing furiously.

"We go after them," Esmé said. "They must have followed Wendy here, and kidnapped Sara thinking it was her."

"What is going on?" Michael asked Chase, the only one of the group that he could actually see.

"Kobolds," Chase said matter-of-factly. "Your sister was kidnapped."

"She was what?" Michael yelled. He looked around the room frantically as if in hope of finding the kidnappers still hiding somewhere.

Esmé shifted back to the physical world and put her arm around him. "Michael, don't worry. We are going to get her back."

"How are we going to do that? What if they've already done something to her?" Michael said. His words were spewing out so fast that they jumbled together. "We have to get her back. Let's go after them!"

"They won't do anything to her until after the circus disaster," Esmé said softly. "I promise. Let's go back downstairs and figure out what to do."

As they went downstairs Red noticed how Michael's hands shook uncontrollably. *Mine would be doing that too if I was in my body.*

Downstairs the group sat in a circle on the recliners and the couch. Chase paced back and forth around the back of the group.

"I say we take off right now and try to catch up with them," he said.

"It's too late," Wendy said. "They took her hours ago. They'll be long gone by now. I'm positive they took her to the cave anyway."

Michael sat silent, cross-legged on the floor beside the couch where Red and Esmé sat. He chewed on the fingernails of his quivering right hand.

"Then let's go to the cave. What are we waiting for?" Chase said. He took his billy club off the holster on his hip, and swung it in circles by its handle as he paced.

"We have to have a plan," Red said. "Look, I'm ready, but if we just show up there without any idea of what we are going to do, then we are just going to wind up getting captured as well."

"I wish there was someone we could go to," Esmé said.

Michael stood up and walked toward the staircase where the telephone hung on the wall. "The police. I'll call the police; they have to help us." He picked up the receiver.

Chase walked over to his side, and pushed the switch down with his club, disconnecting the line. "No police. They don't like me, and they'll never believe us. We have to take care of this on our own."

"We don't have to tell them who took her," Michael said pleading.

"It won't make a difference," Chase said. "If we tell them she was kidnapped, they'll ask how we know. If we just report her as missing, they won't do anything for at least a day. Kids go missing all the time. Ninety percent of the time, they are out with their boyfriends or girlfriends that they don't want their parents to know about. The police don't bother until it has been 24 hours. All we would do is draw attention to ourselves and frighten your parents."

"Why shouldn't they be frightened?" Michael asked. "I'm frightened. Red is frightened." He threw his arms up. "This is the time when being frightened is the exact right thing we should be."

"Michael," Red said trying to calm him.

"Think about it logically for a moment," Wendy said coming up beside Michael. She pushed her glasses further up her nose. "One: Your parents will never believe what happened. Two: Even if we could manage to convince them the spiritual world is real, there is nothing they could do to help. And, most importantly, three: If we do manage to convince them, even to come along with us, we will have lost valuable time."

"Time," Michael said. "We can't waste any time." He placed the phone back down on the hook and sat down on the stairs. "What's our plan then?"

"Tom," Red said. He pounded one fist into his other hand. "He didn't want to get involved before, but I bet if he knew a girl was in danger, he'd have to help us."

"Chase said that he refused to have anything to do with helping you find The Hermit," Wendy said.

"But he has to help," Red replied. "If he knows another girl is in danger, I'm sure of it."

"I hate to tell you, Red, but I think Wendy is right," Chase said. He slid his club back down into its holster. "I don't think he'll help us."

"It doesn't hurt to try, does it?" Esmé asked.

"Right, I think we should at least try," Red said.

"I agree with Red and Esmé," Wendy said. "We can't stay here anyway."

"What do you mean we can't stay here?" Michael asked.

"They are probably watching the house," Esmé said. "It would be safer for us to be somewhere else. I think we should talk to this Tom as well."

"We can all go to my hideout. We'll be safe enough there," Chase said. "If you all are intent on asking Tom for help, go right ahead. I'm going to go check out the circus and see if I can see anything going on there."

"I don't know if you all have noticed," Red said. "But I'm not really in the best shape for jogging, or even riding a bike into town."

"Don't worry," Wendy said. She smiled broadly and glanced at Chase who rolled his eyes. "I planned ahead in case you needed to be evacuated."

IN DARKNESS

Sara bounced off the rock wall of the cave, and fell down on her knees. Between her spinning head and the dim flickering light, it was a challenge for her to bring into focus the figure standing at the open iron cell door. Her mouth filled with a copper taste. She spat a stream of blood onto the dusty gray stone of the floor.

"Let me out of here," she said, remaining defiant. "I don't know what you're talking about."

"Tell me who sent you here?" The Hermit said. He stabbed the tip of his staff back down on the floor after using it to send her flying across the cell.

Sara climbed to her feet, but stayed huddled near the wall. Her pajamas were covered in the dank dirt of the cave. Her face was also covered in the same dirt, except for two clean channels that ran from the corner of her eyes down to her chin. "Nobody sent me, you brought me here."

"You lie," The Hermit said stepping into the cell. Animal shapes, silhouetted by the light of torches in the distance flitted in and out of view behind The Hermit. He blew out a puff of smoke that lazily floated away, and flicked his cigarette at Sara. She didn't flinch as it bounced off her shoulder.

She scanned around the cell for anything she could use to attack the strange man with. The only thing in the cell was a bowl of water they shoved into the cell after her. Her only hope was for him to come further in the cell; maybe then she could get around him.

The Hermit watched her eyes wander around the cell. "Don't bother. There is no way out." He took another step toward his captive.

Sara pushed off the wall and tried to run around the side of The Hermit. He raised his free hand and clenched it into a fist. Sara felt herself pulled off the ground by an invisible force. The Hermit pushed his hand forward, and Sara found herself again thrown against the rear wall. Her head cracked against the rock, and she felt her teeth bite into her tongue. The world spun and grew dark around the edges. The Hermit raised his hand above his head, and Sara was brought back to her feet with a jerk. She panted for breath and spat out another mouthful of blood. The Hermit lowered his hand, and Sara wiped her mouth with her pajama sleeve. It came away with a red streak.

"Tell me what you know about the vigilante," The Hermit demanded. His voice was scratchy, but calm.

"I told you, I don't know anything," Sara said. "You got the wrong person."

"So far, I have been kind," The Hermit said. "But this is beginning to get tedious. I hate to resort to torture, but you are giving me little choice." He snapped his fingers. Two coyotes strutted into the cell, one on each side of The Hermit. They curled their lips and growled at Sara. Saliva dripped off their exposed fangs.

"Why were you spying on us yesterday?"

"It wasn't me," she said. Panic began to replace her anger at the sight of the two dogs. She had never liked large dogs. "I wasn't even at home. I was playing soccer."

A wave of doubt past over The Hermit's face. He looked down at the coyote on his right. "I thought you followed her home. Are you sure this is the same girl?"

The coyote stopped growling. It looked up at The Hermit and whimpered. It cowered a few inches away from its master.

"Turn around," The Hermit said to Sara. She didn't move. He aimed his staff at her. Electric light flowed out of his arm into the staff. "I said, turn around! I only saw the girl from behind when she was running away." He moved the staff forward. Lightning arced from the top of the staff toward Sara. She felt herself forcibly spun around. Her face pressed against the wall.

The Hermit examined her from behind, her black hair was matted against her skull. "You've brought me the wrong girl." The Hermit kicked the coyote. It squealed as it hit the side of the cell. He turned and strode out of the cell. The two coyotes rushed to squeeze out of the cell before he slammed the door shut.

The force holding Sara against the wall suddenly stopped. She turned back toward the retreating figure of The Hermit. "See, it wasn't me. Now, let me go."

The Hermit continued to walk away.

"I won't tell anyone anything," she pleaded. She ran to the door and grabbed the iron bars in her hands. "Just let me go!"

The Hermit disappeared around a corner followed by the two coyotes. Sara watched him leave. The torchlight reflected off the bars of other cells before darkness swallowed the flickering light.

She fell to her knees. She was cold and alone. As the flickering light faded away, so did her defiance. Tears now raced down the tracks on her dirty cheeks. She shook the door, and the metallic rattle echoed in the darkness.

***

Red bounced up and down in the yard trailer behind the four wheeler the entire ride into town. He grasped the sides as tightly as he could and leaned back against the duffel bag he had Esmé bring from his house. His right leg hung out the front of the trailer, each little bump was agony on his bruised and battered body. He thought that the ride would be smoother once they got into town, but the potholes in the alley on the way to Chase's hideout were the worst.

"Ow," he cried after a particularly violent jolt.

"Sorry," Chase said. "I thought it would be a nice comfy ride for you. We're almost there, though."

"I told you we should have let some air out of the tires," Wendy said. Her arms were wrapped tightly around Chase's waist from behind.

"It's fine," Red said through gritted teeth.

They pulled behind a building. and Chase maneuvered the four wheeler and its trailer down a ramp. He jumped off and unlocked the double steel door. Wendy drove the four wheeler into the basement. Michael and Esmé came in right behind them on bicycles, Michael on his own Mongoose and Esmé on Sara's too small, and for Esmé, way too pink, Schwinn. She would have preferred something black, maybe with skulls on it, or at least more exposed gears.

Chase shut the doors behind them and flicked a switch on a breaker box. Lights came on one at a time, revealing a gigantic unpartitioned basement. Four work lights created a bright pool of light in the very center of the expansive room. Several other smaller pools of light flickered to life off to the sides. The rest of the room remained in darkness.

The center section was devoted to computer and other electronic equipment piled high on racks. A half-circle desk dominated the space with four monitors, identical and arranged in a row. The next largest lighted area contained a workout mat, several punching bags hanging from chains, various weights, and a pommel horse. Another area near one wall was a small kitchen. A single cot with a sleeping bag looked stark underneath a single light bulb at the far end of the room.

"Whoa," Michael said.

"How did you get all this down here?" Esmé asked. She laid the bike down on the concrete floor and stepped toward the computer area.

"A little at a time," Chase said. "There are pallet trucks and other equipment over by the entrance. I had a lot of stuff delivered to the warehouse next door, and I had to bring it in here when no one was around."

"Um, can somebody help me out of here?" Red said. "I can't see anything."

Michael and Chase came over to the trailer and together they lifted him out. Wendy wheeled over one of the chairs at the desk and they sat Red down in it.

"This place is cool," he said.

"It must be a guy thing," Esmé said. She leaned over and nudged Wendy with her elbow. "It is too dark and quiet in here for me."

"I feel safer in the dark," Chase said. "I like being hidden."

"What is all this computer stuff for?" Red asked. He scooted himself over to the desk with one foot, then propped his other leg on the desk.

"Police, fire, and EMS scanners," Chase said. He patted the row of computer monitors. "I've even got the city's traffic and some of the street and store cameras streaming through the computers. On this one I have real time updates from social media with keywords like – crime, fire, stolen – stuff like that. I like to be able to keep an eye on everything."

"Look, this is all very cool, but we need to find this Tom guy and rescue my sister," Michael said. He looked over at Red in the computer chair with his foot propped up on the desk. "And Red's dad, too."

"Not just them," Esmé said. "We have to stop the ringmaster as well. Straub wants to kill hundreds of people."

"Right," Chase said. "Let's get down to business. Wendy, what's the plan?"

"I think we should split up," she said. "I think Red and Chase should go to the hospital, since they know Tom. Michael and I should go to the circus to see what is going on there."

"What about me?" Esmé asked. "I want to do something."

"You can't go to the circus, obviously," Wendy said. "And Tom already knows Chase and Red, I figured they would have the best chance of convincing him."

"That is not going to work," Chase said. "Tom and I don't see eye-to-eye. Besides, the circus might be dangerous. I think I should go there."

"Fine," Wendy said. She rubbed her temples with her fingers, trying to work out the logistics. "Okay. Let's have you and Michael go to the circus, Red and I will go to the hospital, and Esmé can stay here and monitor everything and keep Red and my bodies safe."

"I'm not going to stay here," Esmé said.

"You can come with us," Red said. "Maybe you can help convince him about the circus' plans.

"It's settled then," Chase said. He walked over to his practice area, and pulled a leather sheathed knife off a small shelf filled with various weapons. He tossed the long knife to Michael. "I hope you can fight."

"Hold on a second, nobody said anything about fighting," Michael said. He pulled the knife out and looked at it, not knowing what to think of it. It was oiled and shiny; both sides of the eight-inch blade were honed razor sharp. He ran his thumb down one side, and jerked it back at the sharp pain. A bead of blood ran down his thumb into his palm. He put his thumb in his mouth. When he brought it out it had stopped bleeding, but the wound was deep and remained gaping.

"I don't think we'll have to right now," Chase said. He secreted several other weapons into his outfit. "It is better to be prepared. We know they are dangerous, and before this is all over, we are almost definitely going to have to fight."

Michael slipped his belt through a loop on the knife's sheath.

He and Chase walked back to where the group had gathered in a circle during their conversation, unconsciously drifting into the warm light of the work lamps.

"We are just going to leave Wendy and my bodies here alone?" Red asked.

"No one has ever found me before," Chase said. "I think

you'll be fine. Hold on." He left the group and went over to his sleeping area. He pulled out two more cots from against the far wall and placed them next to his own.

"One for Red, and one for Wendy," he said. "Now are we ready?"

Wendy checked her digital watch.

"It is nearly one p.m. now," she said. "We'll all meet back here at three."

"Here," Esmé said. She untied a key from one of her dreadlocks and tossed it to Michael. "It is to my trailer. In case you need it."

"How will we know which one it is?" He asked, examining the key.

"You can't miss it," she said. "It has my name written all over it."

17

HELP WHERE LEAST EXPECTED

Tom was sitting on the bench in the small park when Red, Wendy, and Esmé arrived. They were all in the spirit world. As the three approached the bench, it looked to Red like Tom was asleep.

"I see you've found some new friends," Tom said. He leaned forward and pushed himself up off the bench with his hands on his knees. "Good afternoon, my name is Tom Clack. And what shall I call you two young ladies?"

"This is Esmé, and this is Wendy," Red said hurriedly, nodding toward them. "Listen, we've got a problem."

"Red, I warned you that if you don't let things be, they would only get worse," Tom said, narrowing his brow and crossing his arms.

"I didn't have a choice," Red said. His frustration at Tom's unwillingness to help was getting harder for him to control. "We're already involved."

Tom sighed and sat back down on the bench. "How much trouble are you in?"

"We found The Hermit's cave," Red said. "He followed one of us back to my friend's house, and kidnapped his little sister."

"I'm really sorry to hear that," Tom said. "I suppose you came to ask for my help."

"Yes, we need your help," Esmé said. "You are the only adult not with the circus any of us know who has any idea of the spirit world, much less everything else that is really going on."

"I'm sorry," Tom said, "but you've got the wrong man. I do not want anything else to do with The Hermit or any of his djinn."

"Tom," Wendy said and stepped forward. She put her hand on his knee. "Red told us about you losing your wife to him, and I'm very sorry for your loss. But if you don't help us, a lot more families are going to be broken apart."

Tom looked slowly down at Wendy's small hand. It was the size of his daughter's when she had been taken. She was about the same age when his whole world fell apart. "I can't do it," he said lowering his head. "You don't know how long I've had to live with the mistake of getting involved with The Hermit's affairs."

Wendy pulled her hand back, and Tom traced his fingers across his knee where her fingers had rested.

"People are going to die," Red said. "You said you knew my grandfather, and that he sacrificed himself to save you." His frustration finally coming through his voice, he grew angrier and louder with each breath. "You owe your life to him! Now his son, my father, is kidnapped, Sara is kidnapped, and they plan to kill hundreds of people!"

Tom looked up at Red as he grew more intense. He lowered his head again and placed his hands together in his lap. He wrang them together, unwilling to look up at the three young people. "I promised myself I would never get involved in anything to do with the spirit world again. I'm not going back on my promise."

"You should be ashamed of yourself," Esmé said. She walked up to Tom and looked down at him with her hands on her hips. "What kind of man turns his back on saving the lives of others, especially since his own life was saved."

"Esmé," Wendy said calmly. She put her hand on Esmé's shoulder and gently pulled her back. "Let's just go, he isn't going to help us."

Tom lowered his head again. He wiped his eyes with the palm of his hand. "How are you sure The Hermit is going to kill all those people?"

"It isn't him. It goes above him," Esmé said, a measure of restraint returning to her voice. "It's Rinthim Straub, the ringmaster of the circus. I'm from the circus - or at least I was - and I overheard their plans."

"They are planning to kill the entire audience during a performance," Red said. "Unless we find a way to stop them."

Tom nodded along with Red's words. He still refused to look up. "I've heard of Straub and heard horror stories of what he is capable of doing." When Tom finally looked up at Wendy, his eyes were red. "They are planning to sacrifice their spirits to open up the interstice."

"That's right," Esmé said. "We have to—"

Tom raised one hand. "Let me finish, then you can go on your way." He took a deep breath and started over. "They are going to sacrifice their spirits to the interstice. If you are going to try and stop it, you have to find a way to stop The Hermit. The Hermit is the harbinger for this interstice. No one but him can open it, and there can only be one harbinger at a time.

"Straub, on the other hand, is a djinni himself. He wears the body of a human, but he isn't one. He came into the physical world through an interstice. He is connected to it, and he'll know immediately if something happens either to it or to the harbinger."

"So, what do we need to do?" Red asked.

"The Hermit has to be killed," Tom said. "Either that or find some way to get rid of whatever power it is that has kept him alive all these years and given him the ability to affect the interstice."

"Won't you come with us?" Wendy asked.

"No, I've given you all the help I'm able to," Tom said. He stared at his hands again. "Go on. Leave this old man alone. If you are smart, you'll find a way out of town, let whatever happens happen to other people."

"Come on," Red said and turned back toward the parking lot. He and Esmé walked along the path. Tom didn't look up.

Wendy stood still for a moment, then walked up to Tom and put her hand on his shoulder. At her touch Tom began to sob. He put his hand over hers.

"I understand," Wendy said, "even though my parents don't care for each other or for me the way you loved your wife and daughter. I understand because that is what I have hoped for my whole life." She pulled her hand away and started to follow behind Red and Esmé.

"I wish I could have had a father like you," she said over her shoulder. "I am so sorry you are broken." She ran up the path.

"What was that about?" Esmé asked.

"I just wanted to tell him I understood," Wendy said.

"Since we have some time before Michael and Chase get back to the hideout, can I go check on my mom and dad?" Red asked as they walked through the parking lot.

"Yeah, of course," Esmé said.

***

Red told Wendy and Esmé to wait in the hallway outside of his father's room, and he stepped tentatively into the room alone. Inside, the first bed was now occupied. An old man lay there, unmoving – either asleep or in a coma of his own. Red, still in the spirit world, moved past his bed. Beyond the man's curtain was just enough space for a hospital chair to be pulled up beside the second bed, the bed where his father's body was frozen without its spirit. Red's mother sat in the chair.

Red walked up beside her, and looked down at his father. He looked the same as before. It reminded Red more of a three-dimensional image of his father than the actual person, like he had been perfectly reproduced in wax. Either way, he knew it wasn't really his father, just his shell.

Red looked over at his mother. Her eyes were virtually the same. She stared as blankly off into space as his father. The same dulled expression on their faces. He realized that she must have been hitting the anti-anxiety pills pretty hard. She did it sometimes when things were rough around the house; she thought that neither Red nor Donal knew. Of course they both did, and they both knew the other knew as well. It wasn't something that they had ever acknowledged and nothing they would have openly discussed. It always frightened Red to see his mother this way. He felt that somehow it was his fault, that if he could just be a better son, then she wouldn't feel the need to check out.

Red turned back to his father. He placed his hand on top

of where Donal's were overlapped across his stomach. "I'm coming. I'm coming for you and nothing is going to stop me from saving you."

Red left and joined the others in the hallway. Together they headed out of the hospital and back toward downtown. Red thought about the different ways Tom and his mother had chosen to deal with the reality of their lives. Tom willfully ignored everything, while his mother took pills to help her forget. They didn't seem too different to him. One word from his dream the night before kept coming into his mind, no matter how he tried to forget it: *coward.* Both Tom and his mother's reactions seemed cowardly to Red, but then again, what had he ever done that was actually brave? *Coward.* If he panics while batting in a baseball game, what is going to happen when he comes across something truly frightening and difficult? What will happen if he has to come face to face with The Hermit?

***

The Circus Paenultimus was set up on the largest area of flat land they could find. It wasn't entirely flat, there was no land around Laurel Hollows that was completely flat. In this field the land sloped at a slight grade toward a small creek bed that held flowing water only after a heavy rain. The main tent was erected immediately in front of the creek. Across the thick black mud and shallow pools of mosquito-infested water scattered along the otherwise stagnant creek bed, the land slowly rose back up at a similar grade. Here the circus set up their campers and trailers in tight circles. Hundreds of feet scurrying back and forth had worn down through the dry grass creating hard-packed paths in the few days since their little community had been established.

Along one of those paths, near the far edge, Chase and Michael crouched and moved from behind one trailer to another. They paused at each one, making sure no one could see them, before they too scurried down one of those paths to hide again behind another trailer, always drawing nearer to the communal tents shared by the staff. A brief burst of wind blew the stench from a large pile of animal waste toward them. Michael covered his nose with the crook of his arm. He tried to keep focused on their immediate danger. It was the only thing that kept his mind off of what might be happening to Sara.

Chase held out his arm to prevent Michael from passing ahead of him. So far, even though they had seen several performers, they had yet to be spotted. He didn't want to take any chances. Chase leaned out from behind one of the trailers. The next one had a white wooden sign hanging beside the door. "Director and Ringmaster, Rinthim Straub."

"That's his trailer," Chase said nodding toward the trailer. "Let's lie low for a minute."

Michael lowered his arm. The worst of the dung smell had past. "What I don't understand is why didn't we send someone who could be invisible to do this part?"

Chase looked Michael up and down. "You aren't scared are you?"

"I wouldn't say I'm scared," Michael said. "Nervous, maybe."

"It wouldn't do any good," Chase said. "I've seen a couple of things here only in the spirit world already. Strange things I don't even know what to call, and Esmé says some of the people here are like me, and can see into both worlds at the same time, one of those is apparently The Hermit."

"When did you talk to Esmé?" Michael asked. He didn't want to know what kind of *things* Chase saw, but he was really curious as to why Esmé and Chase were talking in the first place.

"Last night," Chase said. "I walked her over to Red's house to make sure she got there safe. Be quiet. I think I hear someone coming."

Rinthim Straub emerged from one of the tents alongside a young woman. She was jotting something down in a notebook. The two paused outside the door to Straub's trailer. Straub pulled a keychain out of his jacket pocket.

"Will that be all, madam?" he asked. The kinder his actual words were, the more menacing they sounded.

"Yes, Mr. Straub. Thank you," the woman said. She slid her pen through the spiraled top edge of her notebook. "I'll make sure the photographer knows he can only stay for the first part of the show tonight. Sorry it took us so long to get out here for a profile on the circus, but it should be in the Gazette in the morning. In time for your weekend performances."

"You are too kind," Straub said. He took off his hat and bowed low to the woman. "Now if you will excuse me, there is a lot of work that goes into making sure each performance proceeds according to plan. I have some catching up to do."

"Of course," she said. "Break a leg, or whatever it is you say."

"That will do nicely," Straub said. "Good day." He spun on one heel, hopped up the wooden step leading to the door, and, unlocking, it he stepped inside. The woman dropped her notebook into her purse and headed toward her car on the other side of the camp. Once her car was out of sight, a man and a woman knocked on Straub's door.

"It's Luca and Nadya," the man said.

Chase heard a muffled response from inside the trailer, and the two entered. Chase looked down the row of trailers. When he saw no one was coming, he motioned for Michael to follow him.

"There is an open window at the back of the trailer," Chase whispered. He pointed to a window above the trailer's hitch. "Keep low and follow me." They ran bent over to the side of the trailer and flattened themselves as best as they could against its side. They could just make out the words coming from inside.

"Everything is nearly ready for tonight," Luca said. "The ropes will fail and it will all come down as soon as Nadya and I finish our performance."

"Good," Straub said. "Make sure everyone who matters is ready to leave as soon as the tent comes down. We are going to have to gather the spirits as quickly as we can and get them to the interstice before any of the local police get involved."

"Of course," Nadya said. We have prepared a couple of caravans already to transport them."

"What of your daughter?"

"Our daughter?" Nadya said. Her voice was almost, but not quite, free from any tremor.

"Yes, have you found out what happened to her yet?" Straub asked.

"No, not yet," Luca said. "She is still missing. The Hermit says he knows nothing about her."

Chase and Michael looked at each other. Michael pointed up at the window and mouthed, "Esmé's parents? It's happening tonight."

Chase nodded and held his finger in front of his mouth.

"And you are sure she knows nothing about our real purpose?" Straub asked.

"We're sure she knows nothing," Luca said. "We think she just ran away, she hasn't been happy with the circus life for a long time."

"You realize that I can't have her ruining our plans," Straub said. "If she turns out to be a problem, or has been captured by whomever it was spying on us at the cave, it would be best if you dealt with it yourself. Keep it in the family, as they say."

"There is no problem," Nadya said. "We'll bring her back."

"See that you do," Straub said.

A large black bird landed on the roof of the trailer above Chase and Michael's head. Its feathers shimmered in the harsh light. It looked down at the two of them, its talons scrabbling for purchase on the shiny metal surface. Chase pulled his billy club out of its holster and waved it at the bird trying to scare it away. It rose a few inches into the air and squawked at him.

"Shoo, go away," Chase said in a whisper. "Scat."

The bird squawked again and snapped its beak at the club, but it flew around the corner of the trailer away from Chase's swings. Chase and Michael breathed a sigh of relief. The conversation continued inside; they apparently hadn't taken any notice of the brief quarrel. Then they heard the sound of something hard scraping against the metal skin of the trailer. Michael looked around the trailer's edge. The bird was scratching and squawking at the trailer door.

"Open it," Straub said. "Our friend The Hermit has sent us another message."

Michael watched the trailer door open and the bird fly inside. He threw himself back against the trailer wall. "We have to go," he whispered.

"Back the way we came," Chase said and motioned down the side of the camp toward the distant road. Inside the trailer the bird continued squawking loudly. They bent over and rushed across the open space toward the next trailer.

"More spies!" Straub yelled. "Don't let them get away. One of them is the vigilante The Hermit told us about."

The door burst open and Luca and Nadya came running out. Straub stepped into the doorway, and placing two fingers in his mouth let out a loud whistle. The bird flew out from behind him and took off into the sky.

"Run!" Chase yelled. "We'll try and lose them in the trailers." He pulled his club out of its holster, grabbed Michael by the collar and dragged him toward the nearest mass of campers.

A trailer door opened in front of them. Before the person inside could step out, Chase leapt toward it. He hit it with his shoulder sending it slamming shut. Michael fumbled with the clasp on his knife's sheath while running, he couldn't quite get it unhooked.

"Over here," a voice yelled from behind them.

They turned down the next pathway. It led between two trailers. They had to turn sideways to fit between them. Emerging from the other side they saw two large clowns wearing face makeup, but no costumes. The two stood there shirtless in baggy pants. They were smoking cigarettes and drinking something clear out of a mason jar. At the sight of the two teenagers, they threw the jar down and came at Chase and Michael.

The first one lowered his head and tackled Michael around

the waist. The breath was knocked out of him as the obese clown fell on top of him. He reeked of liquor. Michael tried to free himself, but couldn't find purchase against the man's hairy, sweat-slicked stomach. As the other one neared Chase, he spun in place and brought his billy club down hard on the clown's collar bone. Michael heard a sound like a tree branch snapping, and the clown fell on the grass in agony.

"Chase," Michael said as the clown smiled down at him with gapped teeth. He sat straddle over Michael, his legs now pinning down Michael's arms. With one hairy hand he covered Michael's mouth, with the other the clown grabbed him by the neck and started to squeeze. Michael choked. He could just feel the clasp keeping the knife in its sheath with the tips of his fingers, but he still couldn't quite manage to get it open. He gave up trying to get to the knife as the clown's fingers tightened around his neck, completely cutting off his air supply.

Chase ran over to where Michael and the clown were struggling. He planted one foot beside Michael's head and kicked the clown in the face. The clown let go of Michael's neck and stood, belly quivering, to face Chase.

"We don't have time for this," Chase said. He hit the clown in the chest with his anchor-branded hand. The clown flew several feet in the air and flipped before falling face down. He didn't move. Chase wasn't sure whether or not he killed the man, but he didn't have time to think about it. He helped Michael up, and pulled the knife out of its sheath with one flick of his fingers. Spinning the blade deftly between his fingers he handed the blade to Michael. "Here."

The two took off again. They rounded the corner of a trailer and found themselves inside a circle of smaller trailers surrounding a blazing campfire. A whole chicken was roasting above the flames on a spit. It had obviously just now been abandoned. Chase and Michael heard people closing in on the circle from every side. They looked around for anywhere they might be able to hide.

"There. Esmé's trailer," Michael said pointing at a small silver trailer. On the side in bold purple and yellow letters it read 'The Beautiful Esmerelda, the Mystifying Gypsy Sorceress from the Dark Forests of Romania.'

"Come on," Chase said. They ran to the trailer door. As Michael pulled the key out of his jeans pocket, the door opened and Nadya stepped out of the trailer. Luca came from around the side behind Chase, he held a leather strap in one hand. Chase crouched into his fighting stance, waiting for one of them to make the first move.

"Wait," Michael said. He held out his hands palm up between Luca and Chase. He turned toward Nadya. "You're Esmé's parents."

"You know Esmerelda?" Nadya said. "Is she with you? Is she safe?" She scanned the circle of trailers.

"She's safe," Michael said, still holding his hands up. "She's not here, but she is safe."

"What have you done with my daughter?" Luca said. He held the two ends of the strap with one hand. He began spinning it in circles. A metal ball bearing the size of a marble glinted each time the swinging brought the small pouch in the center around.

"Nothing," Michael said. He took a step backward so that he was standing beside Chase. "She came to us. She came to warn us about what the ringmaster and The Hermit are planning."

"Michael, what are you doing?" Chase said. He glowered at Michael.

"It's okay," Michael said. He looked at the hard face of Luca, and back at Nadya. He couldn't find any expression on either face. "I think so anyway."

Nadya turned toward her husband. "What do we do?"

"Michael, we have to go," Chase said and glanced over his shoulder. The circus had organized and were sweeping through the camp. "We are running out of time."

They heard a loud squawk overhead. Chase and Michael looked up and were sure the screech came from the same bird that saw them spying on Straub earlier. Chase thought things were about to get ugly.

"I'll take care of him," Luca said. He stepped toward Chase and swung his slingshot faster and faster.

Chase held out his branded hand waiting for the throw to come so that he could block it. Instead of throwing the ball at Chase, Luca looked up at the flying bird and sent the ball speeding through the air. The ball hit the bird, tearing right through its fragile body. Feathers flew away from it as it plummeted to the ground. It landed at Luca's feet. He picked up the bird and tossed its body into the fire.

"Here," Nadya said. She opened the door to Esmé's trailer. "Hide in here. We'll come get you when it is safe."

Chase and Michael jumped into the trailer and slammed the door behind them. Just in time. They heard the search party arrive at the circle of trailers as the door shut. "I really hope we can trust them," Chase said.

"Yeah, me too," Michael said. He sat on the floor with his back to the door. He reached up over his head and turned the lock.

"Did you see them?" Luca said. "We heard that stupid bird of The Hermit's and thought it came from here."

"Sssame here," Synesteria said. She glided into the clearing around the now smoking fire, and looked around. She picked up a black feather from the ground and turning it between her fingers she flicked her forked tongue out, smelling it. She glared at Luca, and dropped the feather back to the ground.

Luca stared back at her.

"Sssearch the trailers here firsst," Synesteria said. She slithered off ahead of the search party.

Adrenaline pumped through Chase and Michael. Chase sat down on the floor with his arms across his knees, his branded palm toward the door. Michael closed his eyes and leaned his head back.

"This one is clear," Nadya said pretending to pull the door of Esmé's caravan shut.

18

THE WAR ROOM

"They're an hour late," Esmé said. She paced in heavy footed circles around the sleeping cots in Chase's downtown hideout. Each passing minute that Chase and Michael were late stretched out longer than the one before it.

"I think Wendy and I should go after them," Red said. "They don't know who we are. We should be fine."

"If you show up at the circus in the spirit world, they will definitely capture you and take you to be sacrificed with everyone else after the performance tonight," Esmé said. "It's not a good idea."

Wendy sat on the edge of one of the cots, her face buried deep in her hands. "We have to do something," she said looking up. "Chase has been my only friend for years."

At the other end of the long dark room, the double doors leading to the ramp outside creaked open. The figures of Chase and Michael were silhouetted against the bright afternoon light.

"Chase," Wendy shouted. She jumped off the bed, and ran toward him as fast as she could. Her limp, almost unnoticeable when she walked, was clearly evident as she sprinted across the concrete floor, heavily favoring her good leg. She didn't slow down until she ran into him and threw her arms around his neck. "Are you okay?"

"I'm fine," he said. "We're both fine."

Michael took a step to the side away from Wendy's over enthusiastic embrace. "We were spotted."

Esmé looked the two of them up and down, particularly Michael, as the three of them walked across the hideout to where her and Red were waiting.

"What happened?" She asked.

"The Hermit sent a messenger bird to the circus. It saw us, and then Straub and everyone came after us," Michael said.

"Your parents included," Chase said to Esmé.

"What did they do?" She asked. She took a step away from the group and put her hand over her mouth. Conflicting emotions stirred inside her. She had yet to come to grips with the idea that her parents, who always seemed to love her so much, could be involved in such an evil scheme. She longed to be with them, but was terrified at the thought of seeing them again.

"They saved us," Michael said. He walked over to her and tentatively laid a hand on her shoulder. The instant clamminess and sweatiness he had gotten in the past whenever he touched her seemed to have passed. "If it wasn't for them, we would have been captured for sure."

Esmé nodded. Feeling vulnerable at the mention of her parents, she tugged Red's chopped up uniform down, covering her stomach. Michael took his arm off her shoulder after giving it a small squeeze.

"Here," Michael said. He took the backpack he found in Esmé's trailer and laid it on the floor in front of her. "I didn't know what clothes you would want, so I just stuffed as much as I could in your backpack."

Esmé and Michael stared into each other's eyes for a moment. "Thanks," she said.

"Don't mention it."

"So, what precisely happened?" Wendy asked.

"We were being chased through the camp," Chase said. He leaned against a stack of wooden pallets. "We were about to be caught when we ran into her parents. I thought they were going to try and kill us."

"I told them you were our friend," Michael said to Esmé. "And that you were safe."

"They hid us in your trailer until the ringmaster called everyone in the circus to a meeting. Your mother came and told us it was clear for us to leave," Chase said.

"They gave me something else for you," Michael said. He dug in his pocket and pulled out a wadded up yellow scarf. "She said you would know what it means."

Esmé took the scarf gingerly between her fingers and careful unwrapped it. Inside was tiny porcelain top hat. Long rabbit ears, one of which was folded over, stuck up from inside the hat. The rabbit's eyes and nose were barely visible over the rim. She tied the scarf around her neck and turned the figure over in her hands. The rabbit that had always been glued to the inside of the hat fell into her palm. "It means 'goodbye,'" she said. "They called me their little magic rabbit. When I was little I wanted nothing more than to be an escape artist. They said that one day their rabbit would escape forever."

"What are you going to do?" Red asked.

"It doesn't matter," Esmé said. "Right now we have to get to the cave and stop The Hermit. We're running out of time."

"So we're really going to do this?" Michael asked.

"We have to," Red said. "We have to save Dad's spirit, rescue Sara, and stop the disaster at the circus."

"I'll be right back," Chase said and jogged off into the darkness.

"Where is he going?" Michael said.

"Beats me," Red said. With a groan, he managed to sit all the way upright.

"Wendy," Esmé said. "So, do we have a plan?"

"Of course," Wendy said. "I've been developing a stratagem." She stepped into the light and put her glasses on. Pulling a folded piece of notebook paper out of her back pocket, she spread it out flat on an empty cot. "We kill The Hermit."

Her flatly stated intention struck the group dumb.

Chase returned to the silent group. His arms were full of a variety of weapons which he carefully laid down on the cot beside Wendy's paper. "In that case, we'll need these."

Michael looked doubtfully at the array spread out in front of them. "Are you sure you don't have any guns?"

"Guns are too dangerous," Chase said.

"I thought that was the point," Michael said. "If we are going to have to kill The Hermit, a gun seems to me to be the best option."

"We have a couple of shotguns at the house," Red said. "We could stop—"

"No guns," Chase interrupted. "They are more dangerous for an inexperienced person using them than they are for their opponent. People get careless and overconfident if they have a gun in their hands."

"I know how to shoot," Michael said. "I don't know anything about hand-to-hand fighting."

"Michael," Wendy said. "You won't be joining us anyway."

"What do you mean?" Michael asked, his face red. "I know I had a hard time at the circus, but there is no way I'm going to sit here while the rest of you go out to fight. The Hermit has my sister. I'm going."

"You can't come with us," Red said. "We talked it over while you and Chase were at the circus."

Michael turned to Red who stared at his own feet. Michael looked at each of the rest of the group in turn. They all avoided making eye contact with him. "So, you are all just going to abandon me here?"

"We aren't abandoning you," Esmé said.

"It's part of my plan," Wendy said. "We need you here. Somebody has to make sure mine and Red's bodies are safe while we are in the spirit world."

"I'm supposed to be a baby sitter?" Michael said. "Wouldn't it be better if there were five of us instead of four?"

"Michael," Red said. "Calm down. Somebody has to watch over us. It is as important as going to the cave. Both The Hermit and Straub know that we are out here somewhere and will be looking for us. If no one is here and they find this place, then me and Wendy will be killed, and there is nothing we can do to defend ourselves."

"You don't know that will happen," Michael said. "Everything worked out fine before."

"Things have changed," Chase said. "Now we know The Hermit and Straub are looking for me and my hideout."

Michael threw his arms up. "We don't know if they'll ever find this place. We do know that you are going to have to fight at the cave. It makes the most sense for me to come along. I'm sure I'm a better fighter than Wendy." He turned toward her. "I don't mean anything against you, but I'm older, bigger, and stronger." He then addressed the rest of the group. "I think it would make more sense for her to stay here and for me to go."

"That is precisely why you cannot come," Wendy said. "The fact that you are likely to be better at fighting is one reason you need to stay. If we are indeed attacked here, I don't think I could defend Red by myself."

"We also are going to need Wendy's tracking skills," Red said. "Michael, listen. It was my idea. I need you to stay here. I'm relying on my best friend to keep me and Wendy safe." The two lifelong friends looked squarely in each other's eyes. "Do this for me, please."

Michael nodded at Red. "Yeah. No problem," he said. He sat down with sagging shoulders on the edge of a cot, but offered up no more complaints.

"If no one else wants them," Chase said, diffusing a tense silence that had fallen over the group. "I'll take the tiger claws." He picked up a pair of steel knuckles from amongst the weapons spread out on the cot. He held the claws tightly in clenched fists. From between each of his fingers three inches of sharpened blade stuck out, glinting underneath the solitary bare light bulb.

Esmé stepped forward and retrieved a long bo staff that was at least a foot taller than she was. "I know a little about using a bo," she said.

"Wendy, Red. What do you want?" Chase asked.

"I've already got something," Red said. He turned to Michael. "Can you bring me the duffel bag that Esmé brought from my house?"

Michael nodded and, remaining silent, went to retrieve the bag from near the hideout's entrance.

"Chase," Wendy said. Her voice was like the squeak of a

mouse. "I don't know what to take. I'm not even any good with a steak knife."

Chase picked up a small crossbow and a quiver of bolts. He handed her the crossbow and put the quiver over her shoulder. "Here, you can use this. All you have to do is pull back this lever, it isn't hard. Then just put one of the bolts in the slot and fire away."

"Thanks," she said timidly. She held the weapon awkwardly at her side.

Chase looked at Michael as he returned with Red's duffel bag over one shoulder.

"I've already got the knife," he said, patting the leather sheath at his waist.

"We need to get going," Chase said.

Red, with Michael's help, put on his catcher's mask and pads from the duffel bag, lay back down on the cot, and gripped his baseball bat tightly in his hands. "Thanks. I'll see you in a bit," he said to Michael. "I'll see the rest of you all on the other side." He shifted into the spirit world.

Wendy laid down on the cot next to him with her crossbow held in one hand. "I'm shifting."

"Wish us luck," Esmé said to Michael.

"Be safe," he said to Esmé and Chase's back as they faded into the dark, away from the work lamps toward the four wheeler.

19

THE CAVE

As the afternoon light waned, Red, Chase, Wendy, and Esmé walked side by side into the forest. The four, brought together by happenstance and shared experience, each brought their own doubts and fears along with them. As they delved deeper into the forest, the undergrowth diminished and the hard ground beneath their feet gave way to leaf littered moss. Their heels sank deep into the soft growth. Each step brought them further into the forest's dark embrace. They sank deeper into their own thoughts – of failure, despair, and inadequacy.

Red stepped into a mud puddle hidden beneath a layer of leaves. Even here, in the spirit world, the mud sucked at his tennis shoes. He struggled momentarily to pull one foot out. Every step he took drew him closer to his father, but also closer to The Hermit. The mud slurped as he managed to pull his foot free. He tried to keep his mind a blank slate, clear of what may or may not happen when they finally came to the cave. No matter how hard he tried to put the thoughts behind him, he kept imagining himself as the hero. He imagined what it would feel like to have rescued his father, taken on The Hermit and defeated him.

Even as he imagined the victory, there was a part of his mind clinging, like the sticky mud, to an alternate scenario. He imagined failing to rescue his father and to protect those who came with him. As in his dream, he imagined The Hermit separating them from himself. He saw The Hermit raising the staff and attacking his friends while he just stood there doing nothing, like a coward, terrified and unmoving – unable to do anything other than simply bear witness as The Hermit murdered them.

Wendy was unhindered by thoughts of whatever the future might hold. She bounced across the forest floor, enjoying the freedom the spirit world provided her in full two-legged mobility. She was surrounded by three people she now thought of as friends. For the first time in her life, she had more than one friend. The thought gave her a confidence she had never felt. In school, people were usually either mean to her, or they were nice in an obviously artificial way. The people walking beside her knew her primarily in the spirit world where she wasn't handicapped by her physical limitations, but empowered by her innate nature. Each step she took wasn't filled with trepidation, but was an assurance of the camaraderie she had always dreamed of possessing.

Chase barely took notice of the three others walking beside him into the unknown. He kept his head down and plodded along. This moment was the culmination of the last three years of his life. Soon he would face the person responsible for the death of his mother and the separation of his family. Each step brought him closer to that vengeance. He thought only about rescuing Red's father and Michael's sister tangentially to his own goal of killing The Hermit. Beyond that moment, he held no thought. That future, whatever it might hold, was of no concern to him for now.

Esmé led the way through the forest toward the cave. She turned back toward the group and motioned for them to follow her down a hill toward the stream that flowed from the lower mouth of the cave, still a half mile away. Chase, Red, and Wendy made their way down the embankment behind her. Esmé watched as the others descended. She didn't know any of them, not really. She did know that each one of them was here for their own personal reasons. What she was less sure of was of her own reason for being here. Of course she didn't want the ringmaster Straub to kill all of those people, but the only thing she really had at stake in this fight was the balancing out of whatever incidental assistance she might have given to Straub. *Does balancing that out mean I have to risk my own life,* she wondered. In a way, it felt like it was the sheer momentum of the events that were dragging her along.

She crossed the stream, stepping across the slick rocks. She paused halfway across, each foot on a different stone, to make sure that everyone else was able to make it, especially Wendy, the smallest. As they made their way past her, Esmé watched a long-legged spider riding on a leaf down the stream. The spider's raft sailed between her legs. Pulled by the stream's current, it spilled over a tiny waterfall. It was captured by the fall's underflow and was sucked deep into its plunge pool. It disappeared under the falling water. It did not emerge, though Esmé waited for several moments.

"How much farther is it?" Red asked.

"Just a couple of more bends in the creek," Esmé whispered.

"Shh! We need to start keeping quiet."

Esmé looked at the group, their hastily organized and clumsy community. *This is my family now,* she thought. *Their fight is mine.*

As they made their way around the next bend, the group heard muffled voices. It sounded like many conversations overlapping each other. The bank of the creek nearest the voices was over their heads. Chase motioned for them all to crawl up its side. He held his hand for the rest to hold back as he inched his head above the crest of the embankment to get a better look. He slowly lowered back down and shook his head.

"I can't see much," he said. "I saw the tops of a few heads, but that is it. We are too low."

"Let me try," Esmé said. She peered over the edge, laid down her bo staff and, seeing no one around, she crawled the rest of the way up. She wrapped her hands around the trunk of a small tree and pulled herself up, her two feet resting momentarily against the slender trunk. She bounced, testing her weight a couple of times, and then ran up the side of the tree. She leapt backward off the trunk, spun in the air, and grabbed a branch of a neighboring tree like a gymnast during a high bar routine. Without slowing down, she used the speed of her downward arcing descent to carry her to a fir tree where she became lost in the thick evergreen needles.

Chase, who had been peering over the edge of the bank, turned back to Red and Wendy. "Unbelievable, did you all see that? She is really fantastic."

Wendy scowled.

The three lay quietly against the side of the bank. Red tried to make sense of the mumbling he heard in the distance, but the voices were muffled by the sound of the creek beneath him. They were relying on the cover of the creek's constant sound to mask their approach, but that very cover made it more difficult to decipher the conversation ahead. The only words he was able to understand clearly were 'hurry,' and 'get a move on.' It wasn't much to go on.

He gave up trying to eavesdrop. Instead, he held his baseball bat out in front of himself with both hands. He had been trying to use his transmuting ability to change the bat as they had marched through the woods, but he couldn't get anything to happen. He gripped the bat's handle tightly in his fingers. His knuckles turned white. *Be a sword,* he thought toward the stubborn bat. Again and again he thought it: *Be a sword.*

The bat seemed to momentarily lose cohesion, but refused to change. He lowered his head and brought the bat to rest against his forehead. *What is wrong with me?* He thought. *Why can't I get it to work?* He was still trying to force the bat to change into a sword when Esmé fell out of the sky and landed on the ground near his feet.

Wendy immediately rose from her position against the side of the hill. "What did you see?" She asked Esmé.

"There are about a dozen kobolds and people up there," Esmé said. "Some of them are from the circus. They have cleared a large circle in front of the cave that they are surrounding with torches. They also put down two rows of torches, like a path, leading to the cave's upper entrance."

"It must be for the sacrifice," Wendy said.

"Some kind of ritual," Chase said.

Red was barely paying attention to the conversation. He

was still trying to turn his bat into a sword.

"Did you see The Hermit?" Chase asked.

"No, I think he must be inside the cave. One of the men from the circus came out and said The Hermit needed a couple of men to help him inside," Esmé replied.

"What are we going to do?" Red asked looking up. He gave up on changing the bat into a sword, he was just going to have to rely on fighting with a bat if it came down to it. "I don't want to have to fight my way to get to The Hermit if we don't have to."

"Can we sneak inside from the lower entrance you were in?" Chase asked Wendy.

"I'm not sure," she said. "There is at least a small opening between the lower cave and the primary cavern, so there is likely a larger way between them, unless it has been blocked."

"I think we should try that," Esmé said. "I agree with Red. I don't want to have to fight any more than we have to."

"I'm game either way," Chase said. "As long as we get a shot at The Hermit, I don't care if I have to fight through two dozen of his minions, whether they be human or kobold."

"Chase, not all of us have your thirst for violence," Wendy said.

"It isn't about violence," he said. He stared vacantly beyond her. "It is about vengeance."

"Either way," Red said. "We stand a much better chance of coming out of this alive if we can sneak up on The Hermit before anyone else sees us."

"I don't think that is an option anymore," Esmé said looking over their heads.

On the bank behind and above their heads what looked to be a coyote glared down at them. It flashed white fangs between furled black lips and stepped forward. It let out a deep growl and pounced over their heads toward Esmé.

Esmé ducked and the coyote landed in mud at the edge of the water. It struggled, slipping on the mud as it spun around to face them.

"Shoot it," Chase yelled at Wendy. He reached into his pockets to put on his tiger claws.

Wendy struggled to pull up her crossbow, already notched with a bolt. Before she brought it all the way to her shoulder to aim, she accidentally pulled the trigger. There was a 'pfft,' and the bolt sank into the mud, three feet in front of the coyote.

Esmé ran to her staff that rested against the bank. She caught it up with one hand, and spun around to face the animal. Red rose to his feet and brought his bat up over his shoulder.

"I'm sorry," Wendy said. "It was an accident."

"Don't worry about it," Chase said sliding the claws over his fingers and crouching low. "Just get another one ready."

The coyote regained its footing and stared defiantly at the group. It threw back its head and howled.

"That's the same animal from the accident. I'm sure of it," Red said, but no one could hear him over the chilling call as it spread a warning to all djinn and humans within earshot.

Chase took a few running steps and leapt on top of the creature. He swung his steel-clawed fists at her as furiously as he could manage. The coyote dodged each swing, twisting underneath his weight. The two, caught in such a furious embrace, rolled into the creek with a splash. The coyote's long thin snout snapped ferociously, trying to clamp down on Chase's arms. They continued fighting, rolling over each other, and fell into a deep pool.

"What can we do?" Red asked.

Before anyone had a chance to answer him, they heard more voices, now loud and distinct, between them and the cave.

"The howl came from over here," said a man's voice.

Red, Esmé, and Wendy turned around just in time to see two heads appear over the top of the embankment.

"Down here," the nearest one said. "It's that Hibbard girl, Esmerelda, and a bunch of kids. What are you —"

The man was cut short, surprised, as Esmé ran up the bank with her bo held behind her in one hand. She planted her feet firmly on the ground, and using her body as a fulcrum she brought the staff around. Gripping it with both hands, she swung it downward and across the man's kneecaps. The crunching sound was like a large branch breaking off a tree. The man fell forward in agony, his knees bent the wrong direction.

Red scrambled up the hill toward the second man. As he neared the top he could see that there were now several other people and kobolds running toward them. From behind he heard Chase grunting and the pained yelps of the coyote. As the first of their assailants neared him, he recognized him as the strange man from the circus who took their tickets. Red Hesitated. *The man's name was Arthur*, he remembered: *Arthur P. McCoy, the third.*

"I don't know where you all come from," McCoy said. "But I know you are never going back." He pulled a pistol out of the back of his trousers and pointed it at Red.

Red heard a *thwip* from somewhere behind him. One of Wendy's bolts hit McCoy in the chest. He looked down at the seeping blood of the wound, and fell silently forward.

"I told you a gun makes you overconfident," Chase said emerging from the creek. He was soaking wet and blood was splattered across his chest and his face. The coyote lying dead in the creak behind him. He noticed Esmé and Red staring at the blood.

"Don't worry," he said. "It's not all mine." He turned back toward Wendy, who was staring white faced at the fallen man. "That was a good shot."

"He's dead," she said, her voice cracking. "I killed him."

"Wendy!" Chase said harshly. "Now is not the time. Deal with it later."

Wendy nodded and mechanically notched another bolt into her crossbow. Red adjusted his grip on his bat and Esmé spun her bo around behind her, ready for her next opponent.

"Let's do this," Chase said. He ran up the bank ahead of the rest of the group toward the converging men and kobolds with wide eyes and a loud, defiant cry.

***

Two rows of torches formed a pathway through the twisting passages of the cave. They wound through the string of chambers The Hermit had been using as his home. They passed the rock-rimmed fire pit he used to prepare his meals and keep the cavern warm. The twin lines of torches passed the ancient mattress tucked into the recess where he slept. Beyond his chambers, the torches passed between the two banks of prison cells before disappearing into the cave's inner recesses. There were four cells on each side. The cells were empty, save the first two facing cages, a fact only one of the two prisoners realized.

Red's father, Donal Snyder, was that prisoner. To the best of his knowledge, it had only been five days since he was brought here by The Hermit and his minions following the car accident. The first day he raged and yelled for help, berated his captors, and demanded release. There had been no response, only the deafening silence of utter darkness. The second day he pleaded, he begged for release. He would have felt satisfaction with a response. Even that was denied him. No response or even acknowledgment ever came.

The third and fourth day ran together in his mind. Those days he spent wallowing in guilt, reproaching himself for neglecting the duties his father had given him. He knew it was his fault that this happened. It was his failure to take on The Hermit and protect the interstice that brought on his imprisonment, and even ultimately the accident. He didn't even know then if his son was alive or dead. He had thought that by ignoring everything, somehow it would simply go away. He had run from the reality of the spirit world entirely, justifying his decision by believing that the work he did as a photojournalist made up for it. He believed that if he brought the knowledge of injustices and evil to the rest of the world, it would somehow make up for his own unwillingness to take on the evil in his own community. It was during those two dark days that he came to realize it was his own cowardice that let this happen.

Anything dealing with the spirit world had always terrified him. Each time his father had worked with him on learning to perfect his abilities had been a traumatic experience. When Isaiah passed away, Donal knew that he had been in the spirit world at the time, and it only made the entire idea of it worse. He decided then that he would have nothing to do with it; he would turn his back on it and let it sort itself out. There was no amount of war or danger in the physical world that terrified him in such a way. He knew he wasn't really brave, not the way everyone else thought him to be – and especially not the way that Red thought of him.

During the night, while he had been in the depths of that despair, The Hermit along with several kobolds and animals, brought in another prisoner. This one was not in the spirit world however. They threw her into the cell opposite him, and The Hermit began interrogating and torturing her. It was Sara Lagos, Emily and Alexander's daughter. He didn't understand why she, of all people, would be captured and questioned. The Lagoses had never had anything to do with the spirit world, at least as far as he knew. He had screamed at The Hermit, but he was ignored. Trapped in his empty cell, forced to watch as The Hermit tortured the child, Donal felt powerless and defeated in a way he'd never felt before. Even after it was over, The Hermit paid no attention to him. He had walked right past his cell without even a sideways glance. That had been the only time during his imprisonment in the cell that Donal had seen any light until the torches had been placed in position.

During that time, however, he had not taken his eyes away from where Sara was locked in her cell, even though he could see nothing but utter blackness. It helped his focus that she talked to herself during that time. It also gave him the first sprigs of hope he had felt since his own capture. She had mentioned in her mumblings that Red had survived the accident, and that he was staying at their home. Apparently, she had a crush on him as well. It was the first news he had of the outside world. It came as a warm breeze on a cold night.

He heard the commotion in the distance well before he saw the warm glow of torchlight bouncing off the gray walls of the cave. He heard the gruff voice of The Hermit and the whiny growling that kobolds twist into words. Something was happening outside.

***

Wendy stood well behind the rest of the group, firing one bolt after another from her crossbow as fast as she could load them. She was getting quicker and more accurate with each one. It felt to her that her will for each shot mattered more than her aim. The bolts sometimes seemed to change their trajectory as they flew away from her.

Chase was in a frenzy. Each time he knocked back one of the kobold or human attackers, he engaged another within the space of a heartbeat. Unconscious, perhaps dead, men lay motionless on the ground. Kobolds turned to dust in a path behind him and Esmé. She danced through the melee, spinning around and swinging her bo in great arcs. She flitted in and out of the spirit and natural world to dodge attacks, depending on who was delivering them. They were holding their ground, and surprisingly to them, they were advancing toward the mouth of the cave.

Each time Red was about to engage an enemy, either Esmé or Chase got there first. He was thankful for the help, but embarrassed because he felt that he hadn't contributed at all to the fight. A bolt flew over his shoulder hitting a man in the neck he was just about to swing his bat at.

"Thanks," he yelled over his shoulder to Wendy, even

though she was too far behind him for her to hear.

A kobold, hidden behind the man felled by Wendy's bolt, leapt over the falling man toward Red. Red stepped toward it, his left foot falling into his natural baseball batting stance, and swung his bat. He brought his right shoulder down like he was trying to hit a long drive over shortstop. The bat made a wet crunch it struck the kobold's head, like a bag of half-melted ice falling on asphalt. It fell over backward to the ground, dead. The encounter gave Red a sense of confidence, and he surged toward the middle of the fight, the kobold turning to dust behind him.

Dozens of birds suddenly took off from their cliffside roosts and began diving at the group. Chase punched at them with his tiger claws, but they moved out of his reach too quickly. They pecked at his arms and his face, then flew away as quickly as they had arrived. Red swung his baseball bat wildly at them, his face protected by his catcher's mask. It was only by sheer luck that he managed to hit the one he did. It fell stunned to the ground.

Esmé's luck was a bit better. She managed to knock three to the ground before the first one tore a strip of flesh off her arm. She screamed and grabbed the bird by the neck with her left hand and flung it against a tree. She swept the bo around and around her as fast as she could, trying to keep the birds away.

While dodging the birds' fevered attack, Red watched as the men and kobolds they were fighting began to spread out around them. They formed a wide circle around the group and closed in.

Wendy wasn't sure how to help the rest of the group. So far, the birds had not attacked her, but there was no way she could have hit one of them with her crossbow, even if they held still. So, she decided to focus on trying to thin out the men and kobolds. She notched another bolt in her crossbow and brought it up to her shoulder. Before she pulled the trigger, she was hit in the small of her back from behind. The crossbow fell to the ground in front of her, firing uselessly into the air. She landed on the ground beside it and rolled onto her back to see her attacker.

A woman with a thin beard of whisky blonde hair stood over her with a smoldering branch. She was dressed in the purple and yellow of the Circus Paenultimas.

"You killed Arthur," she said. Her eyes were glazed over and unfocused, puffy and pink. "How could you!"

"What? Who is Arthur?" Wendy asked.

"He was my husband," the woman screamed through gritted teeth. She grabbed the branch with both hands and brought it over her head like an ax, smoke trailed behind the blackened stump. Embers glowed red inside the branch, brought back to life by the influx of oxygen. She brought it down toward Wendy's head. Wendy managed to roll out of the way as the branch bounced off the ground inches from her head, sending up a cloud of orange sparks.

Wendy struggled to her feet, only to be knocked down again by a blow to her ribs from the woman's branch. The back of her head hit a root sticking out of the ground, and her vision filled with swirling sparks like those thrown up by the branch. She tried to focus on what to do as the woman brought the branch over her foul, grimaced, and scraggly-bearded head for another strike. But Wendy was too dizzy from the blow to the head to do anything.

"You murdered him," the woman said, her eyes wild and

maniacal. "I'm going to kill you, you stupid little --"

The woman froze. The smoking branch dropped from her grasp. She coughed a spray of blood and fell to the ground. A metal rod protruded out of her back between her shoulder blades.

Wendy stared at the rod, trying to make out what it was and who could have done such a thing as the figure of Tom Clack came running past the now dead woman and knelt at her side.

"Are you okay?" he asked.

"Yeah, I'm okay," she said. She pushed herself up onto her elbows. "What are you doing here?"

"I kept thinking about what you said at the hospital. You reminded me that there are things worth fighting for, things worth risking your life for," Tom said, helping Wendy to her feet.

Wendy's blurry vision finally cleared and Tom's face came into focus. "Thank you," she said.

Tom stood too, still holding her hand. "You remind me of my daughter when she was your age. Her name's Anna. I couldn't sit in that park any longer watching the birds and squirrels play if I knew someone like Anna, someone like you, was in danger."

Wendy picked up her crossbow from the ground as Tom pulled the rod out of the back of Arthur's wife. The rod, she saw, turned out to be an aluminum forearm crutch, broken off near the bottom.

"They don't keep too many weapons in the cancer ward," Tom said noticing Wendy's gaze. "I had to grab whatever I could find. Come on, we still have to get to The Hermit."

The birds attacking the rest of the group suddenly quit the

fight, flying off into the trees. Red, Esmé, and Chase found themselves gathered together, completely surrounded by kobolds and men and women from the circus. The Hermit, his staff in one hand, strode out of the cave's mouth. Everyone turned toward him.

"What is the meaning of all this?" he asked. He stared at the three teenagers standing back-to-back in the center of the circle. His dark eyes were all but hidden underneath bushy eyebrows, yellowed from long years of neglect. He scanned the three of them, coming finally to rest on Red. "Ah," he said looking Red in the eye. "I know who you are; you must be the Snyder boy. You thought you would waltz in here and rescue your father. And look, you brought some friends along as well."

Red glared back at the old man. Snakelike tendrils of energy twisted and writhed down The Hermit's forearm into his staff. Fear and hatred swirled in Red's mind. Red turned, feeling someone fall against his side. Wendy and Tom stumbled into the knot in the center of the circle, pushed there by three kobolds. Red barely registered Tom's presence before turning back to face The Hermit.

"It is good you are here. I can rid this valley of the curse of your family for good," The Hermit said.

"You'll have to kill us first," Chase said.

"That is the plan. But first we have a ceremony to prepare for," The Hermit said. He turned his back on the group and headed back toward the cave. "Bring them inside. We still have a few empty cells that need filled."

20

NEEDS

Hundreds of birds swirled like a vortex as they rose out of the small clearing in the forest outside The Hermit's cave following their attack. They formed a shifting knot over the forest canopy and over the green checkerboard fields of the rolling hills and farms surrounding Laurel Hollows. They dipped and swerved in synchronicity, one mind with a multitude of bodies, as they navigated the unseen rivers of the sky. They had a message to deliver. Below them on the manmade rivers of asphalt, many of the town's residents made their way in the same direction - toward the tents and caravans of the Circus Paenultimus for an evening's entertainment.

Rinthim Straub stepped out of his office, fastening the last button of his waistcoat. He slicked his oily hair back over his ears with long bony fingers and looked off into the distance toward the dark green forest that blanketed the rising hills. His long ringmaster's baton was tucked underneath one arm. Before he could make out the dark cloud of birds, he heard them calling. Their discordant squeals, squawks, and calls told him something was amiss.

The birds spilled out of the sky and landed on every available perch and ledge around Straub. Their chittering continued growing louder and more urgent. Straub's eyebrows furrowed, pinching a deep ravine into the flesh above his long nose.

"No," he said under his breath. "I'm running out of people to spare."

He pulled the baton from underneath his arm, and swung it at a cluster of birds perched on the railing leading up the stairs to his office. The nearest birds took the hit head on and fell dead to the ground; the rest scrambled into the air, their wings fluttering.

"Go, find out where they came from," he commanded the birds. Then, spinning on one heel, he headed into the dining tent, throwing the flaps violently aside.

The tent was nearly empty, the performers had already finished eating and were either getting dressed or otherwise preparing for the evening's performance. The half dozen left were those who labored in the circus' shadow, away from the bright beams of the spotlights.

"Everyone, listen!" Straub bellowed. Every pair of eyes turned quaveringly toward the towering voice. Straub, his face red, took a deep breath, then continued in a more measured tone. "It is time for you to earn these meals. There is a situation I need you to help alleviate. There are some unwelcome visitors at the interstice. It seems they are in the spirit world. Their bodies are somewhere in this pathetic excuse for a town. Go find them, eliminate them, and make sure there is no one else who might come to their aid. I've sent birds ahead, and they'll report back to you if they find anything. Pair off and go find them."

Blank, bloodless faces stare back at Straub. No one moved. "Now!" he yelled. The workers scrambled to their feet, sending paper plates and chairs scattering. They ran out of the tent, their meals unfinished.

Straub rubbed his temples with the tips of his fingers. "This can't fail," he said to the empty room. "We can't lose a single interstice. We have to have them all."

***

Michael sat on the cot with his arms resting on his knees at the edge of a pool of light around the bodies of Red and Wendy. He kicked a piece of crumbled brick back and forth between his running shoes, trying to ignore the faint scratching sounds all around the room. He figured that it must be rats inside the cinder block walls.

"Sit here and guard our bodies, Michael," he grumbled to himself. "You're good for nothing else."

"Sure, it's only my sister The Hermit kidnapped," he said in response. "I couldn't imagine wanting to actually go and save her myself."

He nearly fell off the cot when his cell phone rang. It echoed off the distant walls. He glanced at Red and Wendy as he dug the phone out of his jeans pocket.

"Oh crap," he said seeing his mom's photo on the phone's display.

"Uh, Hi," he said nervously putting it up to his ear. He paced around the cot he had been sitting on.

"Is everything alright?" his mother asked, noting the tremor in his voice.

"Yeah, yeah. Everything's fine."

"You sure?"

"Yeah," Michael said, passing a glance again toward Red's

cot. "I was just worried the ringer would wake Red up."

"He's been sleeping good?"

"He is out cold. He didn't even stir when the phone rang," Michael turned toward the door where he thought he could hear the rats growing louder.

"That's good," Emily said. "I'm sure he needs it. I'm at the hospital and getting ready to see his mother, I wanted to give her an update. I'm not sure exactly when I'll get home. Your dad should be home in a couple of hours, though."

Red began stirring in his cot. Michael hurried over to his side and knelt down. Red grunted, his head turning from side to side. A low moan escaped his lips.

"Was that Red?" His mother asked.

"Yeah," Michael said. "I think I better go in case he wakes up and needs anything."

From behind Michael, Wendy began making noises as well. Turning he saw a trickle of blood running down the side of her face from a nostril.

"Was that Sara?"

"Uh, yeah." Michael said. "I think she must have wanted to watch TV, but Red is still sleeping."

"Let me talk to her real quick."

"Sorry, she just stormed out of the room," Michael grew nervous. He wanted to get off the call as quickly as he could.

"You sure everything's okay?" Claire asked.

"Yeah, mom. Really. Listen I hate to cut you off, but Red's waking up. I'll see you when you get home, okay?"

"Yeah, okay. Love you baby," she said surprised at Michael's curtness.

"Love you too," Michael said. He pressed the 'end call' icon with his thumb and threw the phone down on the cot beside

Wendy.

"What do I do, what do I do," he said.

The scratching sound he took to be that of rats seemed to be coming from all around him now. He walked slowly over to one of the small windows near the ceiling along the walls. Chase had painted it black.

What is going on? He wondered.

He heard a clank at the door. It too echoed through the basement lair. Michael walked slowly toward the door with one more look over his shoulder at Red and Wendy who seemed to have calmed down. *Maybe they're back*, he thought. *I really hope they're back.*

He looked out the peephole on the door, and seeing nothing but a bird resting on one of the rails leading down the ramp to the door. *Of course I can't see them,* he reasoned. *They are probably in the spirit world.* He threw the doors open.

The last light of the day spilled in through the open door along with hundreds of birds. He stumbled backward and, tripping over his feet, fell to the ground. The birds swarmed around The Brand's hideout. In their frenzy they upset a stack of pallets near the cots. The top pallet fell smashing to the concrete floor and onto Wendy's body.

***

Claire ran her fingers unsteadily down the thin hospital blanket covering Donal. Her fingers skimmed limply over the miniature mountain ridges and sank into the valley like folds like dense tendrils of smoke underneath a snow laden sky. She gathered the cloth tightly in her grasp, squeezing it in clenched fists. She reached into herself, seeking to find her determination – that bit of her that wasn't afraid to take action, that decisive part of her that drove her to leave her parents' home and not look back. But she couldn't find it. It had been repressed for far too long, too deep inside her for her to reach it all by herself anymore.

"I can't do this alone," she said to the empty shell of her husband. "I don't know who I am without you." She relaxed her grip, watching Donal lie motionless on the bed. She heard a soft knock on the door behind her as it swung open.

"Claire?" Emily said as she walked tentatively into the room. Claire turned to face her.

"Hi," Claire said, resting her hands in her lap. "I'm sorry I was just sitting here lost in my own thoughts."

"Look," Emily said. She dragged a chair up beside Claire. "I think it's time we had a good heart-to-heart."

"I'm fine, Emily," Claire said. "Really."

"You and I both know that's not true," Emily said, putting her hand on Claire's shoulder. "I don't mean just about Donal either."

The monitors beeped a steady chime as Claire wrung her hands. Nearly a minute passed before she accepted the fact that Emily was prepared to wait as long as she was to speak.

"I don't know who I am anymore," she said abruptly and looked away. "I put everything into Donal, into our marriage. I don't know who I am without that. How can I do anything, be anything without that part of me?"

Around her, machines marked off the seconds as the question hung in the air. Emily took time to prepare her unexpected response.

"You can't," she said. Claire looked around to her.

"Donal is a part of who you are," she said. "He is a part of what it means to be Claire Snyder and will always be a part of you, no matter what happens. To deny that is ridiculous, and belittles the good man he is."

Claire nodded, looking at her hands. "But," she said quietly. She searched her mind for an excuse she hadn't already used to dissuade Emily, but she was too tired to find a new one. The emotions of the last few days had been slowly eating away at the barriers she erected between herself and the rest of the world. Resignation, like a heavy blanket, fell over her, weighing her down. It dragged down the last of her defenses. She opened herself up to her friend. For the first time in decades, she allowed herself to be exposed, raw and vulnerable.

"Will you help me?" She asked.

"Claire," Emily said tenderly. "You know I'm here for you; of course I'll help you do anything. What do you need from me?"

"I need someone who I can be honest with, who'll be honest with me," Claire said. She sat up straighter in the chair, untangling her fingers from each other and gripping the chair's armrest. "I need someone to lean on while I learn to stand on my own again."

"I'm not talking about being your crutch," Emily said.

"That's not what I mean either," Claire said. "I'm going to do it on my own, I just need help getting going." The two women stood and hugged.

"You know, if and when Donal wakes up from this, you are going to have to be strong for him," Emily said.

Claire nodded and looked down at her husband. "What do I do now? Where do I start?"

"I think the best way to find out who you are is to give

yourself to the people around you," Emily said. She pulled back, holding onto Claire's shoulders and looking her deep in the eyes. "I think the best place to start is probably the boy lying injured on the couch in my den."

"Red," Claire whispered.

21

SACRIFICES

Red sat alone in the corner of the dark cell. His chin rested on drawn-up knees, held tight against his body by his clasped hands. He stared at the flickering torchlight on the bare rock wall opposite his cell. He heard the voices of his friends, but forced himself to tune them out until they carried no more meaning than the fleeting and shifting shadows.

I've led all these people to their deaths, he thought. *It's all my fault.* He lowered his head until his forehead rested on his knees, blocking out even the light. *What have I done?*

The longer he sat there drawn into himself, trying to ignore the reality around him, the more the indistinct murmurings began taking on more solid sounds, becoming words his troubled mind couldn't help but comprehend.

"Listen," a voice said. Red recognized it as Chase's. "It's not your fault. You did what you had to do."

Red looked up thinking Chase was speaking to him. He was about to protest, and explain that it *was* his fault, that if he hadn't dragged them all into this, then they would all still be safe. He parted his lips to speak, then stopped short when he heard Wendy's fragile voice. It came in spurts between sobs.

"But, I killed them," she said. "They're dead, and I did it."

"They deserved it," Chase said.

"Did they?" Wendy said. "Are you sure? How do you know they deserved it? They might have just been trying to capture us."

"They deserved it," Esmé said. Her voice sounded cold in Red's ears as it bounced back and forth down the cavern's narrow walkway. "Everyone at the circus deserves that and worse. And don't forget, they are planning to kill us if we can't find a way out of here."

"She's right, Wendy," Chase said. "They definitely got what was coming to them."

"I'm sorry," Wendy said. "I was just firing away, I didn't even think about what I was doing." She paused, sniffed and let out a deep breath before continuing. "I thought I wanted to be like you, Chase, but I'm not like you. I can't just kill people like that. I thought I could, but I can't."

"Wendy," Chase said, more softly than Red had ever heard him speak. "Is that what you think of me? That I'm some kind of killer?"

"No, that's not what I meant. Not exactly anyway," she said, speaking quickly. "I mean, it doesn't seem to bother you the same way."

"You're wrong. It eats away at me all the time," Chase said. He, too, exhaled audibly. "I only killed one person before today, and it was an accident. I didn't mean to do it, but he had a gun, and I just reacted. I did it out of instinct, out of self-preservation. I can't tell you the number of times I've replayed that moment in my mind. Again and again I see him drawing the pistol. Yet, no matter how many times I replay the scene through to the end, I can't figure out any course of action that one of us doesn't wind up dead on that sidewalk."

Chase's last words melted away into the flickering dark. For several moments only the sounds of distant drops of water landing in small pools and the soft static of burning torches could be heard. Wendy finally broke the silence.

"I'm sorry," she said. "I didn't know."

"It's fine," Chase said. "I've learned to live with it."

"I think right now we need to focus on figuring a way out of here, or none of us will live with anything for very much longer," Esmé said.

"You're right," Chase said. "Do either of you know where Red is?"

"I'm here," Red said. He pushed himself off the back wall and walked to the front of his cell. The metallic bars of his cell crackled with energy as he neared them.

"Did you say Red?" Another voice said nearby. Red recognized it immediately.

"Sara? Is that you? Are you okay?" He said. There was no reply.

"I don't think she can hear you," Esmé said. "She's not in the spirit world."

"Yeah," Chase said. "I said Red, who are you?"

"It's Sara," Red said, "Michael's sister."

"Red is here?" Sara asked excitedly. "Red Snyder."

"Tell her I'm here," Red yelled. "Ask her if she has seen my dad."

"Red is here," Chase said. "Are you Sara?" His voice was overpowered by another.

"Red! Is that you? What are you doing here?" Donal Snyder shouted nearby.

271

"Dad!" Red shouted back.

"Yeah, how did you know?" Sara said at the same time.

Everyone, both in the spiritual and physical worlds began talking at once. They spoke louder and louder, drowning each other out in the echoing cave.

Esmé shifted from the spiritual world to the physical. She shouted over the tumult. "Everybody shut up! Be quiet for a second.

"Now," she continued after the last echoes of their excited voices diminished into the distance. "Who all is in here? Let's go one by one. Chase, you keep track since you're the only one that can hear and be heard be everyone else. I'm Esmé"

The rest of the people trapped in The Hermit's cells called out their names: Wendy, Chase, Red, Donal, Sara, and Tom. It was the first time Tom had spoken.

"Seven," Chase said. "Is there anybody else?" After a moment of no response, he decided that was it.

"What's going on?" Sara asked Esmé. "The only people I heard were you and Chase. You said that Red was here."

"He's here," Esmé said. "You just can't hear him. He's in the spirit world, and you are in the physical."

"What are you talking about?" Sara said.

As Esmé did her best to try to patiently explain the physical and spiritual worlds, Red called out to his father.

"Dad! Dad, are you okay?" he asked.

"I'm fine," Donal said. "What are you doing here? Are you okay?"

"I'm fine, I came to rescue you."

"You shouldn't be here. This is exactly what I was afraid would happen," Donal said.

"I can't believe you knew about all this, about The Hermit

and everything, and you never told me anything," Red said.

"I never wanted any part of it," Donal said. "I was afraid, but none of that matters now. Where did all these other kids come from anyway? Who is Tom, and how are you even here in the spirit world?"

Before Red had a chance to answer, Tom spoke up.

"Donal, I knew your father," he said. "He found me one day in the spirit world before I understood what that even meant. He took me under his wing and taught me. I met you once. You were just a toddler then. I can't imagine you would remember me. Isaiah was my mentor, and I was there the day that he was killed."

"How did you find Red, and why did you get him involved in all of this?" Donal asked, anger and confusion coming through his voice.

"He found me," Tom said.

"After the accident," Red said. "I was in the hospital, and then all of the sudden I found myself able to move in the spirit world. I stumbled into Tom, and he taught me what it all meant."

"I'm sorry," Donal said. "This is my fault. I shouldn't have waited this long to find my own courage."

"Dad," Red said. "It's not your fault. You didn't know this would happen."

"No, Red. It is my fault. I may not have known exactly this would happen, but I did know something would happen if The Hermit wasn't stopped – him and those he serves."

"It is as much on me as it is on you," Tom said. "I helped The Hermit find people to sacrifice."

"You did what?" Wendy yelled. "All this time, you have been helping The Hermit?"

"I know you must hate me now," Tom said. "But he let my daughter stay alive as long as I continued to help him. But this has gone far beyond my family now. I can't just stand by and be complicit any longer. I have to take responsibility for my past and stand up to him."

"Listen, everybody, I know everyone is feeling really down on themselves right now, myself included," Red said. "But none of this is going to get us out of these cells."

"I think I might be able to help with that," Donal said. "I don't think that the men who threw you in your cells saw me. I think I might be able to reach some of your weapons. They threw them in a pile next to my cell."

Donal leaned against the bars of his cell. The tendrils of spiritual energy flowed from the metal into his outstretched arm as he reached for the cache of weapons leaning against the wall beside his cell. Pain like he had never felt before raced through his body. Back in the hospital, his body arched violently, Claire jumped out of her chair, sending it skittering across the floor. Emily gasped.

In the cave, Donal's searching fingers finally managed to grasp onto something. He couldn't see what it was as he pulled it back through the lattice of bars. He stumbled backward away from the cell's entrance and found he was holding a baseball bat.

"I got something," he said examining it. "It looks like Red's baseball bat."

"What good is that going to do us?" Red said.

"I think it'll do just fine," his dad replied.

The bat melted in Donal's hand. It grew shorter, and as it

did it took on the shape of a large sledgehammer. Once the transformation was complete, Donal raised the hammer over his head with both hands, held it there for a moment, and then brought it down against the lock on the door. As it arced through the air, tiny bolts of energy began to wrap around its head. It struck the lock on the door. A loud, deafening clang reverberated through the prison. The impact knocked Donal against the back wall of the cave as the cell door swung open.

"What was that?" Sara asked.

"It was Donal, Red's dad," Chase said. "We're going to get out of here."

Donal rushed out of the cell. He grabbed the keys that were hanging nearby. "Red," he yelled. "Where are you?"

"I'm here!"

Donal raced over and unlocked Red's cell. The two of them embraced.

"I thought I lost you," Red said. "I promised I would come find you."

"I'm here." Donal said as he pulled out of the embrace and held Red by the shoulders at arm's length. "It is all going to be alright."

Donal let go of Red and unlocked the rest of the cell doors. All of them, save Red, who stood motionless watching his father, grabbed their weapons from the pile.

"Here," Donal said, handing the sledgehammer to Red. It morphed back into a baseball bat as Red took it in his hands.

"Thanks," he said. "But what about you? Maybe you should take it."

"I'll find something else," Donal said.

"But it is just a bat for me," Red said turning it over in his hands.

Donal put his hand on Red's shoulder. "I'm sure it'll be whatever you need it to be when the time comes."

"Come on," Chase interjected, pulling the straps of his steel knuckles tight. "We have to go. We don't have much time."

The group headed back down the corridor toward the cave's entrance. Red snatched his catcher's mask by its strap, pulled it down over his face, and joined them.

"Sara, just stay behind us," Esmé said.

"Right," Sara said. "I don't have a clue what is going on, I'm definitely not going in front. How do I know Red is really with us?"

"He's here," Chase said.

"Yeah, you keep saying that," Sara said walking behind them. "But how do I know it's true."

"Tell her I was the ghost in her room the other night," Red said.

"This is so frustrating. I hate being the message boy," Chase said before turning back to Sara. "He says that he was the ghost in your room the other night.

Sara stopped in her tracks, she felt the blood rush into her cheeks as she drew her hands into tight fists. "That was him!" As the idea that the ghost was Red sank in, she went through a range of flickering emotions: frustration, confusion, and bit of anger before settling into severe embarrassment. Red had been alone with her in her room. "Oh," she said, trailing behind Chase and Esmé. "I guess you aren't crazy after all. I think I'm finally beginning to understand it a little bit."

She stopped, and turning to one side, spoke into the empty air. "Red, I don't know where you are, but you are going to pay for that! Do you hear me?"

"He heard you, Sara," Esmé said. "I'm sure of that."

They jogged silently down the torch lined passageway as they made their way back toward the cave's mouth. They heard The Hermit's voice barking orders, and the grumbling of his servants before they could see the light from outside.

"Wait," Donal said.

Chase held up his hand, and everyone stopped as he motioned for them to all stand against one wall.

"Tom and I will go out first," Donal said. "You kids wait here."

"Right," Tom said, coming up beside him.

"No," Chase said. He walked in front of Donal and put his hand, palm open, against Donal's chest. "This is my fight as much as it yours."

"Mine too," Esmé said.

Red and Wendy stepped forward at the same time.

"It is all of ours," Red said. "If we don't stop him, everyone in this town is in danger."

Donal nodded at Chase and the rest of the group. "Fine," he said, defeat evident in his voice. He pulled a torch off the cave wall near his head. "I'll admit, you all seem to have done well so far, except for getting captured, of course. We'll do this together. Red, stay close to me."

Chase led the way out of the cave mouth. Donal, Tom, and the others followed after. The Hermit stood in the center of the recently cleared circle. Only a half dozen or so kobolds and men were present. They were busy stacking stones and setting tall torch stands into the ground in a large circle around the clearing. The Hermit turned toward them as they exited the cave. At the sight of The Hermit they all paused.

"Why do you bother?" he said exasperatedly, his staff held firmly in his right hand. "You are just delaying the inevitable. Your spirits would be useful, but after tonight won't be required." He raised both arms and called at the men and kobolds around him. "Kill them."

Before the men around him could lay down their stones or torches, the kobolds leapt toward Red and his compatriots.

Donal and Tom jumped out in front of the younger ones, grappling with the first of the kobolds. Tom wielded his cut-off crutch like a sword, fending off one of the attackers, while Donal swung his torch, now a flaming sledgehammer, throwing fireballs at them with each arc.

Red, Chase, and Esmé ran up beside them. They defended themselves from the first of the human attackers. Wendy stayed behind near Sara, she slotted a bolt into her crossbow, and brought it up to her shoulder.

Sara watched the tumult, everything was confusion and chaos. She was only able to even see half of the fight, only what was happening in the physical world. That was enough though to make her throw herself against the cold wall of the cave. She only saw the man fall to the ground as Red knocked his first attacker to the ground with a solid hit to his head.

Chase fell to the ground wrestling with a kobold. It was too close to Chase for him to swing with sufficient force against it. His blows only scratched the Kobold's thick skin, even with the tiger claws. They rolled all the way over, until the kobold was on top. It looked up and saw Wendy lowering her crossbow at it. The kobold planted his foot on Chase's face and sprang toward Wendy. The kobold's hand came down on the bolt in the crossbow at the moment she pulled the trigger. His viselike fingers held onto the slender projectile, but the force spun his body around, bringing the bolt back toward Wendy. She felt it sink into her side, she dropped the crossbow and screamed in pain.

Chase bounced back to his feet, but was forced back into a tight knot with everyone else near the mouth of the cave. Sara was just a few feet behind them. Several kobolds and men lay injured or dying on the ground.

Esmé dove into the fight, spinning furiously. Kobolds and men falling underneath the wide swings of her bo. She leapt and shifted into the spirit world. She grabbed a twisted walnut branch and swung from it, falling into a clustered group and shifted back to the physical world. Two men fell aside at her assault. As she turned to face the others, she felt a heavy blow against the back of her head. She fell stunned to the ground, dropping her staff.

Wendy grabbed at the pain in her side with both hands. The kobold picked up her crossbow and hit her across the face. The pain in her side - and now on her face as well - disappeared into the back of her mind as she felt the painful tugging coming from her around her bellybutton. First the kobold, then the clearing rapidly fled away from her as she was speedily dragged away from the scene. She struggled to remain conscious as she bounced off trees and was dragged backward through thick bushes and undergrowth by the cord that linked her spiritual and physical bodies.

"Wendy!" Chase yelled, watching as she flew through the forest. As she disappeared, a mountain of a man dumped a barely conscious Esmé at his feet. Donal and Tom put themselves between The Hermit's men and the kids. Neither of them had much fight left in them.

"Enough!" The Hermit shouted. He brought his staff down hard against the forest floor. The moss-covered ground rippled like a still pool suddenly disturbed. The ground heaved in expanding waves. The disturbance knocked Red and his companions, as well as their attackers, to the ground. The Hermit's men and kobolds scurried to their feet and hurried away from their prey, clearing the area between them and The Hermit.

"I don't have time for this," he said. He raised his staff above his head and swung it around in a wide arc. As it swung the dark energy gathered near the staff's base. He stopped the the staff midswing and pointed it directly at Red's group.

My dream, Red thought as The Hermit attacked. *This is what I dreamed about. Everyone is going to die if I don't save them.* A ball of glowing plasma sped toward them.

"No!" he shouted, pushing his way past Tom and his father. Red planted his right foot on the ground with his bat over his shoulder and stepped toward the ball of oncoming dark energy.

***

After the flock of birds made their frenetic examination of The Brand's lair, circling several times over the bodies of Red and Wendy, they flew back out of the door.

Michael grabbed the heavy metal door and tried to close it. Before he could close it entirely, again it was thrown open - knocking him to the ground. Something unseen shot across the large room toward the two resting bodies, throwing up dust in a straight line. He got to his feet and slammed the doors closed, a heavy latch fell into its slot.

Far behind him, Wendy screamed and struggled to push the fallen pallet off of herself. She had fallen on the floor and was doubled over with one hand on her side and the other on her head as Michael came running through the dark toward the pool of light.

"Wendy!" He yelled. "Are you okay?"

She twisted in agony on the floor as Michael slid the last few feet on the dusty floor to her, as if he were coming in to home plate. He looked over her body, trying to see what was wrong. "What can I do?"

Wendy rolled onto her stomach and pulled her hand from her side. She held it in front of her, surprised at the lack of blood.

Michael reached down and helped her as she tried to stand.

"Where," she said, looking around the room in confusion. It took her a moment to take it all in, to recognize Michael. "How did I get back here?"

"I don't know," he said. "Are you sure you're okay?" he asked again.

"Yeah, I'm okay," she said. She took a couple of feeble steps to her cot and sat down on the edge. "I was pulled back, I think."

"Where is everyone else?" Michael asked. "Are they okay? What about Sara?"

"They're in danger," she said. "We were all fighting The Hermit when I was pulled back. We have to go help them." She struggled to her feet, putting all her weight on her full leg.

"But, is Sara okay?" Michael asked. He was breathing hard and his heart was beating faster than he had ever felt it.

"She's with them," Wendy said. "We found her and Red's dad. Listen, we don't have much time, we've got to go help them."

Michael looked over at Red's body lying as still as if he were dead. "What about Red? We can't just leave him here."

"Hopefully, he will still be safe here," Wendy said. "We have to leave him."

Michael looked across the room to the door with the heavy bar across it. "Um," he said. "About that. I think maybe we've been found."

Michael explained how he thought everyone had returned, but when he opened the door, the birds had swarmed through the room and out again.

"I was just trying to close the door when you came flying through," he said.

"That's not good," she said. "Let's get Red and get out of here before they come back with reinforcements."

"How are we going to do that?"

There was a loud bang at the door before Wendy had a chance to respond. Wendy and Michael looked at each other, then a third bang rang through the basement like thunder. The heavy metal door visibly deformed inward after the last hit.

"Grab something to fight with!" Wendy shouted as the doors flew off their hinges - one door landing ten feet from the entrance. Two figures stood silhouetted in the doorway with a small battering ram held between them. A cloud of dust hung in the air obscuring their faces.

Michael unbuttoned the strap holding the knife in its leather sheath at his waist with one hand. He slid it out and held it in front of him. Wendy picked through the small pile of weapons still lying on the nearby cot. She was hoping for a second crossbow, but there were no more, only hand-to-hand weapons.

"There they are," one of the men shouted from the doorway. The two men ran toward the small circle of light where Michael and Wendy were. Red's body still lay motionless behind them.

"Wendy?" Michael said nervously. "Are we really going to have to do this?"

Wendy settled on a small dagger, not much longer than a letter opener. She turned back toward Michael, noticing at the last second a small leather buckler. She grabbed it too and slid it over her left wrist. "I don't think we have any other options," she said as she came limping up to stand beside Michael. "We have to keep Red safe."

Michael knelt down and with a loud yell he took off across the room toward their assailants. Wendy followed behind him, still unsteady.

As the four drew closer to each other, the men from the circus stopped in their tracks, one of them pulled something out from underneath his jacket and held it in front of him. Wendy recognized what it was and picked up speed. Michael hesitated just long enough for Wendy to catch up with him. She dove at Michael.

"Gun!" she shouted. She collided with Michael and the two of them fell to the floor sending up another cloud of dust.

The gun's report was deafening as the man fired it at the spot Michael had been only a split second before. Again, he fired before Michael and Wendy could regain their footing. It ricocheted off the ground in front of them, throwing chips of concrete into their faces. With their eyes burning and ears ringing, they made their way into the darker shadows near the wall.

They threw themselves onto the ground behind a rack of Chase's unused electronics.

"Where did they go?" One of the men said as they strained to see into the darkness.

"Come out, come out, wherever you are. Come out and play with us," the one without the gun said in a sneering sing-song voice. He held a short piece of metal pipe in one hand. He slapped it into his palm, punctuating each syllable.

"What do we do?" Michael whispered to Wendy.

"I've got an idea," she said, absent-mindedly reaching for the glasses hanging from her neck, but they fell apart when her hand touched them. She pulled a small power supply off the rack in front of her. She threw it as far as she could down the room along one wall, the wires trailing behind it as it flew through the dark just beyond Chase's training area and its own pool of light. It landed on a rubber mat, bounced off the far edge and clattered across the floor.

"There," the gunman said, pointing his pistol toward where it landed. The two of them made their way cautiously toward the sound.

"After they get into the light we go after them," Wendy whispered. "They won't be see us until we are right on top of them."

They watched as the two men disappeared into the dark between the lights, and then emerged into the light again near a full-size punching bag.

"Get ready," Wendy whispered. The two stood and started slowly toward the men. "Quietly, until we are on them."

Michael and Wendy half walked, half jogged, crouching toward the men. As they neared the edge of the light that the two men were making their way across, Michael accidentally kicked something on the floor.

"Oops," he whispered, as a piece of broken brick bounced across the floor and into the light.

The two men turned at the sound, unsure of where it came from.

"Now," Wendy said.

Michael took off toward the men. As he ran his body fell into the rhythm that it was used to from years of training. The knife in his hand even felt like a relay baton. The familiarity melted his fear away. He took long graceful strides, pulling away from Wendy. He planted his left foot firmly on the ground, and with the simplicity of muscle memory, bounded over a rack of dumbbells like a hurdle. He leaned his torso forward, his right leg outstretched with his left tucked expertly underneath his body. He emerged into the light as he cleared the weights. He came down right in front of the two men and began spinning as soon as his right foot made contact with the ground.

The man with the pistol pulled it up with both hands to fire, but he was too slow. The blade of Michael's long knife caught him across the wrists. The gun went flying, landing outside the light. Blood sprayed in spurts from the man's wrists. Everything happened in slow motion for Michael. He saw each individual drop of blood arc through the air as they glinted with reflected light. The man held his arms in front of him and screamed, his hands dangled limply from his wrists, his tendons severed.

As Michael continued his spin, he saw the second man bringing the length of pipe down toward him, but everything was still in slow motion, including his reactions. As the blow neared the back of his head, Wendy leapt between them and blocked the blow with her leather shield. The blow was hard enough that it knocked her backward into Michael, and the two of them again fell onto the floor, this time near the dumbbells.

The man who had held the gun fell to the ground, his hands unable even to even grasp his wrists to stave off the flow of blood. Theother man knelt down in front of Michael and Wendy. Wendy pulled herself up against the weight rack, her dagger nowhere in sight. Michael leaned on one elbow, his knife on the ground near his feet. But before he could lean forward to reach for it, the man kicked it away.

He leaned down toward Wendy and Michael, a cruel smile spread across his face. "I'm afraid I am going to have to hurt you," he said. "But it won't hurt for long, 'cause you'll be dead soon enough." He brought the pipe up across his body and swung it again toward Michael's head.

As the man began his swing, Michael threw his arms in front of himself while Wendy's fingers tightened around one of the dumbbells, she threw her body toward the ground, using the momentum to swing the five-pound weight over and across her body as hard as she could. It collided with the man's chin, knocking him unconscious. His body slumped to the floor.

"Thanks," Michael said.

"Come on," Wendy said. "Let's find something to tie them up with before this one wakes up."

***

The ball of energy came slowly toward Red as he stepped in front of his father and the rest of his company. He held his baseball bat over his shoulder, ready to swing. Crackles of electricity slowly rotated around the orb. Red blocked everything else out of his mind. He heard the crackling of the dark purple orb and imagined he could even smell the metallic burning of it as he tightened his grip on the bat.

It was somehow inevitable. Less than a week ago he was worried about the normal things of any other fourteen-year old - winning a baseball game, not embarrassing himself, girls. Now, here, outside the cave with his new friends and his father behind him, he found something inside himself, something sustaining him that he had not even known was there, the courage to do what must be done, despite his fear. In fact, Red realized as he began swinging his bat, it was actually fear that drove him to put himself forward of the group. Fear for the others, not fear for himself. Even if it meant the sacrifice of his own life for theirs.

Red stepped into his swing, the oncoming ball was right in his sweet spot. The bat arced through the air to meet it.

He felt it first in his fingers. The rubber of the grip melted, forming itself around his hands. It fit his hands perfectly. The grey metal of the bat flattened and grew longer. Tiny fingers of steel or iron stretched out from above and below his hands, forming an intricate cage guard around his clenched fingers. As he brought the bat around, the undeniable shape of a sword formed in his hands. The blade, long and slender, was razor sharp. What had been a rubber grip, was now wrapped strips of leather. The pommel of the sword was the head of an antlered deer. The antlers intermeshed around the outside of his hands forming the protective cage on one side of the glowing sword. It tingled with a slight electrical charge of its own.

As his sword made contact with the orb, he became clad head-to-toe as a magnificent knight. His armor glowed silver white and glinted in the fading light. Every inch of the armor was etched in intricate design. Sweat rolled into his eyes as the two opposing forces met. There was a loud crack, then a *thwump,* like air filling a vacuum. For a split second, the separation between the physical and spiritual worlds was ruptured. It was just a flash, but the image of Red as a glowing white knight was visible to everyone in the clearing, regardless of which world they were in. Sara saw him between herself and The Hermit; it was an image that would never leave her mind. It was burned into her subconscious, as it was everyone else's in the small clearing outside the cave.

The ball of energy was transformed. Instead of a twisted mass of darkness, it was now a glowing, golden globe hurling back toward The Hermit at double the speed it had been thrown. The Hermit tried to dodge, but he was too slow. The globe hit him squarely in the chest and knocked him backwards onto the ground. Red alone remained standing in the clearing, his armor like a second sun in the darkening twilight.

There was a moment of silence as Red looked at the brilliant sword in his hands. In a widening circle around him, tiny whirlwinds tossed glittering dust into the air. Piles of stones and still-lit torches were scattered around the clearing. *It's not done yet,* he told himself.

Red strode toward the fallen hermit. He held his sword high over his head, prepared to bring it down in a final thrust. But as he did, The Hermit managed to bring his staff around to block the strike. Around them, the men and kobolds scrambled to their feet. Esmé and Chase, as well as Donal and Tom, took up the fight. Even Sara, still in the relative safety of the cave's mouth, threw rocks at The Hermit's forces.

Amidst the maelstrom of fighting, in the center of the cleared circle, Red and The Hermit exchanged blows, The Hermit with his staff and Red with his sword. It was an ugly fight, neither of them accustomed to fighting. Parry and thrust – thrust and parry. Each time Red believed he had The Hermit at a disadvantage, he was knocked back by a force from The Hermit's hand. Likewise, each time The Hermit tried to bring enough force to his hands to finish him off, Red managed to bring down another strike upon him, forcing The Hermit to spend his built-up energy to block the blow.

Around and around they went until Red managed to knock The Hermit down. He slid back against a crumbled pyre of stone. The Hermit's staff slipped out of his fingers and clattered to the ground at his side. Red stood over The Hermit's prostrate form, looking down on him. For the first time, Red actually saw The Hermit for what he truly was. He was a man aged beyond his years, ancient and pitiable. All that remained of the man The Hermit had been was blind ambition and hatred. Red hesitated to deliver the final blow that would bring the death of The Hermit.

The Hermit took the opportunity to pick up his staff; he gathered as much energy into it as he dared. He rolled onto his side and pointed his staff at Red. Arcing and shifting like electricity, the energy flowed down The Hermit's arm into his staff. A sustained bolt erupted from the top of the staff and hit Red in the stomach. He was thrown, doubled over, to the ground. His sword flew out of his hands and landed far out of his reach.

Red looked up dazed at Esmé, Tom, and Chase, he saw them upside down as they fought The Hermit's men and his kobolds. He even saw Sara at the entrance to the cave. No one had yet reached her as she continued to throw stones. He didn't see his father anywhere as The Hermit rose to his feet. All hope left Red. *I'm going to die, and I'm never going to see Dad again.*

"Dad," Red call out feebly. "Dad?" As his doubt grew, he felt his armor beginning to dissipate around him.

The Hermit, now on his feet, walked over to Red and looked down at him. "You have no idea what you've done," he said through gritted teeth. His narrow lips quavered as he spoke. His whole body sent off tendrils of energy. They circled, crackling and twisting around his body, gathering into a ball at the tip of his staff. "Years," he said. "I've spent decades, lifetimes serving the interstice and the Kindred."

The Hermit stepped toward Red. The ball of energy continued growing and was already at least three times larger than that of the ball he had thrown. He stood just a few feet away from Red's own feet. Even his eyes seemed to glow with maniacal fury.

"You can't take this away from me!" The Hermit shouted. He brought the staff back to thrust it at Red.

Red brought his hands up in front of his face in a futile attempt at protection. The Hermit brought the staff forward, but suddenly froze. His dingy, yellowing shirt stuck forward for a moment before the glowing tip of the sword pierced the decaying fabric. As Red watched, The Hermit convulsed and his eyes darkened.

The Hermit fell forward onto his knees. As he fell, the

sword morphed back into the shape of a baseball bat in Donal's hands. Donal stood behind the fallen hermit and was breathing hard, but otherwise appeared no more injured than before.

The Hermit grasped at the bat sticking out of his chest. He tried to speak, but only dark blood spattered out. He let out one final spluttering cough and sank to the ground.

"Dad!" Red yelled as he tried to stand up.

"Red," Donal said, walking toward his son.

A deep rumble came from inside the cave. The ground began to shake. Everyone stopped fighting and looked towards the cave mouth. It was no longer dark inside. As the sound grew louder and the tremor more intense, a bright beam of light burst from the cave streaming from the interstice. It shone on The Hermit, and swirled around him, raising him ten feet into the air.

As everyone watched, the already ancient visage of The Hermit grew older and more horrible. His white hair lengthened before falling out in clumps onto his shoulders. His skin dried up and drew tight against his skull. His clothes rotted around his body, the extended years of his life all coming upon him at once. He crumbled into dust which spun inside the swirling light like a miniature galaxy. Small crackles of energy were thrown from the spinning swirl outward toward all the creatures and kobolds he had brought through the interstice into this world. They too rose into the air - writhing, aging, and turning to dust.

The earthquake grew more intense, knocking any still on their feet to the ground before the streaming light from the cave and the shaking ground both stopped abruptly. All the dust that had been kobolds fell to the ground. In front of Donal, the particles of The Hermit contracted into a vibrating, glowing mass nearly a foot across. The light was so intense that Donal and everyone else in the clearing averted their eyes. Donal raised up one arm to shield his face from the emanation.

The mass expanded, shaking violently. It engulfed a struggling Donal before shooting up into the sky above the tree tops, dragging him with it. The mass still spun, growing wider and more chaotic. It suddenly collapsed in on itself and exploded, expanding across the sky toward the horizon like ripples in a pond. The very air felt electrified.

Red watched as Donal, a tiny black shape against the brightness, fell out of the sky. He crashed into the ground at the center of the clearing. His arms and neck at unnatural angles.

"Dad," Red yelled. He stumbled to his feet and ran over to his father's body. He threw himself on the ground beside his father, grabbed his hand and squeezed it tightly. "Dad, say something."

Red heard an agonizing groan from his father. Donal managed to twist his head around toward his son.

"Red," he mumbled.

"Dad, everything is going to be okay. We beat him," Red spluttered between his tears. "Everything is going to be okay, right?" He watched as Donal's eyes glossed over. He shook his father's shoulder with his free hand. "Dad!"

Around them, the mere handful of men still left that had came from the circus to aid The Hermit in his preparations, fled into the woods. Tom, Sara, Esmé, and Chase made their way to Red's side.

"What's happening?" Sara said.

Esmé shifted back into the physical world and placed her

hand on Sara's shoulder. "It's Red's dad."

Donal's eyes grew clear again. "Okay?" he said. "Yes, I think everything is going to be okay, it's going to be alright. At least it will be... in your care." He looked around at the people surrounding Red. "But you'll need the help of your friends."

"No," Red said. "We need you, I need you."

Donal coughed as he reached a shaking hand up to Red's face. He cupped it in his palm. "I love you son," he said. "I'm proud of you. You were brave in a way I could never be, in a way I never was."

Donal's upraised hand fell limply by his side as his eyes stared vacantly at nothing.

"NO! You can't die!" Red screamed. But even as he begged, he felt his father's hand become insubstantial. As Donal's form crumbled in his hand, Red's tears fell from his cheeks into the dust that had been his father's spirit.

The sun finally disappeared behind a distant ridge as Red felt someone grasp his shoulder.

"Red," Tom said. "I'm sorry."

***

The earthquake hit the Circus Paenultimas as Luca and Nadya were preparing for their act. It was already going to be a shortened act without Esmé. In moments, Rinthim Straub's plan to bring the tent down on the crowd would come to fruition. At the first tremor, the ringmaster ran out of the quavering tent and looked up at the sky. It wasn't long after the shaking subsided that he saw the ripple of light spread across the sky, disturbing even the clouds on their lazy course. He knew then that The Hermit had failed; he was dead and the interstice virtually closed.

Anger boiled up inside him. He let out a deep roar and threw his baton at the nearest trailer. It sailed straight through the aluminum siding leaving only a small golf-ball sized hole. It hit something more substantial on the other side of the trailer, and with a clattering of dishes and shattering glass, the trailer tipped over on its side.

Straub spun on one heel and marched back into the tent, straight into the middle of the center ring. The crowd was still uneasy from the quake, and many were heading for the exits. In his fury, he remained steadfast on carrying through with the townspeople's deaths, even if it served no purpose in the greater plan. He had to get the crowd back under his control.

"Ladies and gentlemen," he began in his most gregarious voice. He looked up toward the top of the stands where the spotlight controllers stood. "All lights on me," he bellowed over the tumult. The lights spun around the tent, eventually settling on his tall, lank frame.

"Ladies and gentlemen," he began again, more firmly this time, with less patronage. "Please return to your seats. Everything is alright."

Luca and Nadya exchanged a glance as they stood at the foot of the lattice they would climb to begin their routine. They watched the ringmaster intently. Several workers scrambled to secure their safety gear.

"I have spoken with the authorities," he lied, struggling to make himself heard over the raucous crowd. "If you will please be calm so that all can hear this important message." He paused for a moment to see how the crowd responded. Most, but not all seemed to grow calmer. Most returned to their seats. "Please. This is important. I have been asked to relay to you that everything is in order. I have been told to tell you that you are in a safe place, and that you should remain here. And, trust me, you are in a safe place. The emergency services ask that you stay off the roads at this time unless it is an actual emergency.

"So please!" he continued loudly. "Please return to your seats, at least for a few more minutes while the police and emergency personnel deal with the crisis outside of these tent walls." Again the ringmaster paused. He watched the crowd. Everyone in the crowded tent was now either silent or returning to their seats.

"I promise I will keep you as up to date on the situation as I am," he said. "However, until then, please enjoy the show." Straub strode out of the spotlight and hopped over the barrier around the center ring. He grabbed a clown by the scruff of his collar. "Get your people out there right now," he growled.

"What do you want us to do?" the clown asked petrified.

"I don't care what you do, just get out there and distract them!" He nearly pushed the clown to the ground as he made his way past him. At the edge of the tent, he spied one of the men tasked with severing the tent's ropes.

"I think Esmerelda and her friends stopped The Hermit," Luca said to his wife. "I'll be right back." He slipped away from where they were waiting and followed discreetly behind Straub as the entire company of the circus' many clowns filled the three rings in utter disarray.

Straub leaned toward the man standing near the performer entrance. "Now," he said. "Tell your friends we are doing it now."

The man nodded and sank off into the shadows as the ringmaster pushed aside a flap and exited the big top.

Luca followed the man for a short distance until he was sure the ringmaster was well away. He pulled a dagger out of one of his boots, and grabbed the man with both hands around his head, making sure to cover his mouth. He pulled him into the shadows underneath the bleachers.

"Be silent," Luca said under his breath into the man's ear. Above him the crowd was still settling back into their seats. He heard the sounds of clown horns and uneven, nervous laughter. "I know who you are; you're Thom," he said. "And you know me. It's Luca."

He relaxed his grip slightly on the man. "I just need to ask you a couple of questions."

Outside the tent, Straub strapped down his trailer; it was all ready for a hasty departure. "It's about time I put this whole stupid circus act behind me anyway," he said to the empty trailer. He grabbed his truck keys off the hook just inside his office door and slammed the door shut behind him. He walked quickly along the side of the trailer and with a quick kick, knocked away the blocks of wood underneath the trailer's tongue. It fell neatly into place on his truck's hitch. He knocked down the lever with one hand, and not bothering to chain it or hook up the lights, got in the cab of his truck and started the engine. He was doing his best to get away before the tent came crashing down.

Nadya saw Luca emerging from the underneath the stands. His hands were empty, but one of his wrists was covered in blood. "What's going on? Are you okay?"

"Quick," he said. "I'm fine, but we have to warn everybody else." He grabbed her by the hand and ran toward the center ring. Instead of heading straight there, he went to the side rail and snatched the microphone out of the announcer's hand.

"What do you think you're doing?" The man asked.

"Emergency," Luca said, not slowing down.

"I killed Thom, he wouldn't tell me who else was helping him. Maybe we have enough time to get everyone out," Luca said to Nadya as he pulled her along behind him.

The clowns were still doing their best to fill time as the two Hibbards arrived in the ring. They stopped near the far edge. Luca flicked on the microphone.

"Everybody listen!" he yelled into it, waving one arm in the air. His voice was piercingly loud. "Listen," he said again.

The spotlights all turned on him. The clowns, relieved that somebody else was now the center of attention took the opportunity and slunk toward the nearest exit.

"You are all in danger," he said. "The tent is going to fall down. You all need to leave."

For a brief moment everything was silent. He was about to repeat himself when the first people began to scream. There was chaos as everyone panicked and tried to all go down the narrow stairs of the bleachers at once. Some even leapt off the sides or slid down through the space underneath their plank benches.

"Come on," Nadya said. She gripped his hand tightly. "We have got to get out of here too."

Luca dropped the microphone to the ground and the two of them did their best to lose themselves in the mad, frantic crowd. The Circus Paenultimus was no longer a safe place for them.

The crowd poured out of the big top in all directions, even pushing themselves underneath the walls of the tent. The men who were to bring the tent down grew increasingly more frightened that Straub would blame them if the crowd escaped, so they began to cut through the last strands of the heavy ropes holding the tent upright. It didn't take much to bring the big top down. With people pushing their way out any way they could, it was already shaking violently.

First one rope, then two, three, four. They snapped like rubber bands pulled too taught. The whole tent wobbled back and forth, seemingly unsure which way to fall. Despite their intentions, the conspirators were too late. The last of the townspeople squeezed out the tent's egresses into the midway as the giant flag-topped tent and massive poles came crashing down on empty rings and empty stands.

Straub watched in his side mirrors as the tent fell to the ground. It threw up a cloud of dust. He smiled to himself, unable to see that any had escaped. He pulled onto the highway, heading East. He reached over his shoulder and slid aside the rear window that opened into the camper-topped truck bed. "Are you comfortable back there, Synesteria?" He asked. Looking once more in his mirror, he watched as the sun gave a final flash before disappearing behind a distant ridge top.

"We are going to need a new harbinger," he said. "Do you think you are up to the task?"

One Day at a Time

Claire knew Donal was going to leave her the moment she heard the growling rumble that sounded almost, but not quite, like distant thunder. The windows began rattling and the lights flickering even before the tremor shook the floor. As the tremor passed, the slow methodical beeping of the monitors stopped singing their incessant chorus and screamed a high-pitched steady tone.

She had believed there were no more tears inside her, but from some deep reservoir they managed to flow again. Even though she had imagined some relief at his passing, she couldn't find it. It felt like a heavy stone buried deep inside her chest.

Over time, the weight might lessen, but it would always be there inside her, always be a part of her. It was a burden, but it was also a gift – Donal's last gift to her. It would always remain as a touchstone to him. Each time she reached inside herself for strength she would find it there. Each time it would grow less burdensome; the pain less acute. Each time the memory of Donal, who he was and who they were together, would fill her mind, she could draw strength from it, even as the memories reminded her of her loss.

She held one of Donal's hands between hers, leaned over his still form and kissed him tenderly on the lips. "Thank you," she said. "You'll always be my strength. I love you."

As she pulled away, she felt the pressure of gentle hands on her arm. She allowed the nurse to guide her outside the hospital room. Emily followed behind them.

***

It seemed wrong to Red that his father's funeral and burial was on such a beautiful day. It was only four days since the fight at the cave, but it felt to him both like an eternity had passed and like there had been no interval at all. The sun hung white in a clear blue sky. A light breeze ruffled the fringe of the funeral home tent above the family as they sat on folding plastic chairs – except Red, who sat in his wheelchair. He wanted rain and dark skies. He wanted the world itself to grieve as he did. Even the beautiful view from his family cemetery, on top of the hill overlooking their farm and the forest beyond, seemed to mock his pain.

The preacher was talking about souls and heaven and peace, but Red couldn't follow him. The whole experience felt unreal to him, like he was a witness to what was going on around him, instead of being a participant. He felt like he was experiencing the world from several feet behind his eyes, merely spectating. He looked over his shoulder at the small gathering of friends and acquaintances behind them. They stood in the bright light while the family sat in the shade. Sara and Michael were there, of course, with their parents. Behind them he saw Esmé, Chase, and Wendy standing uncomfortably near the back. For the briefest of moments, he shifted into the spirit world, and sure enough, Tom was standing beside them. He shifted back and stared at the flowers on his father's coffin.

The preacher closed his Bible and prayed. *That's it then,* Red thought at the final amen. *My dad is gone.* His mother pushed his wheelchair over the green turf the funeral home had laid out to cover the dirt from the grave. Once they were out from underneath the tent, Michael came up and took over for Claire, and pushed him down the path toward the Snyder's house.

***

"I'm sorry," Sara said. She wrapped her arms around Red's neck. She pulled back, but still held her hands clasped together behind his head. "I don't know if it is the right time or not, but I wanted to thank you too." She leaned close to his face, and kissed him on the cheek. When she finally pulled away from the embrace both their faces were beet red.

Michael glanced at Esmé, their eyes briefly meeting before they both turned away. Wendy looked at Chase, but he was staring at his feet. The six of them were alone in Red's room following the burial. The sound of reserved conversations could be heard coming from the living room.

"Tom came too," Chase said. "He asked me to send his condolences and tell you he'll come see you soon."

"Thanks," Red said.

"He also told me to give you this," Chase said handing him a long iron skeleton key. "He said it should be yours."

Red took the key and turned it over between his fingers. The letters 'IS' overlapped on key's head like a dollar sign.

"Did he happen to say what it unlocked?"

"It was something of your grandfather's," Chase said. "Tom was sure you'd be able to figure out it."

"Tell him thanks, I guess." Red said sliding the key into a shirt pocket. He looked around the room at everyone gathered there. He hadn't known most of them until just a few days ago. *Who should they be to me now?* He wondered. As he looked at them, he noted that they were all reticent to look him directly in the eye. He realized it was just their own nervousness and let it pass.

"So, what are we going to do now?" Wendy asked. She too had been looking around the room at each person; for her there was no ambiguity of what these people were to her. They were her friends, even her family in a way that her mother and father never had been. Even Sara, whom she had only the briefest encounter with, meant more to her than she could put into words. This couldn't be the last time they would be together.

"What else is there to do?" Michael said. "The ringmaster disappeared without a trace. I think it's over. That's it, we're done."

"It's not over," Red said. "There is always going to be an interstice there in the cave. I can't let it open again. Besides that, there are countless others around the world."

"Why you? Why us?" Michael said. "We did our part."

"Red's right," Chase said. "We have to make sure no one like The Hermit ever returns to open it again."

"I agree," Esmé said. She stood up from where she was sitting on the foot of Red's bed and walked over to Red. She knelt down until her head was even with his. "We have to follow this through. I'm devoting my life, right here and right now, to stopping whatever Straub is trying to accomplish."

"Well spoken," Wendy said. "Whether we like it or not, we have seen the way the world truly is. It is up to us to do everything we can to keep it from falling apart."

"I'm in too," Sara said.

Michael gave his sister a glowering look before softening his gaze. "I'm with you too Red, always. No matter what weird dream world you drag me into, you're my best friend."

Red nodded at Michael.

"What are you going to do?" Red asked Esmé. "Where are you going to stay?"

"I'm going to stay at the campground by the river," she said. "Chase helped me sneak my trailer out of the circus' camp the other night. I think the first thing I'm going to do is hunt down my parents. I think they can help us."

"Chase, what about you?" Red asked.

"I'm not sure yet," Chase said. "I still have my family here. We'll have to see." He leaned against the wall and began cleaning his fingernails with a long-bladed knife. He turned to Wendy. "So, what's the plan?"